J. Vaughan Hughes

Seventy Years of Life in the Victorian Era

Embracing a travelling Record in Australia, New Zealand, and America etc.

J. Vaughan Hughes

Seventy Years of Life in the Victorian Era
Embracing a travelling Record in Australia, New Zealand, and America etc.

ISBN/EAN: 9783337209209

Printed in Europe, USA, Canada, Australia, Japan

Cover: Foto ©Andreas Hilbeck / pixelio.de

More available books at **www.hansebooks.com**

BY

A PHYSICIAN

𝕷𝖔𝖓𝖉𝖔𝖓

T. FISHER UNWIN

PATERNOSTER SQUARE

MDCCCXCIII

LIST OF ILLUSTRATIONS.

SERAGLIO POINT.

SEVENTY YEARS OF LIFE IN THE VICTORIAN ERA.

CHAPTER I.

I AM one who has just commenced to traverse his seventy-first year, and can look backward over a life more or less of a checkered character, involving as it does a time spent in actual warfare, as well as in a struggling civil life passed in the metropolis and the provinces of England, with intervals of travel extending over Europe, the Australian colonies, and America. A review of the experiences of such a life may, perhaps, prove to be interesting and even instructive, and I make no further apologies for printing these reminiscences.

My father was a country rector, who had three sons, of whom I was the youngest. The rectory was not a very rich one, and the income was not supplemented to any great extent by private means. Consequently there was no hesitation as to what was to be done with our boys: we were early impressed with the fact that we must work for our own living, and be the architects of our own future position, hence we were to select the three learned professions respectively, and Physic fell to my lot, my brothers choosing Law and Divinity. My father, fortunately for us, was a good classic, having been elected, as a young man, to act as coadjutor with the head master of Rugby School; hence we were well founded in what was then deemed the *sine quâ non* of a gentleman's education, and the pater kept pegging away at us till we reached the age of thirteen, when we were sent off to a public school to continue our plodding with varying success. Our mother was one in a million, and no sacrifice was too great for her to make for the well-being of her sons. She was very beautiful, and descended from an old family beginning with the Crusaders' times. She gave up the world for the sake of her children. She was the grand home peacemaker, and her sons " grew up and blessed her." Our parents were indulgent to a certain extent, but they had their hard-and-fast line, which was firm and unyielding, and which we were taught to respect. We were allowed our fill of field sports as young lads, and took a practical interest in all the work connected with the cultivation of an extensive glebe-land. This laid the foundation of vigorous health. Cricket, tennis, and croquet were not to the fore in those days.

Play over, our schooling was work—work and no mistake—it meant business, serious and attentive, and we were taught to sing in harmony :—

> " When a weary task you find it,
> Persevere, and never mind it."

Whether at work or play there was no nonsensical familiarity permitted, and a gulf of respectful distance was always maintained at such times, and it never entered our heads to nickname either of our parents to their faces or behind their backs—our father as the " Gov.," or our mother as the " Old Lady." In these very enlightened and very much civilised days such a reverential attitude would, I take it, be considered by Young England as too old-fashioned !

When we become men, that is, when we leave behind the restraints of schooldom and pass on to college life, we are supposed to put aside childish things ; but that, in too many cases, is only an assumption by freshmen, who air their littlenesses in strutting about bedecked in full-fledged attire of the most approved fashion, to the sweet delight of the artistic tailor, who will wait patiently any length of time for his extortionate bill, which, when presented after the lapse of two or three years, shocks and confounds the self-denying parents at home, who are in blissful ignorance that such an indebtedness exists ; and yet the young hopeful can face his loving ones, vacation after vacation, without a blush, consoling his conscience that that is the way young fellows act who would assume the right tone and do credit to their college. They are too weak-kneed to resist the temptation of having a change of trousers for every day in the week, &c., and thus to assume the appearance of wealth which they have not. From the stand-point of my bringing up I could see no fun in this sort of foppishness, nor any feeling of satisfaction

in strutting up and down High Street in cap and
gown, the observed of all observers, especially of the
fair sex. My father, if he had been in the commercial
line, would soon have convinced me in technical language that that style of thing would " not pay."
Therefore, without further ado, I tackled to, and
though the harness chafed me a little at first, I
soon found it became easier in the wearing, and that
regular systematic work for every hour of the day as
it came round was a grand stay against the inclina-
tion to swerve from the right track and to join in the
pranks of the pleasure-seeking lot, who would do their
best to bring you down to their level, and do no hard
work till the last year of their curriculum, with the
risk of being " plucked," cramming notwithstanding.
In order to secure a good place in the estimation of
the professors and stand fairly well with college
authorities I determined to succeed if labour and
plodding would do it. I could not command success
of course, but I resolved not to have it on my conscience
that I did not do my best to deserve it, and laying to
heart the principle of the old fable that the tortoise
will overtake the hare if it keeps pegging away long
enough, and does not faint and get down-spirited on
the way, I determined to rise up at 5.30 A.M., light
the fire, make my coffee, and get an hour's start at
thinking and plodding before my more lively antago-
nists were awake. This early rising made it easy to
be punctual at chapel parade at 7.30 A.M., which I
never failed to attend, as it seemed to sanctify and
encourage the day's employment; it was a bright,
cheerful service, so rendered by the students' quartet

part singing, of which I was bass. I seldom went into
society during my first summer's session, which was
assiduously given up to the study of botany, and a
good standard of health was kept up by roaming over
the country in all directions in search of specimens,
of which I made a useful, practical selection, and
arranged four hundred dried ones for the examination,
which I passed, and which resulted in my obtaining
the certificate of honour, an old student taking the
silver medal. Thus I made my first mark, and secured the smile of approval of one of the professors
at least. And what was more encouraging, this, my
first trial trip in science, pleased a relative of mine, a
double-first classman at Oxford, who had risen entirely
by his own unaided efforts to an eminent position in
Christchurch, that he invited me to spend a portion
of the long vacation at his house in Peckwater Quad-
rangle. There I met some of the greatest intellects
of the day—all now gone to their rest. From
their conversation I frequently gathered many useful
hints, which roused my ambition to rise and go
ahead if industry would do it. I was much amused
one day by observing that their enjoyment of a good
dinner did not interfere with the mental labours of
these great men. My cousin, a bachelor, was celebrated for his excellent *cuisine*, and dinners *a la Russe*
were just then coming into vogue, and one evening,
during my stay, twelve of the great dons were invited
to meet round the hospitable board, when sixteen
courses were served ; the constant changing of plates
was amusing, if not bewildering, and one celebrated,
but humorous guest, who sat next to me, had his

plate removed thirteen times out of the possible sixteen, and, what is more, managed to keep talking all
the time, cracking jokes and reciting telling anecdotes,
reminding one rather of the gifts of the late Bishop
Wilberforce in this respect.

Having now to return to college for the winter
session, the crucial question that had to be put to
myself was how much working power I had in me,
and how many prizes were there within measurable
distance of a first-year's student's chance of getting.
I had the hardihood and presumption to decide to
compete for four of these, which were open also to
second and third-years' men. The first was a gold
medal and money, the interest of .£1,000, given by a
well-known philanthropist, for the best essay on a
chosen subject bearing on science, with a view to
exemplify the Power, Wisdom, and Goodness of God
—somewhat after the style of the Bridgewater
treatises. The next plum was a gold medal for the
best report of cases taken at the bedside of the sick
poor in their own homes, being out-patients of the
hospital which we all walked.

Another gold medal was awarded by authorities to
that student who could pass the best examination in
all the subjects taught during the winter session;
but for this " good-all-round " prize it was laid down
as an essential that the student should have been a
regular attendant at morning chapel. This *sine qua
non* reduced the numbers who wished to compete
considerably; but it goes without saying that this
medal was the great cynosure of all eyes!

The fourth prize in contemplation was a medal for

the best examination in practical chemistry; and as the professor had selected me as his assistant to help him in the college laboratory, I stood a good chance of securing this, though the work was very dirty, the furnaces making one's hands like those of a blacksmith; but the analysis (organic and inorganic) were very fascinating and deeply impressive, never to be effaced from the memory. I had, as I say, the hardihood to try and gain these alluring rewards held out to the young men. Some of the elder fellows deemed me very impertinent to dream of such an ambitious scale of work; but I had made up my mind and set to, undaunted and even uninfluenced by their sneers and gibes. Up early, and closing at 11 P.M., shunning society, and resisting gaieties of all kinds, I determined to plod on and win the lot, it self-denial and hard work would do it. But I may remark here, come what may, I had determined not to do any secular work on the Sunday. I closed my books at midnight on Saturday, and did not open them again till Monday morning.

CHAPTER II

I NEED not dwell on the trials and opposition I encountered during my first winter's campaign—it was gloomy indeed, but it all ended in sunshine in the spring. When it was decided that I had been the successful competitor for the four aforesaid prizes, then human nature asserted herself, and those who had been my bitterest enemies generously came forward with their congratulations, and, in the slang of even that time, dubbed me a "brick," and said I was a credit to the college. But the most gratifying day was still to come, when the sessional prizes were to be distributed among the successful students; and when I was called up for the fourth time to receive a medal—and that in a town hall crowded with ladies and gentlemen—the applause was unmistakable; and to enhance the delight of the reception, the prizes came from the hands of a chairman, a peer, and himself a double-first class-man. I could not help feeling rather staggered, as it was such a revulsion of position—from a retired ascetic life in a college room to be the central mark in such a splendid gathering—but if for a time I felt a pardonable degree of elation, it was quickly suppressed by my father's

manner when I took the medals home. Of course he
was pleased with my acquisitions, but he very quickly
gave me to understand that I must not stay my
hand, but go on working—in fact, must be content
to be a student all my life if I would hold my own
in the world. Much to my great grief, my poor
mother had gone to her rest in heaven before these
honours had been conferred on her " dillin," otherwise it would have been a pleasurable moment to
prove to her that her self-sacrifices and her self-
effacement for the well-being of her family were
bearing fruit. Our sorrow was shared by the poor
people especially, for she had constituted herself
for years the parish doctor (we being six miles from
the regular one), dispensing medicines and surgical
appliances and medical comforts to the sick and
needy with a willing and liberal hand unaided, for
there was no rich squire's house to draw upon
in emergencies, the community being made up of
small farmers and miners. The mouldy, dilapidated
state of the church was a constant fret to her highly
wrought moral sensitiveness, for in those days of
religious indifferentism it was most difficult to get
money even to make the necessary repairs. I recollect when the tower was giving way under the weight
of its eight bells, my father had no end of trouble
to collect £10, having to supplement the rest of the
cost out of his own pocket—and this for to keep this
portion of the sacred edifice from collapsing altogether. When I reflect upon and compare the
condition of the national churches of that period
with that of the present day, even in obscure

districts, I am struck with astonishment at the
great change for the better. On entering one of
these, open only once a week, the smell was like
that of a mildewing vault, damp and stuffy, with
fungi growing out between the flagstones on the
floor; the woodwork of the seats worm-eaten and
decaying, and the three-decker itself hardly safe to
mount. Those were the days in which dissent made
much headway with the lower illiterate classes,
roused to a high pitch of enthusiasm by itinerant
preachers chosen from themselves, and who could
speak to their hearts in a phraseology peculiar to
themselves the grand truths in the good old
Book.

Passing on from this bit of digression, we arrive at
the second winter session, which commenced under
most auspicious circumstances. I had made my
mark, and was something more than the mere numeral
on my college room door. Our warden (the chancellor
of a diocese and the son of a bishop who had married
a peer's daughter with a nice dowry)—a man who
knew what hard brain-work meant, having edited
three large volumes on Ecclesiastical Law—was so
exercised in his mind over the fact that any student
could manage to monopolise four college medals in
one year that, at one of his wine parties which he
gave to a select few every week, he surprised us by
saying that he would be pleased to confer £50 on any
student who could accomplish the same feat again.
We forgot the dignity of his position for the moment,
and gave him a hearty cheer for his liberal offer; £50
was great in our eyes in those days, magnified to the

extent of £500 to what that sum would be to us in after life. It must be confessed that I felt much disappointed that I was out of the running : but, pillowing the matter over that night, I reflected over the principle of the proposal, and, calling upon the warden the next morning, asked him if he deemed it an essential to the gaining of his £50 that the prizes should be actually and despotically four medals. His reply thrilled me with hope. "Certainly not," he said. "All I bargain for is, that they should be first class." Then I replied, "Perhaps you would permit the Scholarship on Divinity to stand as one?" "Not only so," said he, "but, being a clergyman, I should feel rather inclined to make that count as two." "Oh, no." I replied ; "pray keep to your original agreement." But he said, with a twinkle in his eye, "Are you going to try?" "Certainly so, if you will allow me." A cordial shake of the hand was his answer, and we parted, he saying it would be fearfully hard work; but there was an encouraging "God help you," unexpressed save in his benevolent face. Well, the winter months were passed in right down hard plodding, on which I relied rather than upon any superior talents I had been blessed with. Those of superior intellects would persist, as usual, in putting off coming into the struggle and the fight till the season was half spent, and then in their flurry got nervous, sleepless, and dyspeptic, and, with brains *suddenly* overstrained, the staying powers of the memory would fail just at the finish. In all my anxiety to win I still kept to my resolution not to do any secular work on the Sunday, but I drew a line there which did not include the study of divinity and philosophy; these I set apart for that day as recreative, peaceful, and inspiring. Butler's " Analogy," Paley's " Evidences of Christianity," and Fénélon's works were the books for the examination to get the scholarship which was good for £20 a year.

To make a long story short, and not to weary the attention of the reader, I will at once jump to the conclusion of the session, which ended in my being the successful competitor for the Chancellor's Prize of £50, which involved, happily for me, the much-coveted scholarship. These secured to me £70 in cash, which for the moment made me feel passing rich, and the vacation would have been spent in undimmed pleasure but for a very heavy black cloud which came across my sunny sky. My father was suddenly taken away from us at this critical time of my career in life, and with him was gone our old home at the rectory, and, what was worse, I was now thrown on my own resources practically to continue and finish my studies and obtain my diplomas.

CHAPTER III.

The real tug of war began in my third and last year, and it was very doubtful at its beginning whether I could find sufficient financial help to remain in college and finish the necessary course of lectures and secure my hospital certificates. As to my very dear relations, some of them boasting of their thousands, I soon found that they could flatter with their lips, but they did not feel disposed to fork out much from their purses. "Put not your trust in princes, nor in any child of man." Assistance came in the nick of time from most unexpected quarters, from strangers, in fact, and it roused the feeling that the loving Father was just chastening, but not forsaking, the newly-made orphan. Circumstances soon proved this as plainly as if an angel from heaven had spoken. I had my £70 intact, and my "commons" in the college hall would only cost me £24. I therefore had a fair balance in hand, but to supplement this I got £10 for acting as tutor to a junior class which the good warden had instituted, and which he entrusted to my supervision. This was very cheering, and a great compliment to an undergraduate. He also con-

fided to me as umpire a prize of £6 to be given to the
student whom I considered had passed the best
examination in these two subjects—ditto, another
compliment. Feeling quite safe as to getting through
my final exams. for the diplomas when the time
arrived for such, I did not stick now so close to work,
but went out to enjoy a little musical society, but
what I greatly yearned for, and had set my heart
upon, was to get if possible a stained glass window
at the east end of the college chapel. This I set
myself out to accomplish, and having first obtained a
beautiful design—the subject being our Saviour heal-
ing the sick at the Pool of Bethesda, which was given
to me by a rising young artist as a gratuitous contri-
bution—I found that the cost of putting in the window
would be £120, the manufacturers waiving their
claim to any trade profit. So far so good. Now
began my first begging-letter experience, and as my
application was a good and disinterested one, it gave
me boldness to persevere. Subscriptions came in
nicely, and in order to square the deficit I gave a
demonstrative course of lectures on chemistry in the
college hall, to which outsiders were admitted by pay-
ment. This was also a success, and ended with a
surplus, which delighted the professorial staff, who
were in fears that the hat would have to go round
among them after all. And though they considered
me in an irresponsible position, the whole affair from
beginning to ending was a striking proof to them and
to all the students what could be done by pluck and
perseverance, provided the object to be attained had
sound moral and religious bearings, and this even by

an individual poor and humble who had only made his mark by taking a few medals, &c.

Nothing very worthy of note took place till the end of the session, when all my certificates, necessary for my final exams., were filled up and signed by the respective professors, and I was ready, with feelings unruffled, to undergo those trying ordeals so fearfully dreaded by the student who has become perhaps nervously and tremblingly anxious because his accusing conscience whispers to him that he has not made the best use of his time and opportunities, and has put off till the third year, and to his trust in " coaching," to cram into an unprepared and an unexpanded mind and memory that amount of knowledge which ought to have been *gradually* acquired over the course of the three years allotted to him. Sleeplessness and sinking dyspepsia overtake him at the eleventh hour, and as the solemn day arrives he throws up the sponge in sheer fright at the idea of being " plucked," so he retires into private life and private study for six or twelve months, involving additional expense to his self-sacrificing relations or friends, whom he has cajoled into believing that he has broken down from a legitimate strain of over-work—a deception his tutor could at any moment prove to the contrary. The above description is truly typical of those young men who have been cursed with a little independence of their own, and which they have magnified in their worldly inexperience into something of tenfold its value, and have been induced under this false notion to lead a life of *dolce far niente* during the first two years of their college life, and have thus trifled with

opportunities which can never be recalled. Such
instances are very pitiable and sorrowful when the
subject is a married man who is trying to enter the
profession later in life than ordinary. An instance
of this kind I recollect very well. I was coaching a
gentleman whose wife had the means of starting him
in a profession, and she was very ambitious that he
should succeed, and he, on his part, was equally
anxious to show her that she had not married a fool,
but one who could soar far above the mental calibre
of a tradesman, from whom she had originated ; consequently the man's mettle was up, and I must admit
he made the most courageous efforts to succeed. He
was a strong, athletic fellow, · and loved practical
surgery, in which he was well up, having been an
assistant to a surgeon in the " Black Country " for
several years, but when we came to abstract theories
and abstruse occult subjects, he was stupidity itself,
and my labours to drill him into something like
decent shape was prodigious, and my stock of
patience was sorely tried ; but what annoyed me
much was this—when he stumbled a little in his
replies he used to get so guiltily red in the face, which
was of the full-moon size, and made him look so
intensely stupid and deficient. I was consoled, however, by the knowledge that he really was thoroughly
well up in practical surgery, and that it was to the
College of Surgeons he was going for a diploma, but
I knew the examiners there were not content with
manual skill only—they will have a man liberally
educated in the bothering 'ologies as well ; so I kept
pegging along steadily until the awful day arrived,

and I actually coached him up to the very doors of the college, and as he entered its gloomy portals wound up with one final warning, viz. : " Should the examiners tackle you on a subject you are not quite at home in, pray go on talking, and don't blush and hesitate as if you did not know, and in the confusion the question may be changed to one your jabbering has suggested. Of course you were a little deaf and did not hear exactly what was asked, do you understand ? " " Oh, yes," said he, " I twig your meaning." I waited in some trepidation till his examination was over, and when he presented himself with a beaming countenance redder even than usual, I plainly perceived that all was well, and that he had passed the fiery ordeal, he remarking, " But for your last warning at the entrance I really do believe that I should have been ' ploughed.' The examiner took me on the hip, and I began to feel I was getting hot and confused, when, remembering your hint, I stumbled on and said something about the femoral, when the examiner, smiling, said, ' Oh, yes, what about the femoral ? Do you mean the artery or the hernia ? ' ' Either,' said I, promptly. ' Very well, let us see what you know ? ' Thanks to you, I was at my ease directly, and getting through the descriptions satisfactorily, I gained confidence and passed the remainder comfortably." " Now," I replied, equally gratified, " won't your wife be pleased, and won't she give you such an affectionate hug as you have never as yet experienced, and if she never prayed heartily before I am sure she did to-day for your success. And now you deserve her respect as well as her love. Go forth

and prosper, my dear fellow, and don't forget the
cheerful saying from the good old Book : ' Oh rest in
the Lord, and wait patiently for Him, and He shall
give thee thy heart's desire.' "

As my last session was closing in upon me, and
everything was prepared for my examination, the
only difficulties which stared me in the face were
those of a pecuniary character. I could not see
where the money was to come from to pay the necessary fees for the diplomas ; £35 would be required
for the degree of M.D., reducing the expenses to the
lowest figure. But taking a retrospective view of the
past three years, and the wonderful way in which I
had been upheld by so many unforeseen and unexpected interpositions, I did not lose faith in the continuous mercy of a kind overruling Providence, nor
yet in the power of prayer, which my good mother
never ceased to instil into us. I was not kept very
long in anxious suspense. Our good warden, and his
equally good countess, with whom I had been staying
for some weeks to recoup my energies, which had run
down from too close teaching, informed me that the
founder of the so-called Bridgewater Treatise, which
I had succeeded in gaining, hearing of the fix I was
in, very kindly offered to pay my M.D. fees as soon
as I had passed, which I did at once. This benevolent act of a person I had never seen was so unlooked
for that I was astonished beyond measure, and it so
exercised my thoughts that it implanted in me more
than ever a very lively faith in the Divine ruling,
and Heaven's supervision of the orphan, who was

evidently not going to be deserted. About this time
I was introduced to an honourable and reverend
divine, who came to my aid by advising me to apply
to the " Sons of Clergy Corporation " for assistance
to pay the fees of the College of Surgeons, which that
admirable institution of bicentennial goodness agreed
to do, and I became a full-fledged surgeon.

CHAPTER IV.

WITH the aid of my prize-money and that of the scholarship my cruse of oil was again replenished, which enabled me to accept a pressing invitation from my old professor of chemistry who was staying in Paris, to pay that lively city a visit. This I did by taking a river steamer at Havre and going up that lovely portion of the Seine between that town and Rouen, where I got off and took the train for Paris, which I crossed from west to east to reach the students' quarters. Here I found the professor located in a cheap hotel, the whole expenses of which were met by an expenditure of thirty francs a week. Those were palmy days when the prices for everything had not been run up to the same extent as they are now by crowds of rich Americans and wealthy English merchants, aggravated by an increased octroi in consequence of the expenditure of many millions for Hausman's improvements—the wholesale sweeping off of the old rookeries, and in their place the erection of huge highly decorated mansions which have made everything cent per cent dearer for every class of lodgment in this gay city. I did not pass my time in

20

amusements only. I was advised by the professor to
take a two months' course of practical surgical operations on the dead subject at Clamart, where a public
certificate would be given as soon as the pupil could
perform the whole series of operations as quickly and
skilfully as the teacher, authorised and selected by
the French Government, could do them. This boon
I acquired at the end of the two months. I also
attended the practice at the Hotel Dieu, a Government
chemical laboratory, and other public educational
establishments open gratuitously to the student,
where I picked up some useful crumbs not easily
got at in England. I may here state that Paris
was at that time the resort of men in pursuit of
science from all parts of the world. There were five
different languages spoken in the saloon of our hotel,
each nationality seated at separate tables. They
were a godless lot, and one French count, a more
zealous infidel than the rest, was exerting his talents
to show, by the chemical experiments he was making,
that the Mosaic order of creation was a series of
scientific blunders from beginning to end. However,
it served to arouse my interest on the subject so far
that when I returned to England I spent much time
and some expense in exploring the matter for my own
satisfaction, which involved some delicate manipula-
tions to show the influence of light on the surface
of vegetation, and the wonderful circle of interchanges
between that world and the animal creation through
the medium of the atmosphere. It took several
months to complete, and in the end it convinced me
more than anything I could have gleaned from the

most logical abstract theories, however plausible, that the order of creation as laid down by the unscienced mind of Moses was, on the whole, a marvel of accuracy and replete with truths which modern man, with all his wonderful aids from the perfect instruments for research in the eighteenth century, could not upset or gainsay!

This analysis, though wearisome and trying to one's patience, resulting in regulating and setting my thoughts and convictions on the two grand cardinal points—my faith in the Scriptures, and the Omnipresence of the Deity.   Therefore I am thankful for my first visit to Paris, now forty-four years ago, for implanting in my heart these deep religious impressions which have never forsaken me.

The last of the "three days' *fêtes* of July" at the public expense which had been annually held to commemorate the restoration of the monarchy under Louis Philippe took place when I was in Paris, and the contemptuous way in which everything of a Napoleonic character was treated was quite remarkable—for instance, plaister casts of Napoleon in his cocked hat and riding coat, and Marshal Ney and such like noted personages connected with their glorious wars, would be set up, like so many Aunt Sallys in the booths to be shot at for a sou.   But this *fête*, in which the people seemed to run wild, was not powerful enough to divert the attention of the populace from certain wrongs which agitators kept dinging into their ears, and the king would not budge an inch from those privileges which are supposed to hedge him about by divine right, notwithstanding, it is said, the intercession of Madame Adelaide, his daughter, who prayed to him on bended knees that he would make some concession to the people before it was too late; but the king was stubborn, and could not realise the truth of the position till he heard shots fired into the windows of the Tuileries, when he fled almost penniless to the coast and took refuge in an English yacht and made his way to England, the safe refuge for those in political trouble.

Before this crisis, the undercurrent of murmuring discontent among the democracy was apparent to every one except to those in the palace. I could—every one could—see in every street and in every *café*, knots of men collected together talking politics and discussing openly the situation. The fire was smouldering for months and giving fearful warnings, but the executive took no heed—none are so blind as those who won't see.

I now took my leave of the gay metropolis of fashion, and having some cash to spare I returned home by way of Belgium, visiting Brussels, Antwerp, Maline, and doing the Rhine from Cologne to Strasbourg, which previous hard work enabled me to enjoy the more. On reaching London I got a letter from one of my old college professors requesting me, if I had made no other engagements, to join their staff as tutor, offering me one hundred a year, with rooms and free commons, and any fees I could pick up by private coaching. This offer came upon me quite as a windfall, and I gladly accepted the appointment, as it gave me an opportunity of prosecuting my studies

in order to get the license to practice medicine from
the Royal College of Physicians of London which, at
that time, required one to submit to five or six days'
examination, and to have reached the age of twenty-
six years. The winter session passed off uneventfully,
saving the materialistic impression which began to
prevail among the more advanced students, and
which I endeavoured to combat with all the forcible
arguments I could muster, and having made an
unusual mark myself as a thinker and practical
demonstrator, I perhaps exerted more influence
and weight in counteracting this deadly influence.
At least, our relative positions as tutor and student
were such that we could unreservedly and dispassion-
ately discuss the metaphysical arguments together
without quarrelling and without compromising our
independence.

In April I went up for my examination at the
College of Physicians, and as the windows over-
looked Trafalgar Square we had a full view of the
celebrated Chartist meeting which took place on one
of the days. We were much amused at the fussy
attitude of the hundreds of special constables who,
" bedecked with a little brief authority, played such
fantastic tricks " by shoving about defenceless women
and children; while the Duke of Wellington had
had secreted in St. Martin's Church the Guards and
some shotted cannon, and in the Strand the sacred
buildings near Somerset House were ready to rake
that thoroughfare from end to end in case of a
popular uproar, and the risk of looting the shops;
but the scare collapsed quietly and peace was not

disturbed, and it all ended in the classes learning a lesson from the masses!

Though our time and attention was much diverted from our examining papers during this day's excitement, we finally satisfied the censors that we could be entrusted with the lives of Her Majesty's subjects, and our diplomas were duly handed over to us, headed by the signature of old Dr. Paris, a physician of eminence of a bygone generation, and whose knowledge of the then progress in science, especially analytical chemistry, was rather foggy. My health gave way about this time, and I spent several months at the seaside to recruit it. And as I rallied picked up a five-pound note now and again by giving a practical lecture on chemistry and botany to young men at mechanic institutes.

As another phrase of my life will soon commence, I will defer the same till we are *en route* to the next chapter.

CHAPTER V.

When recruiting at the seaside, I heard of a vacancy in the medical staff of a large infirmary in a midland county town. A physician was required to fill the post of attending, not only to this infirmary with its hundred beds, but also to a fever hospital with another fifty. As there were only two physicians to do the work, the duties seemed rather onerous even to me, but I was pressed to try my luck, as a lady voter said. And on visiting the town for the first time as a perfect stranger to every one, it was discouraging to learn that there were already four candidates in the field, three being well-known local practitioners, and the fourth an elderly physician from London, a stranger like myself. It seemed rather a hopeless sort of struggle, especially so with the three former, but a clergyman of position and influence in the county, and a large subscriber to the funds of the institution, was won over by his wife to my side, and he surprised me by saying that there was a great deal of political feeling in connection with the election, that there was in fact a Whig and Tory side in the matter. I being a clergyman's son was regarded as necessarily belonging to the Con-

servative section, though I had no political bias one
way or the other, for my mission in life was one of
mercy to all ranks and conditions of men. I
chartered a dog-cart, and canvassed the county
thoroughly, and was introduced to about sixty good
families, but a great duke and the founder of the
infirmary were hot against me, but I was told not
to lose heart for all that. On the day of the
election the three local candidates retired, because
the body of governors present unanimously decided
that the appointment would not allow them to continue in general practice.

The choice then rested between me and the elderly
physician from town, and when it came to this narrow
pass one of the local doctors handed over to my side
twenty-four ladies' proxies, which he held blank in
reserve, and filled them in with my name, this astute
movement brought me in at the head of the poll with
a majority of sixteen, much to the vexation and disappointment of the founder and his rich Whig party,
including his Grace, the high and mighty duke.
When the chairman complained of my youth, a
popular clergyman present retorted by saying that
it was just possible a man might be a wee bit too
old, alluding, of course, to the elderly candidate with
his bald head and grey hair, who was said to be
seventy, clenching his remarks also with the further
one that we should have lost the services of Pitt, the
prime minister of England, if we had rejected him on
account of his age, which was only twenty-one years
when the king made him his premier.

However, the legality of the disposal of the twenty-

four proxy papers in my favour cropt up, and it was
finally decided, after a very stormy discussion, to put
us to the trouble and expense of another canvass, and
poll the county once more ; but my party insisted that
I should be acting physician at the infirmary during
the interval of two months, which gave me a very
good innings, and I lost no opportunity of ingratiating
myself with every person concerned, so that when the
anxious day at last arrived I came in with a trium-
phant majority of two hundred in lieu of sixteen.
Thus only good came out of an apparent evil.
Friends rallied around me in every direction, and
the second election diverted much attention to me as
a persecuted individual, which tended to rouse a sort
of general sympathy, very beneficial to a young physician making his way among strangers in a strange
land.

The result was what might be expected. I rapidly
got into a practice, and in two years had set up a
pretty little phæton with a pair of ponies, backed by
a smart " tiger." Financially I was aided by taking
three young men into my house, who were preparing
for their examinations, and who were very useful to
me in taking down a report of my cases at the
hospitals and enlivening my evenings.

I think the above record of difficulties and trials
and depressing circumstances ought to encourage
young professionals to keep a good heart and never
to say die, even when the outlook seems very black
indeed !

For the first time in my life I began to feel what it
was to bask in easy circumstances, and the pleasurable

repose from anxiety involving ways and means was the none less enjoyable because the change was the outcome of my own exertions. The only thing I had now to fear was the danger of becoming too much of a diner out, as the county families were over kind and pressing, and the constant acceptance of their courteous invitations would lead me into expense, and withdraw my mind from study and close attention to practice. It required no little tact to steer clear of giving offence when so much disinterested kindness was being shown towards me on all sides, but very often I could plead that the distances were too far, and the nights too dark to venture out ; thus by one excuse or another I managed to keep my social pleasures within reasonable and conscientious limits. I was perfectly convinced that a society man was not the one to gain the professional confidence of the people : hence I defined my boundary and kept to it.

I was startled one morning at breakfast by one of my pupils saying that he and his fellow students had been scheming how they could get up to see the Great Exhibition (1851)—the one grand novelty and talk of the whole civilised world, being the first of its kind ever organised on such a prodigious scale; but Prince Albert had set his heart upon its accomplishment, and the glittering work was done. I had been contemplating the possibility of getting to see it, but the expense of lodgings deterred me. I had heard of a party of Germans taking a beautiful West-end suite of drawing-rooms, and paying twenty-five guineas a week, which were surreptitiously occupied by thirty or forty men, who huddled together on the floors, cooked, slept, and smoked in them, and left at the end of the season, leaving the decorations, carpets, and furniture in a filthy state. After a little correspondence, we, that is, myself and three pupils clubbing together, negotiated for rooms in a small public in High Street, Kensington, close to the Gardens, where the charges were moderate for the occasion, being those of a first-class hotel in ordinary times. We had a high gala life of it for three days. The wonderful sights in the world's fair served us as a topic of conversation for several months. We were amazed at the two huge elms, one hundred and twenty feet in height, inclosed in the glass roof of the transepts, and the birds flying about and chirping in their branches. Then came the life-like statuary of the renowned Gibson, especially his Greek slave and tinted Venus.

Then our attention to the rows of bottles with the lovely aniline dyes of every conceivable colour, all extracted from sticky, stinking coal tar !

Amid the din of voices of thousands of people, nothing startled us so much as to hear the numerous languages spoken as coming from all nations under the sun, and the quaint picturesque costumes of every hue and from every clime. These elbowed one in every direction, and when the scene was viewed from the galleries a most charming sight was presented — a restless, surging panorama of heads and bodies clothed in every conceivable fantastic form, and glistening under the sunlight with all the dazzling colouring of a rainbow. It was a fascinating wondrous display of shape and colour, and only to cost one shilling! Yet the committee cleared £200,000 after all expenses were paid. We had heard previously a great deal of French and Belgian lace and Lyons velvets, but the first prize for these exhibits were taken by Great Britain. Much of this success was doubtless owing to the schools of design which had been started in our country by Prince Albert.

CHAPTER VI.

NOTHING very eventful occurred till the summer of 1854, when an opportunity presented itself of a trip to New York. A steamer of 2,000 tons, shiprigged, with an auxiliary of 200 horse power, was chartered to make its first voyage to commence an Anglo-American trade in opposition to the Yankee clippers which were very jealous of any competition. We had a very rough passage, occupying nineteen days, the sea running mountains high, and I thought we should have lost a young girl of sixteen, who was such a bad sailor that she could not retain anything fluid or solid from the beginning to the end of the voyage, and the application of large hot poultices was the only thing which gave her any relief at all. This girl with her two elder sisters were returning to their home on a slave estate in South America, and were in charge of a black woman who had been entrusted to go all the way to Paris to fetch them. I never saw such devotion as I witnessed in this negro woman. She was unwearied in her attendance night and day, and the salvation of her young mistress was, humanly speaking, due to her loving-kindnesses. I had read some harrowing tales of the cruelty of the Southern slave-

holders towards their people; but after what I had
seen on board that ship I began to doubt much of the
truth of such statements. We had as a passenger
a celebrated black woman called the "Black Swan,"
who sang divinely, giving us now and again a treat
in the saloon. She had been to London, where the
Queen and Prince Consort had taken her up and
patronised her with a pecuniary result very satisfactory to herself. When she was singing in her
cabin it was difficult to believe that such sweet
thrilling sounds could issue from the throat of such
a repulsive looking individual.

On nearing what is called the "Banks of Newfound-
land" we got into fog of white cloud, and we slowed
our engines to two miles an hour, and just as we had
passed safely through the mist we saw facing us a
brig at anchor, about a cable's length, and we had
just time to port our helm and clear her stem; it was
a close shave indeed, and I shall never forget the
consternation depicted upon our good captain's pale
face: he seemed petrified for the moment to see danger
so near, for had the fog not been cleared, he said, we
must have sent the brig to the bottom, and probably
come off with a hole in our bows. Why this vessel
was anchored at this particular spot was this—immediately in the vicinity, fishing for cod, were a number
of boats, and the brig was present acting as their
depôt to receive their catchings. As the sea was
calm the skipper sent one of his boats with some cod,
and asking for some beef in exchange, which the said
crew were out of. One of the Yankee passengers said
we Britishers did not know how cod should be cooked,

4

and very officiously demanded that he should go to the ship's galley and give instructions to the *chef*, which the steward good-humouredly allowed; but when the fish was placed on the saloon table very few would touch it, it was so flabby, tasteless, and slimy, hence the connoisseur got pretty well joked by the English party. Another fellow of the same bumptious type vowed we slow-going ones from the old country did not even know how to enjoy the luxury of tobacco in a proper way, and began at once to show us how this was to be done, first by taking a quid from the hollow of his cheek and clearing his throat of its dark nauseous saliva, secondly by taking a pinch of snuff from an elaborate gold box, and thirdly producing a Havannah cigar which he began to smoke with great gusto, thus illustrating the three ways the weed may be used and enjoyed (?) by the same individual. I need hardly say that the European ladies present turned away in disgust from this vain display of our brother Jonathan, but I am writing now of what occurred thirty-seven years ago, the rising generation of young people in America though still rather fast are not vulgar withal. After the war between the North and the South a crowd of Americans overran Europe and picked up in their travels some most useful lessons which mollified their manners immensely, and they returned to their country wonderfully toned down and less offensive in their style of address, and with a gradual dropping of their constant impertinent interrogatives. One never hears now in anything like decent society such salutations as, " Well, stranger, your hat shineth gloriously ; I guess

that beaver cost a lot, where does it hail from ? " Or
if in a train they would be quite restless till they found
out where you were going. " I am steering south,"
one would say, "and I calculate you are on the same
track ? Where shall you cast anchor to-night ? "
And they would gradually worm out of you whether
you were going to join a ranch, or bent on speculation
in pork and lard at Chicago, or whether your inclina-
tions were in the corn or oil line ; and it is an easy
transition from the quality to the quantity, from which
it would be soon found out whether you had a large
pile or not to foot up with. Now if you were wide
awake and endowed with much patient tact a quarrel
would be avoided, and all would end well with the
usual invitation to cement the passing friendship by
liquoring up.

As we were nearing Sandy Hook, and the sea calmed
down, we were enabled to carry up our little sufferer
and place her flat on a mattress on the deck and give
her a sun bath which seemed to revive her much, and
the knowledge that her dear native land was in sight
still more so. With our auxiliary screw we did not
get on very fast, and we were not warped up to the
quay till near midnight ; it was a dark night, and no
one was allowed to go ashore before the mails were
delivered, and these were not to be disturbed till
the morning, and so we betook ourselves to our berths
to sleep the rest of the thankful in heart, for I don't
think there was a soul on board but who was most
grateful to a kind Providence for preserving us and
the vessel from foundering in the bottomless deep.
It was a most boisterous trial trip, though perhaps

not a prolonged one for those days of comparative slow steaming. I for one awoke refreshed the next day, though the heat and smells were anything but agreeable. I was anticipating a pleasant ramble in the world-renowned Broadway and its side avenues of huge mansions, but when I presented myself on deck I saw there was an unusual commotion among the officers of the ship with the captain in their midst, holding a most vociferous harangue with two or three Yankee officials : and on coming to inquire into this turmoil I found that a dead negro had been placed in a boat alongside our vessel during the night, and no one was allowed to disembark till an inquest had been held on the body. Of course the verdict of the jury was in our favour, for it was readily proved that no one on our ship had anything whatever to do with causing the death of the black body, and it was made very clearly apparent by what came out at the inquiry that the disgusting annoyance originated in an opposition set up by the American marine to English interference with their shipping trade. A sort of revenge and spite in fact, which we had to put up with as an instance of their narrowmindedness in those illiberal days. Afterwards we were left at peace, and I roamed over the busy and money-making city, teeming with a restless excitable people whose one sole aim and object in life seemed to be business, eternal business, for which they have the keenest eye, the men leaving to their womenkind the acquisition of all the refinements of art and literature, and to whom they instinctively turn for all the current information whether social, political, national, or European, and all other topics not directly connected with trade which engrosses all their attention. Thus the American women took a high position at that period, especially the young girls of the family, who were very liberally educated and indulged in foreign travel, and who acted quite the queen in their mother's drawing-room. These were they who were thoroughly well posted up in all passing events at home and abroad, and thus did away with the necessity of any reading or study by their fathers, who cared for little beyond the limits of business transactions in which they were absorbed morning, noon, and night. Here I think lies the explanation why the young American ladies are such charming society in these days and so much sought after by English noblemen and other men of position and brains, though, I dare say, many of them being linked to a pile of dollars have this to thank perhaps for playing no secondary part in the drama of life!

I had a few letters of introduction to some good families who treated me with marked hospitality, and I was surprised at the extreme abstinence at the dinner table, no wine or spirits were present, and I understood the young ladies never took anything of the kind, hence I could easily understand why they had such beautiful complexions.

The atmosphere was, at this time, most oppressive, the thermometer registering on the shady side of Broadway 105° F., and as my time was limited I had to be about in it a good deal. The smells near the quays were very offensive, and I should say that the air was fully charged with microbes, at least there were more than I could contend against, and I was knocked down suddenly with an acute attack of dysentery, which so prostrated me that I could not rise from bed, and no remedies seemed to have any effect in checking it ; and getting alarmed I ventured on an heroic dose of chloroform, which sent me into a sleep lasting off and on for twenty-four hours, and when I came to my senses again the complaint had gone and did not return. I was so bad for a time that I had given up all hopes of ever seeing dear old England again, hence I was only too glad to be well enough to return home in the same vessel which took me out, besides I felt quite an attachment to our good captain, who was not only very skilful, but was a man of strong religious senti-ments, and who preserved an unspotted character among his officers and crew. His Sundays at sea when he conducted his own services was a sight to see. Every man who could be spared was regularly cleaned up and present, and the whole day was kept as sacred as possible, most refreshing to those who had any serious feelings at all.

Nothing worthy of note supervened on the passage home, and the sensation of seeing again the shores of our dear country can only be realised by those who have been away from them for the first time and returned in safety.

CHAPTER VII.

I HAVE now arrived at a very important epoch, not only in my life, but in the history of Europe also. War was declared in this year of grace 1854 against Russia by England and France, who joined their forces to those of Turkey who had been fighting on the Danube single-handed against the great Autocrat of the North, and subsequently Italy joined the Allies with some thirteen thousand of her picked troops. The origin of this bloody war may be very briefly described. The Greeks disputed the exclusive rights of the French to twelve "Holy Places"—the four principal of which were the great Cupola of the Holy Sepulchre, the Tomb of the Virgin, the great church at Bethlehem, and part of the Garden of Gethsemane. The French Government instituted a commission of inquiry into the dispute, and the verdict of this commission was in favour of the French Catholics, who considered their claim established because the Sultan had specially confirmed their rights by a firman, and here probably the row would have ended if the Emperor of Russia had not interfered, and in a very despotic manner sent the Sultan an autograph letter claiming for the Greeks all their

ancient privileges in Jerusalem, and condemning the
Turkish ministry for countenancing the pretensions
of the French Catholic party. The Sultan got
alarmed, and fearing to offend his great domineering
neighbour, dismissed the " mixed " Commission, and
got a new one formed composed of Turks only. While
this commission was sitting the Emperor Nicholas
proposed to Louis Napoleon that they should settle
this question themselves, leaving the Sultan to carry
out their wishes only. To this request Napoleon
returned a decided negative. Well, the Turkish
Commission sent in their report proposing that the
great Cupola should be common property, and that
the French Catholics should have access to the
Tomb of the Virgin, and a key to the church at
Bethlehem. This decision the French accepted under
protest, but Nicholas demanded that the firman
should be published throughout the Sultan's domin-
ions, which gave great offence to the French, who
demanded the recall of the firman unless it was
promulgated with as little publicity as possible. On,
however, the Turkish official in charge of the document arriving at Jerusalem, the Greeks clamoured for
a public reading of the firman with the usual pomp
and parade, and on receiving further instructions, the
document was read publicly. Then arose the question
whether the French Catholics should have a key to a
side door or enter by the great portal of the Church of
the Holy Sepulchre, which the Latins could not but
feel to be humiliating. Nicholas was not the man to
brook resistance to his wishes, so he sent to Constantinople Menschikoff as a special ambassador with

specific demands, and he acted so insolently towards the Sultan that he claimed a Russian protectorate over the whole of the Greek subjects of the Ottoman Empire, who constituted four-fifths of the entire nation, so that from one squabble to another matters assumed such a pitch that England, France, Austria, and Prussia, felt compelled to interfere, especially when Nicholas ordered an Army Corps to take possession of Moldavia and Wallachia as "material guarantees." The four Powers tried hard to make a treaty of peace at Vienna, which, however, proved a nullity, for the Turk would not concede an inch, and declared war on the 5th of October, 1853, sending their celebrated general, Omar Pasha, with 120,000 troops to defend the Danube against the passage of the Russians, thus showing how—

"From very small beginnings sad issues did arise."

It was an illustration of the old fable of the wolf and the lamb, or rather the Bear and the Lamb, which wanted an excuse, however flimsy, to attack an innocent victim, and then overrun and annex its country. The great Northern Bear had been for a long time casting longing eyes on the possessions of the "Sick Man," and yearned to fulfil the prophecies of Peter the Great, that sooner or later Russia would be master at Constantinople. Active fighting had been going on at Shoomla on the Danube during the winter of 1853-4, the Turks displaying their usual courage behind their breastworks, and keeping in check the attacks of their powerful foe—the weak against the mighty—thus rousing the indignation and

sympathies of the nations of Europe, in the expression
of which feeling the Englishman was most demonstrative, hence our Queen came forward on the 27th of
March, 1854, and announced to both Houses of
Parliament, "that she felt bound to afford active
assistance to her ally the Sultan against unprovoked
aggression," and war was declared against Russia by
the English. The Emperor Napoleon about the same
time made a similar announcement, and the fleets of
both nations anchored in Besika Bay at the entrance
to the Dardenelles—part of our flotilla going to block
the ports of the Baltic. The English and French land
forces were on a large scale, and considering that we
had been at peace for forty years, our contingent was
magnificent, and to all appearances well appointed.
The command was given to Lord Raglan, a Peninsular
officer, and a pupil of the "Iron Duke," who was sup-
ported by such bravos as Sir Colin Campbell and Sir
George Cathcart. The war was a popular one, the
people being exasperated beyond measure by the publi-
cation of the remarkable "Secret Correspondence," in
which Nicholas proposed that the Turkish Empire
should be partitioned off—England and Russia to take
a division. And the anger of the public was not
lessened when they heard that the same proposition
had been made to Louis Napoleon, in which bargain
England was carefully left out in the cold. Hence
the departure of our troops was hailed with the
greatest enthusiasm, English and French standing
side by side, forgetting completely their old hereditary
feud. Parliament suspended its hostilities, and the
" opposition " its grievances when its members heard

that the Czar Nicholas had tried to bribe English statesmen, in order to get them to conform to his wishes. They unanimously denounced this Russian aggression as dead against European freedom and civilisation. Little Lord Russell, a scion of an old historic house of liberty, quite surpassed himself with heroic grandeur when he took up the challenge so insolently given, and cried, "God defend the right!" which Englishmen of all ranks echoed most heartily.

Having now finished a description of how this vexatious and bloody war originated, I will devote several separate chapters to a rehearsal of the manner in which it personally affected my life.

CHAPTER VIII.

HAVING obtained letters of introduction from Sir Andrew Smith, Director-General of the Army Medical Department to Sir John Hall, Chief of the Medical Staff in the Crimea, I took passage with the 46th Regiment on the unfortunate steamer *Prince*, a beautiful new transport, this being her voyage out for the first time. We had a splendid time of it till we reached the Morea, when having to change our course for the north we encountered a regular mistral, against which our good ship could make no headway, as she had only a small auxiliary screw power, so we had to lay to till the morning. The sea ran mountains high during the night, and our deck getting washed with some heavy seas, the stabling, with eleven chargers on board, got shaken from its fastenings, and the horses getting frightened, began to plunge and tumble about. The colonel's horse, a valuable thoroughbred, fell and began kicking the others, to save which the colonel himself cut the animal's throat and had him hauled overboard. We all thought this a plucky thing to do, especially at night time, with the ship rolling and tossing in a downpour of rain. The next day it calmed down somewhat, and we were able to

14

proceed slowly through the lovely Greek islands, passed Athens, and then we were compelled to pull up again in a bay off the island Negropont. From the deck we could plainly see the natives ploughing with the same primitive machine described by Virgil, and drawn by an unequal yoke, an ox and an ass. The head wind moderating we were enabled to steam northward once more, and soon found ourselves passing up the Dardenelles, which Byron swam across, though the current is very strong in its centre. Then came our passage through the sea of Marmora, with its picturesque Prince's Islands, and our entrance into the Bosphorus at seven in the morning, when we beheld one of the most glorious sights in the universe—surpassing anything the imagination of the most lively mind could picture to itself, namely, a brilliant morning sun shining upon Constantinople with its gilded minarets, and many white palaces rising one above another, interspersed with domes, and gardens, and cemeteries, with the everlasting cypress peeping out everywhere. We were all on deck enjoying this brilliant and never-to-be-forgotten scene, which to us, haling from sunless England, looked like fairyland! We cast anchor off Scutari, and I disembarked to get orders, and these were to proceed to the Crimea; but as I was returning to our steamer, the channel had taken on a rough aspect, and the boat could not proceed but slowly, and I could not catch up the *Prince*, which, having a patent windlass, weighed anchor quickly, and steamed away without me, to my no little chagrin. I had no idea what the future would bring forth, for this very circumstance saved my life, because had I remained on board I should most likely have gone down with the vessel when she foundered in the bay of Balaclava on the 14th of November, when she and seventeen other craft were wrecked. The *Prince* had on board a most valuable cargo of warm winter clothing and a fresh supply of electric apparatus. The captain, crew, and some military not yet landed, were drowned, only six were saved out of 150, and these were drawn up the cliffs with cords. After this digression I will hark back to Scutari, where I experienced my first great shock arising from the horrors of war. While I was conversing with the medical superintendent, who should come in but Dr. F——, with a very distressed face, saying that he had just arrived with a large cargo of wounded from the Crimea; that in the Black Sea they had encountered a fearful gale, and that for three days it was impossible to dress a third of the cases, and that several were delirious with pain and nerve shock. There were about 150 wounded on board, many having died on the rough passage down. In his dilemma he asked the chief for the assistance of two or three surgeons to help him to get this shipload of misery ashore, then to dress them and to operate, as several limbs required to be amputated. To this modest request the perplexed superintendent replied, " I am sorry to say that I cannot afford to give you the aid you ask for, we are so wofully short-handed ; " but pointing to me he said : " Here is an experienced hand just out from a home hospital, who will, I dare say, be of great help to you." Then Dr. F—— and I left the office and were soon hard at work till our backs

ached again with stooping and carrying and endea-
vouring somewhat to relieve this mangled mass of
humanity. The wounds, not having been dressed for
so long, were in a most horrible state, and the foul
odours were almost unbearable, even to one accustomed to such. A few more shiploads of like horrors
followed, and then the outcome of the wounded from
the three battlefields of Alma, Balaclava, and Inkerman, were duly landed and placed in comparatively
comfortable quarters in the two huge hospitals at Scutari and the one on the Bosphorus, while the Russian
prisoners were accommodated in a hospital at Pera.
The two Scutari buildings were of immense size, and
were originally intended to hide away 20,000 Turkish
troops to suppress instantly any rebellion among the
Sultan's subjects in Constantinople. The corridors
were very lofty and wide and well lighted, and they
made admirable wards for the sick and wounded,
which numbered at this particular time 4,600, including the Russian prisoners. Mr. Bracebridge took
the trouble to measure the flooring on which they
were billeted, and found that it extended nearly four
miles !

Miss Nightingale arrived out from England the beginning of November, bringing with her about twenty-
four experienced nurses of her own selection, and they
were indeed of great service in dressing and attending
the wounded, and seeing that they were properly supplied with medical comforts. Miss Nightingale, on her
own responsibility, and in defiance of all red-tapeism,
ordered over from Constantinople bazaars hundreds
of mattresses for the poor fellows to lie upon. And

though she was sorely distressed to find that she
could not get sufficient laundry work done to give
such a crowd of sick and disabled men even one clean
shirt a week, she might well look puzzled when the
medical chief asked her where she thought four
thousand shirts could be washed—even supposing
the men had a change of flannels, which scores had
not, and many were torn, and would go to pieces if
exposed to rough handling. Notwithstanding such
drawbacks as these, I soon perceived that she and her
aids had produced a great and beneficent reform
before I left for the Crimea, which I did in about
six weeks, after having shared actively in scenes of
distress, disease, and bloodshed, such as it is impossible to depict with pen or pencil, but which Lord
Panmure did me the great honour of appreciating by
rewarding me with an extra six months' pay amount-
ing to £230. There was a great outcry sent home
with respect to the dearth of medical attendants, and
then the authorities sent out to Scutari a lot of raw
young surgeons, who were of little use in severe cases,
and worried one's life out with questions as what was
to be done here and what there, they would not take
any responsibility on their inexperienced shoulders,
and were not of much more use than Miss Nightingale's skilled nurses, but it proved to them an excellent
school of instruction. On my arrival in the Crimea I
went off to head-quarters to present my letters of
introduction to Sir John Hall, the head of the Medical
Department, who received me most kindly, and
arranged for me to take up my quarters at the Balaclava Hospital, formerly a large Russian Government

school, which was filled to repletion with six hundred patients, suffering principally from rheumatism and dysentery, arising from exposure in the trenches, and want of proper nourishment. Here, also, the medical staff were very short-handed, and I sadly overworked. Besides this heavy duty, I was asked to act as a temporary sanitary officer, and while thus engaged I had to condemn a shipload of Turkish loaves of black bread which the Sultan had sent up as a present to our troops, but which had become fermented and mildewed in the hold, and thus rendered unfit for human food, hence I had to condemn this life-giving cargo, and it was ordered out of harm's way by being thrown overboard into the Black Sea. They were so long on the passage, thanks to the sluggish Turk, and on our part we were slow to order the loaves (3,200) out and get them distributed, red-tapery in the shape of check and counter-check being so dilatory. Our regulations for times of peace were not in keeping with the rapid demands of active warfare. Again, I was told off to attend any sick ladies who might arrive in the harbour, and thus I was brought into contact with Miss Nightingale once more, who would come up to see how the nursing was going on in the Crimea. Before she could return to Scutari she was attacked with camp fever, and laid up in one of the transports. For her recovery she relied entirely on good nursing and nourishment, and objected all through her attack to take either stimulants or medicines. When she recovered she was a mere wreck of her former self, and how to get her back to Scutari was the difficulty, as she was a very bad sailor; so I petitioned Lord

Dudley for the loan of his yacht, which was lying idle
in the harbour. He received me very graciously, but
thought my application rather an astounding one.
Miss Nightingale was now however one of the cele-
brities of the position, and his lordship yielded with a
good grace, and not only that, but said the doctor
attached to the steamer should accompany her on the
voyage, which was a great boon, considering we were
so shorthanded. Though her cabin was most luxuriously fitted up with every possible convenience, and
the berth was slung by elastic webbing to the roof-
floor and sides, and thus every lurch was provided for,
she had a dreadful passage, and the doctor had great
difficulty in keeping life in her, but, God be thanked,
she was spared to do much good work afterwards.
How well the following lines apply to her courageous
deeds !

> " Oh woman, thou art not the weakly thing some
> Would deem thee, light and wavering,
> Thine is no vulgar strength, thou canst not wield
> The warrior's weapon in the battle-field,
> Thou canst do more than this, it is thine to
> Breathe, without a sense of fear,
> The sick room close and tainted atmosphere."

Though many years have elapsed since that memor-
able occasion, the warmth of my gratitude has never
cooled down when I call to mind the great kindness I
received from that inestimable and self-sacrificing
lady, when I in my turn was laid low with Asiatic
cholera in the Crimea. She supplied me with a
continuous relay of experienced nurses, who gave me
their invaluable services both night and day, and

carried me safely through one of the most fatal of scourges, in which ordinary remedies are of no avail, but close attention to minutiæ is of the utmost importance.

In January, February, and March, 1855, the physical strain on our troops began to show itself in a very marked manner; what with twenty-four hours at a stretch in the cold damp trenches without a wink of sleep, stagnating in the snow and sludge with holes in their boots and similar ventilation in their trousers, with food consisting of too much salt junk and pork, biscuits rather mildewy, with green coffee which few could roast before it burnt a hole in their tins, which rendered them useless for drinking, and though last not least of the evils, too much rum taken on the empty stomach and excited brains. It is no wonder they succumbed to rheumatism, diarrhœa, and dysentery, which filled the hospital marquees in front, from whence they were sent down in batches in snow or sunshine to board ship, for anything was better than keeping them in the atmosphere of these canvas charnel lodgings, the air of which was simply abominable and death-giving. The men thus sent away in the four winter months *hors de combat* were ten thousand in number, the cream of our small army, and the place of these old-seasoned soldiers was taken by raw young recruits from home. It was not till February that tinned milk and arrowroot, and suchlike medical necessaries, came out in sufficient quantity to treat these cases properly, for medicines were of no use whatever since the patients were simply dying of starvation. Scurvy was rife from the excess

of salt food, and it was impossible to get vegetables
at any price. I remember paying myself £2 for a
small sack of potatoes given to me as a favour by the
captain of a ship I knew, but before I could get them
hidden away in my diggings, an army chaplain met
me and implored, as I valued his life, that I would
allow him to have half, and being an Irishman, his
eloquence prevailed, and with many blessings on my
head, walked off with many meals of my murphies!

At this time such were the difficulties of keeping
body and soul together, and preventing the encroach-
ments of disease among officers and men alike, that
to constant inquiries as to what they could do for the
best, my reply became a stereotyped one, namely,
"Avoid the tendency to death," and this saying
became a camp expression among the troops. Such
is the hardening influence of the horrors of active
warfare on man's heart, that the selfish remark often
heard at home, "Every one for himself, and God for
us all," would not be inappropriate under such dire
circumstances in which heavenly aspirations seem out
of place, because man's nature is so thoroughly out of
joint! To give an instance of the heartlessness and
want of feeling of even the men towards their officers I
may mention, that a man who had been shot through
the chest had, wonderfully to say, recovered, and I
gave him light work to do by making him an orderly
nurse at the hospital. A very distinguished Italian
general was at that time under my care, and I was
very anxious to save him if possible; and one night I
could not sleep thinking of him, so I got up at 2 a.m.
to see how he was progressing, when to my horror

and disgust I found the poor fellow stretched dead on the floor, and the orderly in the bed with his clothes and boots on, drunk with the port wine which he ought to have given to his patient. With this harrowing incident I shall pass on to another chapter.

CHAPTER IX.

OUR troops were employed in January, February, and March, in hauling up to the batteries in the front, a distance of six miles, shot and shell, preparatory to another, the second great bombardment. This six miles had no regular road, but a beaten track of loose stones and deep ruts, filled with a sticky sort of compound resembling a mixture of clay and glue which sucked off the horses' shoes with a thud, and had no mercy on the soles and heels of the ill-fitting boots of the men, which were a mile too large, so that it was not an unusual thing to meet a fellow with his soles facing inwards. The drudgery and discomfort, and the wear and tear both for man and beast in the slow process of getting up this ammunition to the front was inconceivably painful to witness day by day. Picture to yourself, fair reader, if you can, a long file of dirty-faced beings with unkempt hair, wearing a close-fitting cap with flaps over the ears to keep out the intense cold, wearing a cat's-skin mufti coat of faded material, and showing no uniform except a pair of patched trousers with the red stripe hardly visible, and walking in a slouching manner like a country bumpkin at home; and you have then the appearance of those engaged in this miserable sickening occupation. What a transformation from the smart and trim aspect of the soldier on parade in Hyde Park. The servant girls in Belgravia would turn up there noses at such unlovable and wretched-looking creatures. Just stop these gallant fighters and ask them what they now think of the pomp and glory and circumstance of war, such as the recruiting sergeant dinned into their ears when enlisting ; methinks they would have scorned the proffered shilling with a sneer. If simple Tommy Atkins had been taught Latin, he would have said, " No, no : *Experientia docet.*"

The time at last arrived when it was considered that sufficient ammunition of shot and shell had been stowed away in the magazines to serve the three hundred cannon which were to deal destruction to the devoted town. On the 9th of April, 1855, therefore, Lord Raglan gave orders to open fire. The morning opened with a grey mist, and with a wretched outlook, and one could not see fifty yards in front. Notwithstanding this unsuitable weather, the mandate had gone forth the night before, and the bombardment commenced with a roar of noise never to be forgotten, and the shots were sent haphazard and without aim into empty space, and the ammunition expended recklessly, regardless of the immense labour it took to haul it up. This useless firing went on for two or three hours, till the order to " cease firing " was sent from headquarters. And when the atmosphere cleared up we could not see that we had done much damage. I had obtained a pass to the front from our Quartermaster-General, expecting that there

.would be a great carnage, and many wounded to
attend to, and few to do it; but when I got to the
trenches I found that the wiser Russians had reserved
their fire, and had not replied to our early morning
salute till the atmosphere had cleared and they could
see their enemy and his batteries; hence there were
no more than the usual amount of casualties. But I
was rather horrified at seeing the headless body of an
officer carried by me on a stretcher, whom I had
previously known as a splendid athlete, upwards of six
feet high. This is the way he was killed: he and
two other shorter comrades were standing up, chatting
away and lighting each other's cigars, when a round
shot came over the parapet and took my friend's head
clear off, being the taller one. Now had he taken the
precaution of sitting down in the trench, this sad
accident would not have happened. Many a fine
fellow lost his life by thus incautiously exposing himself. In the following month of May took place a
most desperate series of sorties on the French left—
the scene of these bloody combats being in front of the
central bastion, a space of about six square acres, in-
closing a cemetery with a church in it, and surrounded
by a wall which was loopholed for musketry. These
sorties were obstinately persisted in for three nights,
and may well be regarded as regular battles, for there
were thousands of Russians and French engaged on
each side. The onslaught began by several battalions
of the enemy taking the French by surprise, by a
vigorous rush into the two front parallels, which they
actually succeeded in getting into, when a most
murderous hand-to-hand encounter occurred for the

mastery, and these two trenches became piled up with
the dead and the dying. A report soon reached the
French reserve forces, distanced about a mile off, ten
thousand of whom came up at the double to succour
their overpowered comrades, with the result that
these sprightly fellows, with their usual dash, soon
turned out the Russians, and not only out of the
approaches, but pluckily followed them over the
parapet into the open ground, honeycombed with
rifle-pits, surrounding the cemetery, where, "war to
the knife," the most bloody scenes took place, neither
party budging a yard. On this small area and in the
cemetery itself, "no longer God's acre," now the
devil's, a regular series of hard battles were fought
between these two sturdy combatants, with their
small arms only.

Hearing that the carnage on both sides was
something awful, and exceeding that which had as
yet occurred during the war, I and a friend obtained
a pass from the French commandant, and one of
his sergeants as our guide, in order to get safely to
the seat of the struggle and to be present at the
burying party. When we ascended the front breastwork and looked down upon this field in such a
circumscribed space, the sight that met our eyes
was something ghastly in the extreme. The heaps
of the dead lay thick and high, not only on the open
grass sward but between the stone crosses in the
peaceful-looking cemetery. Even to me, now an old
hand, this small plateau, as an evidence of the
fierce and sanguinary contest between two brave
peoples, was blood-curdling. To look down placidly

on human forms divine, without heads, legs and
arms torn asunder ; bowels protruding ; brains oozing
through skulls shattered by musket shots ; faces
blackened by powder and besmeared by blood
issuing from mouth, nose, and ears ; human heads
mixed up indiscriminately with cannon balls ; arms
in one place, legs in another—and grim death everywhere ! These commingling with broken swords and
rifles, and remnants of tattered uniforms, presented
a spectacle which some would deem unfit for publica-
tion, but which is here given, though as a shadow
of the reality, as a warning to those in authority,
sitting at their ease at home, not to make war till
every other possible means has been exhausted to
arbitrate for peace ! In contrast to this painful outlook, was such as one would expect to see among a
lot of clubmen in Rotten Row. The French and
Russian officers met in the most friendly and non-
chalant manner, as if a burying party of thousands
was a thing of every-day occurrence. They smilingly
exchanged cigars and drank each other's health
out of their spirit flasks, making witty remarks on
the funny aspect of the mangled dead ! Such is
the hardening effect of actual warfare in deadening
the conscience of man, and brutalising his better
nature. To mix with this crowd of well-educated,
and at other times refined men, one might have
exclaimed, " How these Christians love one another!"
but such an impression soon vanishes when the bugle
recalled the several parties behind their breastworks
and the firing commenced as fiercely as ever, and I
and my friend were glad to get away in safety ; but

in turning the angle of the first approach, which was
in the line of the fire, we drew back hesitatingly,
when the sergeant, seeing us linger, said, " Come
along, there is no danger ; " and the words were
hardly out of his mouth when three balls struck the
bank with an ominous thud, which would have taken
us in the shoulder if we had unthinkingly followed
the advice of our impulsive guide. Thank God, we
escaped a wounding which might, or might not, have
been fatal. Our past experience was of some avail
to us on this occasion.

About this time a little incident occurred. A
small streak of silver edging to the dark cloud
of horrors which had overshadowed us so long,
but brought to the fore the kindly benevolent
character of the commander-in-chief of the English
army. In describing this circumstance to various
groups of ladies in my travels round the world, I
have styled it as " the Baby Incident." It came to
pass in this way: A mandate went forth to the
effect that a certain suburb of Sebastopol was to
have a raid made upon it by a select body of our
men ; the attack to take place at midday, when the
enemy were at dinner. The surprise was so complete, and the rush so sudden, that the venture
turned out a perfect success. On entering the
cottages they found that the occupants had
skedaddled, leaving their dinners untouched on the
tables, the canaries in their cages, and various
articles of domestic use littered about, but in one
cottage was left behind, in the heedless flight, a
child about six months old, clothed, and asleep in

its cradle, wrapped in innocent and blissful ignorance
of its future. An officer took up the little one in his
arms and carried her out as a prisoner of war. On
reporting the success of the raid to headquarters and
the capture of the little mite, the question was very
naturally asked what was to be done with this
helpless prisoner ? The reply came back from Lord
Raglan ordering a flag of truce to be sent out the
next morning, which was responded to, and when
the staff-officers met on the neutral ground to have
a parley, they were moved to laughter at the novel
procedure over so trifling a matter as that of the
well-being of a little child, but they politely consented to the demands of our chief, namely, that the
mother of the child should be sought for. Hence
a careful search was made for the woman, but in
vain; no mother was forthcoming to acknowledge
her lost babe. Such is war. On the aides-de-camp
bringing this fact to the knowledge of his lordship,
the next question was what in the world could be
done with this little mite of humanity? And here
cropped up the benevolent thoughtfulness of good
Lord Raglan. "Go," said he, "and make inquiries
among the women in the camp, and find out if there
be any nursing mothers who would be willing to take
charge of an enemy's child." The messenger returned and stated that he had fortunately discovered
that the wife of one of the men of the rifle brigade
had a baby a few weeks old, and was willing to
undertake double duty—and thus relieved us from a
perplexing dilemma.

After three weeks had elapsed, the staff at head-

quarters were startled one morning by Lord Raglan
asking them if they had heard anything lately of
this now remarkable child, but the incident had
vanished clean from their memories, not so with
Raglan the Good. " I wish," said he, " one of you
would go down and see how the mother and her
twins are getting on." The reply received was to
the effect that the two children were thriving
admirably well, but that the poor woman herself
looked weak and thoroughly washed out. " Oh,
indeed," said his lordship ; then inquired how many
cows there were, and on being told that they were
all dry except one, " Then," continued our self-
denying chief, " send down a bottle of milk to that
woman every morning," a requisition which struck
them with dismay, as they would have in that case
but a scanty supply for their teas. I need hardly
say that after this notice the *protégé* of his lordship
became quite popular, and might have been styled,
not a *fille du regiment* merely, but a *fille de l'armie*,
for every fellow in the vicinity of the woman's tent
took to nursing with singular delight, in fact, there
was quite a *furor* as to who should have the honour
of caressing the little enemy. Then an army chaplain took her in hand and christened her Alma, and
so renowned had she become at the end of the war
that the Queen adopted her and gave her a liberal
education, suitable for the position of a governess,
which post she took up in a family going out to the
Cape, where she in time was married very well to a
German, who had been one of our mercenary legion,
and had, among others, an allotment of land given

to him instead of money, and I believe this German
colony did prosper well eventually. And here we
will take leave of our dear little Alma.

I may here relate another anecdote in connection
with our worthy chief, who was one of the coolest
men under fire that ever wore the Queen's uniform.
His figure on horseback was well known throughout
the camp. Dressed in a plain frock coat, with one
sleeveless arm, and wearing a forage cap, he was
riding down to see how the batteries were progressing, especially the one on Inkerman ridge,
which was such a fearfully contested point at the
celebrated battle bearing that name.

One morning, as he was going down as usual, he
met an artillery sergeant on his way to the rear,
after a night's watch. Just as the man was about
to salute his commander, a round shot came over
and knocked the busby off his head, and passed
over the stern of his lordship's horse, but the
sergeant, unmoved, coolly completed his salute, as if
his life had been in no danger whatever. Lord Raglan
was so struck with the man's wonderful presence of
mind under such trying circumstances, exclaimed,
" Well, my man, that was indeed a narrow miss ; "
and the sergeant, with lively promptitude, replied,
" Yes, my lord, it was ; but a miss is as good as a mile."
And so they parted, but our chief was not the man
to forget such a splendid and valuable gift even in
an uncommissioned officer. Hence we were not
surprised to hear that the lucky fellow had been
promoted to a commission in the service. Speaking
of promotions, some very singular ones took place

from the ranks after Inkerman. I was acquainted with a Captain B——, a gentlemanly fellow, who was born in his regiment, became first a drummer-boy, then gradually ascended the scale till he rose to be a colour-sergeant, in which position he entered the battle of Inkerman, where every officer in his company was killed, and he brought the remainder of his men out as their senior officer, and was subsequently promoted to be a lieutenant and captain in the same *Gazette* and in his old regiment.

I will now rest on my oars awhile, as my next chapter will be a heavy one, as it reveals my doings with the Italian contingent.

CHAPTER X.

When the Italian contingent joined us in the spring of 1855, it was brought out in English transports under a pecuniary arrangement with our Government, which guaranteed also to provision them for some time after their arrival; but in consequence of our own defective commissariat we could not meet our engagement so to do in anything like a satisfactory manner. What we wanted so badly ourselves we could not give to them, however much we might sympathise with those new-comers. The Italian troops of all arms of the service numbered about 15,000 all told. They first of all encamped themselves in an unhealthy part of Balaclava valley, and what with this mistake and the short commons we could spare to them, Asiatic cholera attacked these splendid picked men, the very cream of the Italian army, a body of magnificent athletes, but grand physical development was no barrier to the insidious inroads of this black plague—the very scourge of scourges, the effects of which drew tears of agony from their brave and sorrowing general. In this sad and distressing plight La Marmora appealed to Lord Raglan for some experienced English officers to help

him out of his dilemma. Hence it came to pass that
I was selected to aid them in their sanitary and
medical organisation, and a commissariat officer, of
considerable experience and aptitude, was sent to do
all he could with the limited means then at his disposal. Notwithstanding the improvement in their
position and supplies better regulated, cholera of the
worst possible Asiatic type attacked them, and continued to baffle all our efforts to check its ravages. A
man, for instance, would be, to all appearance, in
perfect health at breakfast time, and afterwards be
struck down, and in a few hours of awful agony would
be dead by the evening, and buried before the morning dawned in solemn silence and secrecy, in order to
prevent the knowledge reaching the ears of his comrades and causing depression of mind, a state of
feeling certain to invite an attack. Oh! it was indeed
a tearful and heartrending sight to behold a long file
of these splendid fellows sown up in their blankets,
the soldier's shroud, carried off to an ignominious
trench to be buried side by side, packed away like
herrings in a barrel, then a few inches of soil thrown
over them till the next lot came in unwept over by any
bereaved mother or sister, *sic transit gloria mundi*.

Thus were disposed of thirteen thousand men of all
ranks from the general to the private in about six
weeks. Among the many brave commanders who
were lost to the Italian army at this time, none was
more lamented than the intrepid, stern-looking
Alessandro della Marmora, whose jaw had been frac-
tured during the war of 1849, and who was brother to
Alphonso the chief. Alessandro had organised the

rifles (Bersaglieri), renowned for their quickness, precision, and powers of endurance, and these fine military qualities he soon began to put to the test in the Crimea by making a reconnaisance to the north side of Sebastopol in order to ascertain the exact strength of the enemy's forces in that direction. Four days' provisions were dealt out to the men and this trying expedition took place with a satisfactory result. They all returned well and in good spirits considering the hardships they had undergone — except their plucky leader who was attacked with acute dysentery which he treated at first with indifference, insisting on marching on foot with the rest of his men till he fainted away from exhaustion ; then they lifted him on to a horse, the only one with them when he swooned again, then they were obliged to resort to a stretcher, on which he was brought back much to his great chagrin, for he had boasted that he could outmarch any man in the army. On arriving at his hut I received a telegram from Sir John Hall ordering my immediate attendance at his side. Though he was kept alive for three days, the case was hopeless from the beginning, and he gradually sank from loss of blood, and died in my arms at two o'clock one night ; and when I went up to inform his brother of the death he wept over this favourite leader like a child, and his men mourned for him as a friend as well as a general. He had married an English lady, and the frequent muttering of her christian name in his sleep was rather trying to one's feelings reminding me of home. He had a heavy, twisted, long moustache like his king's, which I had cut off and sent to the widow with his Bible; for, wonderful to relate, a large number of Bibles in the Italian language had been given by one of our colporteurs to the troops, and they used to sit round the camp fires when one would read to others who could not the pathetic tales of mercy, forbearance, and love in the grand old Book. Their Roman Catholic chaplains were furious and ordered the men to deliver them up, but they one and all refused point blank to do anything of the kind, and even their officers' commands fared no better, and in fear of a mutiny the subject was allowed to drop and each knapsack contained the precious jewel to the end of the campaign, and how far this wonderful influence had to do with furthering the completion of Italian unity subsequently it is not for me to say, at any rate *their* first battle for *religious* liberty commenced in the Crimea.

On leaving poor La Marmora late one dark night I met a couple of French Zouaves with two horses in tow. I could just see clearly enough to be satisfied that all was not right, for I had heard of their tricks of stealing stray horses, killing them and then cutting steaks out of their loins; so I challenged them, and they pretended not to understand French, mumbling some gibberish between themselves, but when I threatened to summon the Provost-Marshal, they quietly yielded up the animals with a grumble. When I took them to La Marmora's where I got a light I then found one of the horses belonged to an English battery, and so I took him at once within its proper boundary much to the relief of the sentinel on duty, who said he had broken his tether and jumped over the breastwork. The other was a fine racer-looking fellow, a bright chestnut with white stockings, having a smart head collar on, not English or French I knew, so I took him home to my stable, and advertised him in the *Hue and Cry* at headquarters, but only one subaltern came to inquire, saying he had lost a fine brown charger with black points ; hearing this my groom allowed him to see the horse, which did not tally with his description in the least. He turned out a most useful companion till the end of the campaign when I sold him for £3, the Government allowing us £40 for each charger not taken to England, so I made a good thing of my friend the chestnut.

The strain upon my mental and physical powers was now very great indeed, inasmuch as all this worry with Italians was additional to my other ordinary duties at the Balaclava hospital where I had a lot of Italian officers under my care, and we were still deplorably deficient in medical aid of the right standard, hence just as the horrid plague was on the wane, having exhausted itself as it were, I fell ill myself with cholera, and placed on board ship in the harbour where I received close and unremitting attention from a regular relay of Miss Nightingale's nurses, and with them and the kindness of my male friends of every class I was in danger of becoming quite a pet patient, and I fear a subject of no little envy to other sick officers on board, for I could boast of a whole cabin to myself with the exception of some huge rats which paid me a visit every night to quench their thirst in my water jug ; but I was too languid to heed such trifles, indeed I was so paralysed with pain

and weakness that I felt perfectly indifferent whether
I lived or died. I had sense enough left, however, to
remember how fatal this disease was to all those
patients who had drunk regularly their ration of spirit,
and more if they could get it, that I begged of my
attendants none should be given to me ; so I had my
way, contrary as it was to the prejudices in its favour
in those ignorant times. So I was nursed instead of
physicked through the fiery ordeal, and I was one of
the very few who ever recovered. God, indeed, was
gracious and merciful, and permitted the tree to
remain for several years longer to bear its humble
fruit. When convalescing I was much cheered and
benefited by that good religious officer, Colonel L——,
who was on sick leave on the same vessel. On meeting some of the working staff after my recovery, they
were rather surprised to see me on my legs again ;
exclaiming : " Well, old fellow, we prophesied that you
would kill yourself sooner or later, the pace was too
fast to last you know. For the future you had better
be guided by our wise motto." " And pray what may
that be ? " " Simply this : *Moderate your zeal and
draw your pay !* " " But how about your consciences ! "
I asked. " Oh, our consciences indeed, how can you
expect us to have any when the authorities at home
show so little ? " The reply was not amiss when one
recollects how the hearts of many men were then
boiling over with indignation at the cruel apathy and
neglect with which the troops were treated by the
English Government. Such is the low standard of
religious aspirations in times of actual warfare !

We have now arrived at the day in which the grand

assault was to be made on the Redan, the 18th of June, 1855. Not that we had the faintest hope of holding it, supposing it could be captured. No, the sacrifice of life was to be made for the purpose of diverting the attention of the enemy. The French were to attack the Malakoff the same day, and we, on our side, were to make the most hopeless of assaults, as our allies had not the remotest chance of succeeding, but were beaten back with the most awful slaughter, while our loss was proportionately great. The strength of the Redan was something prodigious. When I examined it after it was relinquished by the Russians, I found it to be a singular construction. Running the whole length of its earthworks was a subterranean gallery supplied with a plank platform for the soldiers to sleep upon, and in the floor were sunken ships' tanks to hold water, which were replenished every night by women; thus the enemy were in comparative comfort and safety too, while we were exposed in open trenches. We had the same kind of loose chalky ground to work in, and there was no reason why our engineers should not have constructed such underground shelters, but then we were not blessed with having such a skilled scientist as Todleben on our side! After peace was proclaimed General Luders and I became very friendly, and he told me, that when we were hammering away at their batteries and flattered ourselves that we had silenced them because they did not reply, the artillery-men retired for the time into these underground barracks till the firing ceased or we had exhausted our ammunition; and this was the case at the Malakoff as well as the Redan, thus very many lives were saved

from the bursting of shells. After the bombardment
of the 18th of June, I was very much struck with the
unusual number of wounds below the knee, and
Luders told me his men were ordered to fire low in
order to secure as many as possible of our fellows
being put *hors de combat*—not to kill outright, as these
wounded would be of no further use in that war, and
yet would be an enormous expense and worry to us by
crowding our hospitals and transports, thus acting,
as our enemy knew only too well, as a most obstruc-
tionable impedimenta on the field of battle.

In our hurry to reach the wounded three of us
thought we might venture to cross the open between
two of the approaches, but we had reckoned without
our host the lynx-eyed enemy ever on the alert, a
13-inch shell was sent at us, which came with its
usual whistling noise, describing an arc in the sky as
visible as a cricket ball. We fell immediately on our
faces, the safest position to take, and watched its
course. When it sank into the earth and burst up
with a tremendous noise, throwing its fragments with
stones and soil 200 feet into the air, it was a grand
sight, and we were not struck by the descending
pieces, wherein lies the great danger at such times :
but one portion of the shell did come so near that I
brought it home to remind me of another narrow
escape from death, and to convince me that a
merciful Providence was still guarding me.

Nothing during the summer months particularly
occurred except Lord Raglan's death, and, as far as I
was concerned, the despatching of the wounded down
to Scutari as soon as they were able to bear the

voyage, but the whole of the army were secretly
sapping up nearer and nearer to the Malakoff and
the Redan, especially the former which was now
400 yards in length and seemed impregnable. So
that when the 5th of September arrived the French
sappers could almost touch the base of abattis of this
most formidable earthwork bristling with cannon.
When the assault was made they had not far to run.
All was kept a profound secret till the morning of the
5th when a fierce cannonade from many hundreds of
guns was made upon the Malakoff, which ceased at
the dinner hour when the sprightly French took it by
surprise and a rush ; and a hand-to-hand fight with
any weapon went on for some time each side bringing
up their reserves till regular battles were fought for
this most important commanding point, which had
at its mercy the shipping, the forts, the Redan, and
the south side of Sebastopol with its churches and
mansions. The tricolour flag floating on the Malakoff
was to be the sign that the English were to assault
the Redan, which they proceeded to do, and failed as
before to hold it because our reserves did not back up
the assaulting column as they ought to have done.
It was the same mistake as was made on the 18th of
June. When the French secured a footing in the
Malakoff they filled up the trenches and turned the
works towards the enemy, but for three days the
Russians were employed in vacating the south side
and going over the harbour on a poontoon bridge to
the north side, blowing up their ships and forts and
magazines, making an infernal noise. They left their
large hospital with a thousand dead among the

wounded for us to take care of. By the ninth they had all gone clean away to the north side. And thus ended this portion of the siege after a most eventful year to ourselves and our allies who had most - laboriously excavated 70 miles of trenches, made 60 thousand fascines and gabions, and fired away 1,500,000 shot and shell. We will now rest awhile and then begin our second year with a fresh chapter.

CHAPTER XI.

At the commencement of the second winter's campaign there was a wonderful transformation from the wretched aspect of affairs which prevailed during our first winter. Some remarkable specimens of civil engineering works were brought to our aid. A railroad was made to the army divisions on the front from Balaclava, and the old roadway by its side was properly macadamized, so that the building of wooden huts and the transport of supplies went on merrily. During these operations the English navvies showed the lethargic Turks the right way to use the pick and the spade, and to trundle a wheelbarrow along a plank. Some very amusing scenes occurred at the expense of the sleepy Osmauli. But let us proceed. No one doubted but that we should have to pass another winter on the plateau before Sebastopol. The Russians after the fall of the south side had fortified themselves strongly on the north, erecting huge earthworks and batteries along the Mackenzie heights bristling with hundreds of cannon, which frowned down on the Tchernaya valley and its river, the dividing line between the two opposing armies, which stared at one another, showing their teeth like a couple of bull dogs but never firing a shot.

There was no doubt, at this particular time, that the Russians were in an awful predicament and yearning for the bare necessities of life. They had at least 200,000 to feed, and the provisioning of such a mass of mouths must have been difficult indeed and costly beyond calculation, inasmuch as the country in the war had become denuded of every blade of corn and all the draught animals had been sacrificed months ago by bringing down food and ammunition from the mainland of Russia; while we were receiving supplies comfortably by sea though at exorbitant prices. It is no wonder, then, that the Emperor of Russia when he paid his visit of encouragement to his troops in the Crimea, and saw for himself some of the horrors of war in the overpacked hospitals at Backsheserai, in October, 1855, became convinced that the best thing he could do was to sign a treaty of peace as soon as he could do it without humiliation. He could see that it was impossible his army could carry on the struggle much longer, without succumbing from sheer exhaustion. Soldiers like other men cannot fight without food in their stomachs. and how was this to be conveyed to them if they continued the suicidal process of killing for meat the draught bullocks as they came into camp, and then burnt the arabas for firewood, instead of sending them back for further supplies! The commissariat had requisitioned the farmers for miles and miles up the country till there were no more animals or arabas left to cultivate the soil. It was a crying shame, and men, women, and children must have died from famine if this cruel war had not been brought rapidly to a close in the spring of 1856. The Emperor, too, a man of peace, so different to his father, must have seen on his way down the barrenness of the land—its desolation, its misery, the half-starved looks of the peasantry, and the dead animals lying thick on the roadside, and other signs, enough to bring the tears to the eyes of many a more hard-hearted man than Alexander was. In contrast to all this deplorable picture we, on our side, were basking in the sun of reaction, and revelling in all sorts of luxury supplied by the patriotic and other funds, the generous gift of a loving country which had at last awakened from its slumbering indifference.

At the beginning of the winter 1855 I was transferred from my position at Balaclava, to take charge of the Monastery of St. George, where about a dozen of the old monks' rooms were furnished with single beds, constituting a little hospital for the reception of those home-sick gentlemen, who were pleading all sorts of illnesses with a view of getting back to England on the ground of *urgent private affairs*, an indulgence which was becoming scandalously abused. Hence a mandate had been issued from headquarters that a check should be put to this bit of weakness on the part of some of the officers, who were well known not to relish trench duties, and who were yearning for the flesh pots of Egypt in their own luxurious homes. When, therefore, an officer pleaded some physical infirmity as an excuse for decamping, he was first sent off to the monastery and placed under my care in one of the little wards,

in order to test his incapacity for further active duty
in the trenches or elsewhere. Various were the dodges
practised upon me to get a medical certificate of
permanent invalidism which would justify a departure
for Scutari or England. The eyes were the favourite
organs of complaint, these appearing unaccountably
red, and even continuing so, notwithstanding the
remedies employed. No amendment taking place in
a few days I would put on a savage look and threaten
them with all sorts of pains and penalties. An
interview would take place somewhat after the following manner : "Now, old fellow, if you cannot keep
your fingers from your eyes I shall be under the
painful necessity of blindfolding you, and placing an
orderly in your room at night to keep watch over
you, and to certify to me that justice is done to my
remedies." This would stop any further tampering
and malingering, and after trying every possible
device to get over me would throw up the sponge,
and quietly go back to their duties again. It was a
very unwelcome and disagreeable position of trust to
be placed in, but I was not going to commit a breach
of that confidence reposed in me by the commander-
in-chief to please any one be he nobleman or com-
moner.

It must not be supposed that the monastery
occupied all my attention at this time. About a
quarter of a mile away, a large corrugated-iron
building had been erected for stores. It did not
long continue occupied with such. A body of
troops had been sent off to attack and occupy the
Kinburn Fortress, situated on a sandy plain. What

with the glare of the sun and the clouds of fine
sand which blew over the fort, the garrison became
attacked with Egyptian ophthalmia, a most conta-
gious and destructive disease of the eye. Those
afflicted were sent back to the Crimea, where it
began to spread immediately. I was at once sent
for by Sir John Hall our chief, who was in an
awful fix. A few were already blind with the complaint and the hospitals were full. I suggested that
all the cases should be collected and isolated without
an hour's delay. "Just so," said Sir John, "but
where can we place them?" I then brought to his
notice the store building and recommended that it
should be emptied of its contents and beds placed in
it. "Go back," said he, with evident relief, "and
do what you think is necessary; this is not the first
time I have given you a *carte blanche*." Seeing there
was a foot of snow on the ground and that it was
falling fast he continued, "How can you get them
together such severe weather as this?" I replied,
"that I should carry them on stretchers covered
over face and all, with a couple of blankets. The
position was a desperate one, and isolation imperative.
The removal or otherwise was a question of sight or
total blindness!" We parted, and on my road back
in a blinding snowstorm I should have gone over the
cliffs into the sea but for the sagacity of my old
chestnut, who saw the danger, which I did not, and
he would not be urged a step further. The track
being obscured by the snow, I retraced till I got to
some huts when I found I was a good mile out of my
bearings. My compass now helped me home where

I arrived with feelings of earnest gratitude for another providential intervention. Having the command of plenty of labour I soon got the building into shipshape and the patients settled down in their beds. The cold was so intense that some nights it was below zero and the poor fellows suffered dreadfully. There was one small stove in its centre, a sort of make believe which did not prevent the tea and milk, &c., taken from freezing into lumps when spilt on the beards of the men. My own hair became a mass of ice from my breath congealing when passing to and fro from my quarters. It was a hard life doubtless, but one's health, like that of the army generally, was most excellent. Our mortality during the second winter did not exceed ¾ per man per cent. Thanks to a better commissariat, plenty of warm clothing and an abundance of wholesome good food, and though last not least, no nerve excitement from the constant apprehension of an onslaught from a wide-awake and heroic enemy. What a pleasant change from our first winter's experience! Then, again, what work we had was varied with play. There was a great deal of dining out, and where we dined we slept, for it was not safe to pass the different sentries of our gallant allies at night, because if we did not give the pass word rightly they would as soon just put a bullet into one as not—no parley was their order! My friends in the Black Watch had really the only mess worthy of the name, and it was a fine sight to see old Cameron, like a father, seated at the head of the table, surrounded by his sturdy comrades,

intermingling the toasts with humorous remarks on
the situation. Kamara was their post, and it was
conveniently located for a pleasure trip into the
Baida valley, which we undertook one day, and
entering a Tartar gentleman's house we were
hospitably entertained by his wife who said her
husband was in prison on suspicion of having
supplied us with provisions. She was a beautiful
woman, and gave us some sad stories of how the
Cossacks robbed them of food, and even violently
assaulted them if they were refused ; no position
was respected by these soldier robbers. The most
diverting amusement was the institution of amateur
theatricals got up by the officers, and another of
a lower grade by the non-commissioned officers.
Both parties succeeding in rousing side-breaking
laughter by their serio-comic performances. The
get-up of the lady-gentlemen being most creditable
considering they had not the advantage of a Bond-
street milliner in the Crimea. The following bill,
which I have preserved and which was printed at
the local press of the *Hue and Cry*, gives the
names of the play and the actors :—

Theatre Royal, Fourth Division. This Evening, April 10, 1856,
Her Majesty's servants will perform—

LITTLE TODDLEKINS!

Mr. Jones Robinson Brownsmith ...	Capt. Earle, 57th Regt.
Mr. Barnaby Babicombe ...	Major Garnet, 46th Regt.
Captain Littlepop ...	Capt. Nicholas, 46th Regt.
Amanthis ...	Mr. Clarkson, 68th Regt.
Annie Babicombe	Mr. Saunderson, 68th Regt.
Susan	Mr. V. Stuart, 68th Regt.

To conclude with—

GOING TO THE DERBY.

Mr. Jeremiah Twiddle	...	Capt. Earle.
Mr. John James Chucks	...	Lieut. de Lacy Lacy, 63rd Regt.
Captain Nobble	... ...	Major Lord A. G. Russell, R.B.
Sam (waiter of Spread Eagle)		Lieut. Harrington, R.B.

Mrs. Twiddle, Mrs. Chucks, Mrs. Plummy, and Gipsy Woman, by Lieuts. Saunderson, Clarkson, and Stuart, of the 68th, and Lieut. Prior, 48th.

Doors open at half-past seven o'clock: Performance at 8.

God Save the Queen.

The foregoing fun was interlarded with some pony races, of which the following is a copy of the " Card of the Races " :—

SEBASTOPOL SPRING MEETING.

Monday, March 24, 1856.

Stewards :

Viscount Talon and Marquis de Spinola, Major Astley, Major Dewar, Major Brown, Lieut.-Col. Campbell, Capt. Chapman, Col. Hale, Mr. Wilkin, Capt. Connel, Major Nicholson, Col. Hay, and Capt. Ponsonby.
Honorary Treasurer and Secretary—Major Wombwell, 46th.

The first race was a handicap sweepstakes of £1 each, with £25 added, for ponies of fourteen hands and under. Half a mile on the flat. There were forty entries, which Capt. Cornat's gr. p. " Bignot " won. Then came a steeplechase of two miles for £50. This was won by Viscount Talon's " Paddy Boy," ridden by the owner ; followed by three other races, won respectively by Capt. Morant's g. g. " Clinker," Capt. Price's, 11th Hussars, " Lillington," and Capt. Brabason's, R.A., " Chutney."

Again, for the benefit of those of a more literary turn of mind, a series of educational lectures were given in the library and reading-hut of the Third Division. The following programme, which I have kept by me for the last thirty-five years, will convey a good idea of the subjects selected to instruct and amuse :—

The " Pursuit of Knowledge under Difficulties," by Rev. B. Harris, Chaplain.

" Places of Interest in Old Testament," by Rev. H. Wheeler, Chaplain.

" Mohammedism," by Rev. H. W. M. Egan, Principal Chaplain.

" On Temperance," by Sir James Alexander, Col. of 14th Regt.

So much for our minds : now to show that our bodies were well cared for at the same time. I will here insert a copy of an old list I have by me which gives the following quantities—they seem large, but then I had five mouths to feed beside myself :—
" Bread, 9 lbs. ; meat, 6 lbs. ; coffee, 6 ounces ; rice, ditto ; sugar, 12 ounces ; rum, 3 gills ; potatoes, 1½ lbs. ; onions, ¾ lbs. ; pepper ¼ ounce ; and 3 ounces of salt."

Now I am on the subject of victualling, it may be mentioned that during the second winter I had got from home a man-cook and a cooking range, with a set of tins as fittings, which enabled me to give my friends quite a *recherché* spread of five or six courses,

made more dainty-looking by being laid on a white
tablecloth, supplemented by the additional refinement
of snow-white napkins. Such a civilised appearance
had not been seen by us since our departure from
board ship, and it drew tears from some of my guests,
because it reminded them so forcibly of the happy and
luxurious surroundings of their homes in dear old
England, where they would be enhanced, maybe, by
the sunny smiles of wife and children, or mother and
sisters. I need hardly say the Monastery of St. George
became not a little popular, and various were the visitors of both sexes who did me the honour of calling
in the afternoons, and patronising the luxuries so hard
to collect, I being six miles distant from the suttlers'
camp, where those landsharks charged a most exorbitant price for everything. When the migratory birds
came flocking over from the north, and settled down
exhausted in the snow, there was no difficulty in
securing a larder full of wild fowl, especially the
golden plover, which were as plump as our partridges,
and in such crowds did they come that I killed one
day eight of them at one shot. This windfall was a
welcome addition to one's ordinary diet. My cook
made these birds into delicious pies, larding them with
fat pork, and placing them over a basis of fresh beef
or mutton. These pies were quite a *pièce de résistance*,
and while they lasted became quite the talk of my
visiting circle for many a day after. My friends came
in the afternoons, not only to taste the luxuries I
could place before them, but to admire the beautiful
view from the Terrace, and to listen to the chime,
rung by old Peter in the Greek church. Peter was

quite a character, rather crippled in his limbs, and was the only one left behind by the church community, but too fond of rum, which in his sober moments he called "No bono, Johnny."

CHAPTER XII.

THERE were discussions and disputes as to whether
we had shattered Fort Constantine at the north
entrance of the harbour when it was bombarded on
the 17th of October, 1854, by our ships, especially the
three-decker *Albion*, which went so close in, and got
herself such a battering. Hence, when peace was
concluded, we made up a party and rode round by
the Mackenzie heights to see for ourselves. We found
the fort was occupied by the Russian commander-in-
chief, General Luders, who received us very kindly,
and treated us most hospitably. When we told him
the purport of our visit, he smiled, and said, "Come
and see." He acted as our guide, and took us round
the whole of the parapets, explaining every circumstance in connection with the attack, and how they
were protected by gabions. On a close examination
we could not discover hardly a place where the stone-
work had been chipped. This review of the outside
finished, the general asked us to see the inside. Here
we found, in a large casemate, a table laid out with
sumptuous refreshments, in fact, six delicious courses
were provided, to which we did ample justice, and to
two or three different wines, finishing up with a glass

of that well-known delicacy, Crimean champagne, in which our host drank our healths at the shrine of Peace. The cannon was in position in this casemate, and such a toast struck us as somewhat ironical and seemingly out of place, but we parted most excellent friends, and he promised to return the visit by coming to see me at the monastery, which he did shortly afterwards, coming in a droski drawn by five splendid ponies. So wonderfully drilled were they, that they would start or stop, deviate right or left, by word of command. The general tried to induce some ladies to take a drive with him, but seeing that we had no regular roads, and that the vehicle bumped about unpleasantly on the uneven plateau, they declined ; but such trifles not troubling my mind, I took a seat at his side, and was amazed at the wonderfully skilful way in which he handled his team. The heads of the ponies were decorated with foxes' brushes and a regular chime of little bells, which seem to excite them to gallop at a great speed. The general paid the Greek church a visit, and old Peter honoured him with one of his best peals.

My cook, hearing that so distinguished a guest had paid me a visit, tried to surpass himself by laying out as fine a luncheon as his limited supplies would permit of, and my visitor, being an old campaigner, took in the situation, and determined to enjoy himself accordingly. To give zest to the entertainment there was seated at the table, a very handsome lady, to whom he gave a cross of Siberian gold, which hung from his watch chain. This generous act did not arise from his having imbibed too much Crimean champagne, for I had none to give him ; it must have been due entirely to the lady's fascinating appearance and address.

When the genial general took his leave, he carried away with him all our warm good wishes, leaving behind the golden cross to remind us of one of the pleasantest days we had ever spent in the Crimea. Little did we think a few weeks back that we should be spending so soon such a happy time with the commander of our enemy's forces on the north side of Sebastopol—but *tel est la vie.*

When the treaty of peace was signed we heard that each plenipotentiary was desirous of preserving the pen with which he subscribed the important document, but these great men were obliged to yield to the expressed wishes of the Empress Eugénie, who supplied them with a beautifully jewelled eagle's quill which she desired to retain as a memento of the momentous event. When this treaty reached the Crimea it brought with it to some of the old stagers the realisation of hopes long hoped for, namely, an early opportunity of getting home alive, and to tell in person terrible tales of battles and sieges, the loss of some friends and the making of others, while to many who came out at a later date it was a source of disappointment—subaltern officers, for example, who viewed the army as an instrument towards worldly prosperity, trusted that peace would not supervene till they had an opportunity of distinguishing themselves, and winning a place in the records of glory! Oh, vanity of vanities, they did not take to heart the saying in the good old Book, that "they who live by the sword

shall die with the sword." I heard an anxious mother
on one occasion exclaim, in simple ignorance of what
the horrors of actual warfare were like, "Oh! my
poor boy, I am so sorry, he had just got to the head
of the lieutenants, and I was in hopes of hearing any
day of his becoming a captain, and now the war is
over he may have to wait ever so long." She, with a
mother's natural instincts, did not stop to reflect that
her son's promotion would have been accomplished
through the further shedding of much human blood
and the cruel display of the worst of passions. How
thoroughly selfish we are, even when our precious
lives and souls are at stake! Talk of Christianity
and its peaceful influences, I should like to know how
many men were brought to think of the Saviour while
this horrid carnage was going on, when, I take it,
half a million of lives were ruthlessly sacrificed on
both sides in order to gratify the vain ambition of one
man, who prosecuted this prolonged warfare under the
cloak of religion. Picture to yourself, dear reader,
the following incidents associated with the cessation of
hostilities. Though thousands of soldiers in the spring
were employed in road-making, building of huts, and in
drill, there was nevertheless much spare time, which
was spent scandalously in drinking, card-playing, and
gambling. The English were better paid than the
troops of our allies, and they did not know what to
do with their money ; hence scenes of drunkenness
and debauchery prevailed at Kadikoi, where suttlers'
booths were kept by most disorderly traders, who en-
couraged all sorts of vices, winked at acts of violence,
and even murder. Night was made hideous with

their brawls, and it was not safe to go near their
squatting ground if you at all valued your life!
It was a blessed day indeed when the post-office
authorities instituted a mode of sending gold to England by means of money orders. Many men then
availed themselves of this easy means of forwarding
their spare cash to their wives and families, or to
their aged parents, thus securing themselves against
the indulgence in their besetting sins—drunkenness
and gambling. It may well be said that idleness,
backed by riches, is the mother of many miseries.
The time had now arrived when we were to bid farewell to the Crimea, and the recollection, if that were
possible, of all its horrors, its dangers and worries,
only too thankful that we had escaped with our lives.
The beautiful month of June, 1856, found us on board
a steam transport bound for Constantinople, where I
landed, and went off to pay my respects to my old
patient, Miss Nightingale. I found that noble creature looking very pale and slender, and delicate in
appearance, with her beautiful black hair cut short,
but still retaining her wonted stock of fiery courage
and activity. She was simply worshipped by the sick
and wounded, who romantically kissed her very
shadow as she noiselessly glided along the corridors,
lamp in hand, when all was silent and quiet at night,
to satisfy herself that all was going on well among
her eyeless, armless, footless, shot, sabred, and
bayoneted devotees. There, within those dismal
walls, was to be seen this refined, highly cultured
lady, going the rounds of her wards two and a half
miles in extent, among thousands of uneducated men,

rough, rugged, bloody, dirty, wounded, sick, hungry, and miserable, undertaking painful and arduous duties with every possible deficiency in the necessary supplies, for she had to deal with men wrapped up in departmental formalism called " red-tapeism," whereby living wounded sick soldiers, the defenders of their country's honour, were treated as so many bales of goods, to be packed aside in heaps and then forgotten. To correct such crying and shameful misdoings was Miss Nightingale's heavy task, almost singlehanded. She might indeed be well defined without any exaggeration a " ministering angel " in these hospitals.

Calling to mind the real luxury of a Turkish bath, I could not leave Stamboul without resorting to that bodily refreshment. The building is like a huge church, with a dome in the centre, in which 150 people can walk about comfortably, and enjoy the delicious balmy heat, and get a good rub down by a small boy, who after lathering you all over, will grinningly show you what an incredible quantity of black scurf he has managed to scrape off your apparently white skin, but there it is on his hands, and you have to believe him. This desquamation will account, perhaps, for the inexpressibly soothing sensations one feels afterwards in the cooling room, where a feeling of heavenly peace and rest takes possession of one. Such a physical and mental paradise you will not find in the puny baths which have been set up in England, and which are a mere sham in comparison with those in Constantinople.

In taking leave of Scutari and its hospitals, I may just mention an incident which presents to us a very forcible picture how warfare with its horrid sequences

and debasing surroundings deadens man's heart to
all those refined susceptibilities of a moral and religious nature, and suppresses that sympathetic kind-
liness of feeling which dominates and exercises our
minds when we behold our friends and companions
ruthlessly snatched suddenly from us in times of
peace. Read, and believe if you can, gentle reader,
sitting at your ease in these "piping times of peace,"
the following plain and unvarnished truth. When
the sick and the wounded had collected in their
thousands at the Scutari hospitals, and even in the
cavalry stables near thereto, they began to die off in
scores daily, not so much from actual wounds as from
dysentery and fever occurring in broken-down, starved
constitutions — hopeless cases. An insupportable
gloom overspread the place like a black pall, which
affected the spirits and courage of the noble nurses
terribly, but their heroism was something wonderful
to witness. The cemetery, therefore, at such a time,
became the centre of melancholy interest. The
private soldiers were buried *en masse* as I have already
described they were in the Crimea, simply stitched
up in their blankets, and laid side by side in a large
grave, while the officers were interred in a small
cemetery overlooking the sea, each with a wooden
tablet at the head of the spot. In this resting-place
are lying eight doctors, the victims of hard work and
disease! The bodies of the dead were collected
together in heaps in an empty ward, then a string of
invalid orderlies would form a procession and carry
the bodies on stretchers through a long corridor filled
with patients who had become so accustomed to this

melancholy looking train, that they would go on chatting, reading, or being read to, or any other amusement going on, without their attention being diverted in the slightest degree by this touching spectacle of their dead comrades going to their last home!

Oh! war, war, with all thy pomp, glitter, and glory! How dost thou in thy very bitterness of trial curse our race, sowing penalties and pains broadcast over us, heaping up poverty on the very poor, recklessly deriding the widow in her bereavement, making her husbandless, making her childless; thou begettest orphans; in the very wantonness of thy cruelty dost thou seek victims from every grade; reckless of all social distinctions, bringing down to one dead level the heartbroken and the desolate! Shortsighted, ignorant, and vain men crown thy triumphs with laurel; but the cypress of the cemetery and the yew of the village churchyard would be more fitting emblems of thy accursed work! I will now draw down a veil over this harrowing picture. May the time be not far distant in this era of the world in which the saying in the Book of books shall be verified, namely, " They shall beat their swords into ploughshares and their spears into pruning-hooks. Nation shall not lift up sword against nation, neither shall they learn war any more " !

I now proceeded on my journey homewards, which I hoped to accomplish so as to spend my thirty-sixth birthday in my own country. On board I found an officer whom I had met formerly at Malta on his way up to the Crimea. He, like many others on furlough from India, had diverged and gone to the fighting

field to volunteer his services in order to see what
war was really like; he never having seen a shot
fired in anger while in India. He appeared then very
impatient to have a go at the Russians, and was
vainly boasting of what he would and could do when
he had a chance, flourishing in the air his six-shooter.
I had now an opportunity of asking him how he had
succeeded, and whether he had left his mark behind
him. As soon as I mentioned the subject, his
countenance fell and he looked rather gloomy.
When I reminded him of his remarks about potting
the enemy with his revolver, " Well," he said, " I
had my chance, it was at Inkerman, and I will tell
you all about it. I got entangled in a *melée* as the
duke did, and it was during a hand-to-hand fight
when a fellow was about to cut me down, I fired my
revolver at and missed him, and then I lost my nerve
and self-possession so far as not to let go the trigger
for the next shot, and thus was in imminent danger
of being killed had not a private soldier come to the
rescue and parried the cut with his bayonet. I need
hardly tell you that such a narrow escape will never
be forgotten, and that it took all the bounce out of
me for the future."

> " Man, proud man !
> Dressed in a little brief authority, ...
> Plays such fantastic tricks before high heaven,
> As make the angels weep ! "

Nothing of any great moment occurred before we
reached Malta, where we landed and were made
much of. One officer struggling along on two crutches
came in for quite an ovation ; he had been shot in the

stomach and the bullet had made its exit at the side of the spine, and yet, wonderful to relate, he had survived and was doing well. Another poor fellow, walking on one crutch, was shot in the heel; the bone had become a mere shell, the interior having crumbled away. He was suffering a good deal, and the leg would be eventually shorter than the other. Both these officers would be compelled to give up the service, much against their will, and become pensioners for the rest of their lives upon the nation's bounty. The latter case is still alive but lame, and has been well cared for by a grateful country, and in his old age comfortably berthed by the Queen at Windsor. Our reception at Gibraltar was equally pleasant and agreeable. One vied with another, ladies and all, in showering kindnesses upon us, and introducing for our comfort all sorts of delicacies to make our voyage more congenial and health-giving. I myself, besides suffering from the effects of cholera, had had three scurvy ulcers on the leg, which had exceedingly reduced me, and so shattered my general health, that I should have to look out for a sanitorium on arriving in England where I should have to remain two or three years to re-establish my constitution. As to further service in the army that was quite out of the question. Arriving at Portsmouth, my luggage, which was something considerable, was allowed to pass the custom house without examination and my store of Turkish tobacco was admitted duty free. From Portsmouth I made my way to Brighton, which I had selected as my future headquarters. And here I will stay my hand for the present.

J. Vaughan-Hughes, Esq., M.D., L.R.C.P., London,
Knight of the Royal Order of St. Maurice and St. Lazarus of Italy.
Surgeon-Major, retired, Crimean War, 1854-5-6.
Author of "Seventy Years of Life in the Victorian Era.

CHAPTER XIII.

Except to those who have experienced the fiery ordeal of having passed through an active campaign of two years' duration in such a war as that of the years 1854-5 6, none can realise in the faintest degree the blessed calm and blissful peace in which the soul reposes when once more one is safe at home again in the midst of every luxury and refinement, and rejoicing in the congratulations of relations and friends at the many narrow escapes to life; cheered also at being honoured with the country's approval and recognition of one's services under fire. In due course the King Victor Emmanuel forwarded to me through the Foreign Office the Cross of a Knight of the Royal Order of St. Maurice and St. Lazarus, "for distinguished services before the enemy," which I received accompanied with a royal warrant to accept and wear the same, signed by Her Majesty herself. This Order with the English and Turkish war medals enabled me to appear at Court with three decorations on my breast. Such an occasion was glorious enough to elicit a sense of pride and vanity in most men's hearts, but to me all such feelings were swallowed up in the one grand predominating reflection that I had

escaped with my life, which idea, at all times, brought
to the fore such a deep sense of gratitude to the
Giver of all mercies that all the other superficial and
mundane thoughts were totally eclipsed. Though
many years have elapsed, this condition of mind still
exists, and when a gallant volunteer for instance,
in the full pride of his new uniform, exclaims, "Oh
how I should like to appear at a *levée* with such
decorations," I would reply, "My dear fellow, you
little know at what a risk to life and health they were
obtained, or you would not think so much of them!"

The first regiment which arrived at Brighton after
I took up my residence was the 4th Dragoon Guards
which had distinguished itself in the Crimea, hence
we soon cottoned together. I became officially
attached to the *depôt* there, and thus kept in touch
with some of my old campaigning friends. Consequently joined in the festivities which the good town's
people were not slow to indulge both to officers and
men. The first fancy-dress ball ever held in the
picturesque old Pavilion was a grand success, there
being upwards of eleven hundred present. Nearly all
Shakespeare's characters were represented. It was a
part of the programme that all the party should be
presented to and passed by the Doge of Venice, who
was seated on a throne in the long corridor. This
was a very dazzling sight, the glittering uniforms and
quaint old dresses were superb. A Queen's Drawing-
room reception could not have come up to it. A
friend of mine went in as Falstaff, and his broad front
was bejewelled to the tune of £2,000, and he was
obliged to pay two guineas each for two of Nathan's

men in plain evening dress to safeguard them and
him from loss or robbery. There were three or four
dressed as Shakespeare in silk velvet with point
lace collar and cuffs. Two pretty sisters, beautifully
figured in pink tights and tulle skirts with wings
on the shoulders representing angels, were much
admired. Everything was conducted with the utmost
decorum, and the committee strictly forbad any
objectionable get-up. The return ball by the 4th
Dragoons to their friends was brilliant in the extreme,
and the Pavilion suite of rooms was decorated with
great taste and lavish expense. Dancing was just
possible in the crowded rooms, and when the supper-
room was thrown open at midnight it was quite
impossible to get near the tables sitting or standing,
groaning as they were with every luxury in season
and out of season.

After remaining a few years at Brighton, and my
health having, thanks to its fine bracing air, become
thoroughly established, I came to the wise conclusion
that that pleasure resort was very well for amusement and to spend money in, but that it was not the
place to get into a lucrative practice unless one
obtained a *locus standi* in partnership with some old
practitioner, resident in the town for years. Hence
my ambition was to fix myself in London as soon as
I could afford to settle in some fashionable street in
its West End, for there is no city in the world where
a professional man can get on so well as in London
if he can patiently abide his time, undisturbed by a
sense of fear or favour.

But before this move took place, I had an opportunity of visiting Italy, where, in consequence of my having received their order of knighthood, I was received with distinguished favour. I was present in Florence when King Victor Emmanuel made his grand *entrée* into that city, and made it for the time being the capital of United Italy. There were great festivities to celebrate the event. I got an invitation to the first royal ball at the Pitti Palace, when there were present 5,000 of the *élite* of the nobility of the land, parading its long suite of twenty-four reception-rooms. The Queen of Portugal was mistress of the ceremonies. I was permitted to enter the compartment where the royal quadrille was being danced, in which were engaged the king's daughter and three of his sons. When I entered the refreshment room, I was surprised to see the tables spread with the most harmless and costless delicacies. The king said neither he nor the country could afford to give expensive entertainments—their war debt was too heavy. There was a huge ormulu inlaid punch bowl, out of which a servant was ladling cupfuls of something of a brown colour, and as it was much patronised by the ladies, I came to the conclusion that it could not possibly be punch, so I went in for a cup of it, and lo! behold it was nothing stronger than clear beef tea—a nice innocent beverage to dance upon truly. At that time the cholera was raging at Naples, and nothing would satisfy the king but he must needs go down, contrary to advice, and pay the hospitals a personal visit. Of course it was considered a very brave self-sacrificing thing to do, and when he returned in safety to

Florence the people were half crazy with delight, and he was received with an uproar of cheers.

Patti was then engaged at the opera house, and though very young was rapidly becoming a great favourite. Hence, on the king's return he went to the opera; Patti had just been before the curtain to receive the applause of the audience three times when the king entered the royal box; then it commenced again more furiously than ever, and poor little Patti, not being aware of the royal presence, came forward again to be applauded, but soon discovered her mistake, but was consoled by receiving a handsome bracelet from His Majesty.

It is not often one finds a foreign order of much service in travelling from place to place, but a very pleasant exception occurred to me on one occasion when visiting the north of Italy. A party of ladies requested my escort from Venice to the river Po. One had been laid up with inflamed eyes, to whom I had been of some little service. They were English, and did not know any other language than their mother tongue; under these circumstances I consented to take a seat in one of their carriages—for two were required. Thus we posted down to the banks of the river. When we arrived our luggage was to be examined at the custom house; but when I showed the official my credentials he very politely permitted our baggage to pass free, and we got at once into the ferry-boat and were taken over to the opposite side before another large party could clear the customs; thus I was enabled to secure the only vehicle standing there, on which our luggage was

placed. While I was chatting with the man in charge
of the office on the south side, the other party had
got over, and had bribed our cabby with a napoleon
to take our trunks off and put theirs on. No doubt
the wealthy English heiress with her suite of man-
servants and maid-servants, courier and doctor, looked
very grand and imposing; but when I appealed to the
official to give me precedence on account of my order
of knighthood, he immediately reversed the position
of things, giving the driver a good rating. You can
better imagine than I can describe it the looks of
this rich domineering English party, when they saw
their fine boxes taken down and placed uncere-
moniously on the muddy shingle, and watching us
drive off to Ferrara, a distance of five or six miles,
which we reached in time for *table d'hôte* dinner;
while the great lady and her companions were
obliged to wait till carriages were sent from the town
to convey them to the hotel, which they reached
about midnight, when no meals could be had.

One more instance in which I found the Italian
order of social service was in Rome. In that city
there were at that time several private galleries of
painting and sculpture, and valuable libraries, possessing ancient collections of manuscripts of great interest, in the mansions of the decayed nobility. The
old Hotel d'Angleterre had then a large number of
visitors under its roof, by some of whom I was
solicited to get them an introduction to see these
treasures, which I had no difficulty in doing. When
a sufficient sum of money had been collected as a
honorarium for the great but impoverished owner,

whose scanty income was considerably augmented by these tolls, then, and not till then, would I consent to be the guide to the party.

A rather singular bet was made by some friends in the hotel on the eve of our attending the *levée* at the Vatican. I must first say that the Pope, in those palmy Church days, was temporal sovereign of the estates of the papal dominion, and at bitter enmity with the king, who wanted Rome to be the capital of United Italy. The bet was this. That I would not dare to appear in the Pope's presence wearing the Order of St. Maurice and St. Lazarus, because if I did he would thus have to bestow a blessing on the king's decoration. I did not let them into the secret that I was going to place the cross between two war medals. Hence, when I entered the Audience Chamber, Monsignor Howard came up to me, and seeing the order, said, "I presume that is a war decoration, and has nothing to do with any political or religious matter whatever." I replied, "Certainly not," that it was for service in the Crimea. "Very good," said he, "then you can have the *entrée*." Pio Nono then entered, and walking down the long corridor, speaking to one, then to another in his well-known, kindly, genial way, came opposite to where I stood, and just glancing at the decorations, said, "Do you think the cholera will travel from Naples to Rome?" "I thought not, if the authorities would look well to the sanitary condition of the city." He then continued on, addressing the company, touching their strings of crucifixes and beads till he reached the further end of the long gallery, when he turned round, raised his hand, and blessed Catholics and Protestants alike. Thus the bet was won ! When I arrived at the hotel, the disappointed ones said, "When His Holiness stopped opposite and spoke to you, we certainly thought he was giving you a good wigging for appearing with that order upon your breast, but you have done us thoroughly."

When the war was over in the United States, the Americans, especially the ladies, came over in swarms " to do " Europe, and give their daughters a polish. It was not only the fashion, but a regular craze set in to cross the Atlantic " to see the wonders of the world abroad," notwithstanding that their greenbacks were exchanged at a discount of 40 per cent. They lavishly spent their money broadcast. They secured the best rooms in the hotels ; gave the best prices in the shops for articles *de vertu*, completely swamping the English buyers by giving double the usual charges for copies of the old masters. They excited quite a sensation in the coral, cameo, and mosaic stores by the free-and-easy way in which they spent their money. Some of their countrymen pretended "to do" Rome in a couple of days, rushing about like madmen from museum to church, and hence to ruins, hardly giving themselves time for meals, at which they would read their Murray or examine the maps. I was crossing the country one day when two young American girls were of the party, who delayed our starting not a little by two huge trunks which they insisted on having chained up behind, making our conveyance dangerously top-heavy. So I asked them why they travelled about with such monstrous impedimenta. "Oh!" they said, "they were obliged to do so, because if they did not trouble them a bit at the hotels they would be thought nothing of, and be snubbed as 'nobodies.'" I could not help seeing that there was some wise forethought in their plans, and that the usual acuteness of the Yankee was to the fore in this instance, and they could, as they say, "whip the English into fits." Here were two unprotected young girls travelling alone thousands of miles from their own land, perfectly at their ease, yet possessed of a shrewdness and tact quite characteristic of Brother Jonathan's family.

Again I came across an American gentleman in charge of four pretty young ladies travelling about in style. He was the envy of all the bachelors, who regarded him as a most fortunate man, and did not fail to express their sentiments. "Oh! you innocent and simple young fellows: you who don't look beyond the surface," said he. "I only wish any one of you had my place for the next trip, and then I should see how you would like to look after four ladies and nineteen trunks and packages. Just try it at one custom house, and then tell me I am a most fortunate man, if you have the cheek to do so." "But what in the world do they want such a lot of boxes for?" "There you are again, you greenhorns. When you are married you will quickly be installed into such mysteries. Don't you see, if ladies change their dresses four times a day, that the gowns must have plenty of space to themselves to avoid crump-

ling." They might have ejaculated, "Truly we live
and learn," but were lost in surprise, and said
nothing.

Mr. Parker, C.B., the eminent archæologist, being
a friend of my family, I had an unusual opportunity
of seeing and studying the ruins of ancient Rome
under his guidance. He had spent quite a little
fortune in excavating different portions of the city,
and possessed a fine collection of large photos, from
which he lectured to his numerous friends. One of
the underground prisons he discovered had been
utilised and converted into a *dépôt*, a sort of refrigerator,
for butcher's meat. What dramatic changes hath not
time wrought !

There were a great many assassinations in Rome
at that time. It was not safe to go out at night
except in company, and with lanterns and sticks.
The streets were not lighted with lamps. I was
at an evening party in a suite of rooms on the
third story (the fashionable and healthy one, high
above the stench of the streets) when a gentleman
was steathily followed up the dark staircase to the
top landing, then stabbed in the neck, just missing
the jugular vein. We heard the shriek and a rustle
down the steps, but before any of us could get outside
the assassin was gone. We were much grieved, for
this gentleman had been forty years in the city, and
had shown many acts of kindness towards the poor.
We heard afterwards that he had been mistaken for
somebody else. This wanton act of cruelty roused
a good deal of indignation in the English colony,
and a deputation was formed to call on Antonelli,

the foreign minister, stating the case, and asking to be allowed to carry revolvers in self-defence. All the consolation we got was this sarcastic and ominous reply, " Oh, yes! certainly," said he ; " but you must take the consequences," and we knew what that insinuation meant.

The populace hated their French protectors, and many officers on patrol were stabbed, and one died of his wounds while I was there. The Pope would now and again come in his carriage, surrounded by his noble guard, and get out among the promenaders in the Piazza di Spagna, when the ladies would gather round him like a flock of pigeons, and kneeling down on the dirty flags, in their splendid silks, would seize the hands of His Holiness and salute them, or failing that would kiss the hem of his garment. There was no Protestant place of worship allowed within the walls of the city in those days : we were obliged to attend a most un-church-like building outside the gates. We were not allowed to congregate even in a private room to read and expound the Scriptures, except on the sly ! All this bigotry is now dead and buried, and religious liberty prevails. Hence the Americans have erected a splendid church in the very heart of Rome, with a lofty spire pointing heavenwards, and not towards the Vatican, where everything inclines good, bad, and indifferent. We will now stop, and then proceed with Chapter XIV.

CHAPTER XIV.

Before we finally take leave of Rome and its renowned antiquities, we must just climb up into the brazen ball crowning the grand dome of St. Peter's, and get a peep through its bull's eyes of the magnificent panorama of the Campagna, backed by its distant hills, and on the other side the meandering Tiber flowing down to join the Mediterranean Sea. Again, let us take a farewell turn on the Monte Pincio of sunny fame, where do congregate the *élite* in their smart carriages and still smarter dresses, where some American ladies would outshine in splendour those of any other country, and did not fail to attract to the sides of their hired equipages and liveried servants the young impecunious Italian nobles, heirs to large estates mortgaged up to the very hilt for generations past ; these handsome, plausible gentry would leave no stone unturned to secure the affections and the money of these rich women, in order to restore the social position of these fallen but proud old families. But—and there is always a nasty but in the fulfilment of these selfish schemes—when the case had advanced so far as to elicit the reply, "Ask papa," the worthy noble

finds that dear papa is showing off at the sacrifice
of capital, and not living in the usual way on his
income at all, and can make no settlement on his
beautiful and fascinating daughter. Then the disappointed—one cannot say disinterested—lover slopes
away, and is no more seen on Monte Pincio for the
remainder of that season. Then you ask a Chicago
merchant, rich in pork and credit, how he dare act
in such a prodigal way, his answer was, twenty-six
years ago, "Well, I can go back to my business and
make as good a fortune, and as quickly, again," and
so he would, for money was made rapidly in the
metropolis of hogs in those days.

We will now pass on to Naples—shining beautifully in a cloudless sky like a white-washed sepulchre
without, but inwardly stenchy and offensive. Vesuvius, slightly smoking in the distance, first attracts
the visitor's attention, and when we get to it we are
told that the feat to accomplish is to take some raw
eggs in your pocket, climb unaided up its steep side
knee-deep in loose lava and cinders till you reach the
crater; then if you have not already fallen and
broken your eggs, you descend into its mouth and
thrust the eggs into the hot dust to be cooked, which
takes about half an hour, then you take them out
and eat them. This I performed safely, but at the
expense of a pair of boots, the soles of which were
burnt off. Of course Pompei and its wonders were
duly done and studied *à la* Murray, then we proceeded *via* Castella Mare to visit lovely Sorento,
basking in its orange groves. We made the Tre-
montana Hotel, on the edge of the cliff overhanging

the bay, our headquarters, from whence we rowed over to Capri in order to enter its celebrated "blue cave" in the waters of which reflecting the sky, a man will plunge in and swim about looking like a silver fish, amid ripples of phosphorescent light—a curious dazzling phenomenon, decidedly worth a visit provided the weather is fine. Returning to Sorento we next took a journey inland to Amalfi, and thence by very good road cut out of the cliffs overlooking the seas on one side, and bounded on the other by terrace upon terrace of orange gardens, till we reached Salerno, the whole ride singularly wild and picturesque. Not being safe to visit the ruined temples of Pæstum in consequence of the roads being infested with brigands, we returned to Naples where I gave myself up for a time to the study of the original statues of the heathen gods, unearthed from the temples in Pompei by Government excavators. Some, especially the colossal statue of Hercules, seemed as fresh looking as if they had been sculptured yesterday. The various surgical instruments taken from a doctor's house interested me very much and tended to confirm the old saying, that "There is nothing new under the sun." While the wonderful preservation of the loaves of bread with the baker's stamp, the coffee-berries, currants, and spices were no less attractive from a domestic point of view to the ladies.

It is not my intention to act as a peripatetic guide to the "lions" of the places I happen to stay at, unless I can point a moral now and again. I shall make a return visit to Italy in the course of ten

years, and then I shall describe the changes, social,
moral, and religious, which shall have taken place in
the country's condition when it has become happily
united and cemented under the liberal government
and free under the auspices of a large-hearted king;
and throws off the yoke of the Austrians, who were so
hated in Venice when I was there, that when the
officers entered a restaurant, the Italian gentlemen
would walk out.

To economise my time I took a berth in a coasting
steamer and left Naples for Genoa, which we reached
in forty-eight hours, touching at Civita Vecchia and
Leghorn *en route*—trade poor, and people half asleep
in each town. Genoa may be defined as a city of
marble palaces of a bygone golden era, when their
owners could afford to keep them up, but in modern
times tenanted by a poor and squalid lot of people,
who tramp their marble halls and staircases with
perfect unconcern and contempt as to their former
grandeur. Such are the changes which a declining
commerce has produced, not only at Leghorn and
Genoa, but also all along the Riviera till one reaches
the large and prosperous community of Marseilles.
I therefore early took my departure from Genoa,
chartered a carriage, from which I enjoyed, on a
lovely bright day to my utmost fill, the varied beauties
of the world-renowned landscapes along the celebrated
Corniche road. The day's journey terminated at San
Remo, a health resort not thought much of at that
time. The town runs up a spur of the Alps at an
angle of nearly forty degrees. is well wooded, and is a
very pretty sight from the sea, and *vice versâ* from its

summit. The streets are narrow and bridged over
here and there by solid masonry to give the houses
stability against earthquakes. The fruit was very cheap
—I bought twelve apples for a penny, and as to oranges
they were a glut in the market. How will this be in a
dozen years hence, when the railway is completed along
the coast and its crowds of English and Americans
appear to spoil the primitive simplicity? Leaving
San Remo and its cheap hotel at seven francs a day,
I continued along the *route à la Corniche*, which, if
anything, becomes more bewitching as one nears
Bordighera and Ventimiglia, up and down hill on a
perfect roadway, passing bold and lofty promontories
and well-wooded hills; then skirting the bases of
precipitous and frowning cliffs washed by the angry
waves of the blue sea, crowned here and there by the
ruins of venerable towers of bygone ages to protect
the residents from pirates. Again we descend into a
richly cultivated plain with its curiously shaped olive
trees, luxuriant growth of vines, figs, citrons, oranges,
oleanders, myrtles, aloes, and even palms, and though
last, not least, the showy mimosa with its feathery
blossoms and delightful perfume. Passing by the
model estate of Mr. Hanbury, a paradise of beauty,
which he kindly allows visitors to see, our road
ascends and curves round a spur of a pine-clad
mountain, when there suddenly bursts upon the sight
a splendid panorama, consisting of the town of
Mentone, with its eastern and western divisions
lying at one's feet, with Roccabruna, Monaco, and
the l'Estérel hills in the distance, and the wide
expanse of the sea with its ever-varying shades of

blue and green. Such a view in a flood of sunshine
is a treat indeed, and not to be forgotten by any
tourist, however apathetic. As we descend into
Mentone the road is cut out of the solid rock, and
a deep gorge is crossed by the Pont St. Louis, a fine
specimen of masonry, which forms the boundary
between France and Italy, and where I had to
submit to my luggage being examined, my Italian
privileges having now ceased. I put up at the
Hôtel de Londres, a small place, but the cooking
was excellent, as I was informed by a Leicester
clergyman, who had ministered there for some years.
My first visit was to my old friend, Dr. Henry
Bennet, at the Hôtel des Anglais. Ill health had
compelled him to leave London every winter and take
up his residence and practice in Mentone, which
became through his influence and that of his book
" Eastward Ho and Westward Ho " the most popular
resort for invalids with delicate chests along the
whole length of the Riviera. The natives regarded him
in the light of the founder of its prosperity, and styled
him " the King of Mentone," and frequently pressed
him to assume the office of mayor, though a foreigner.
He was a perfect Frenchman in thought and speech,
and he carried in the muncipality great weight as far
as sanitary improvements were concerned. He had
a fine suite of rooms in his hotel, where he reigned
supreme ; the landlord and servants obsequiously
submissive to all his orders. He filled the hotel with
his patients. In the large dining-room there was a
T-shaped table at which he presided, and insisted on
having the windows open at the cross part, much to

the alarm of those delicate ones who thought too
much fresh air would kill them. Those, however,
who were obedient to his will were privileged to have
seats at the cross portion of the table, which was
called the "House of Lords," while the tail part was
styled the "House of Commons." I had breakfast
with him in his elegant apartments full of knick-knacks
and presents from grateful visitors, when he offered
to drive me in his handsome carriage and pair as far
as Monaco to hear the celebrated band of musicians,
the pick of all nations, and to witness the play at the
gaming tables, which I accepted in anticipation of
much pleasure, for the road had lovely scenery all
the way, and the Casino had acquired wide-world
renown for the numbers of people it had ruined
and the constant suicides that had taken place in the
first moments of despair and bewilderment at having
lost all. A bright sunny afternoon favoured our
delightful drive, and we both enjoyed the visit
exceedingly, returning in the shades of evening in the
glow of a setting sun with keen appetites for dinner.
After struggling up the mountains with a party of
ladies on mules to see the magnificent prospect from
S. Agnese one day, and on another to make an
excursion to Castellara, and not forgetting to note
the immense commerce in flowers going on per post
between Mentone and England, I regretfully took my
leave of this beautiful health resort, and made my
way to Nice.

The Corniche road continued still to present some
splendid bits of scenery *en route* to Nice, especially
as one approaches Villafranca Bay, and taking the

high road over the promontory which in its descent
looks down on the town nestling in the hollow. Nice
is said to have three distinct climates according to your
position in the city, whether this be in the old town,
on the Promenade des Anglais, or in the sheltered
situation of the "Strangers' Quarter," lying back
some distance from the sea front. Here one meets
in the winter season crowds of Russians, Germans,
French, and English, who congregate together as
much for pleasure as for health; and as money flows
freely, living is dearer in comparison with other
places on the Riviera. Therefore, after mounting
Castle Hill and doing the Public Gardens, there is not
much to see, I departed by train for Cannes, instead
of travelling by road along the coast which is flat
and uninteresting. Cannes may be defined as a
city of detached villas, snugly embowered in their
own detached grounds, which extend for miles on
each side of a splendid wide road, and having a
centre made up of fifty fine hotels, the outcome of
its well-deserved popularity as a sheltered wintering
place for delicate persons with weak chests. A
tourist may spend a very pleasant week there. The
islands of St. Marguerite and St. Honorat are well
worth a day's visit. The quaint old fortress and the
fortified monastery are fine specimens of middle-aged
strongholds in the days of bows and arrows. It is
well also to ascend to see the old parish church and
pottery works on Mount Chevalier, from which a fine
bird's-eye view of the town at its foot may be had, with
the bright sea in front and the Alps in the rear,
which afford such a protection from the dreaded

mistral wind from the north-west. Cannes is a quiet
family place, where home-life predominates over
fashionable display, and does not pretend to compete with her more flashy neighbour, where high
life reigns supreme, and boasts of its "Battle of
Flowers" as not second to that held in Rome.

Leaving Cannes I take rail to Hyères, another
health resort, well worthy of a short visit, because its
climate is so mild for invalids. The graceful large
palm trees lining its public promenade, bearing fruit
which actually ripens, is a truthful testimony to
its warm sunny aspect. Being three miles from the
station and the same distance from the sea is rather
against it; still it is much frequented by families seeking quietness and moderate living expenditure. The
natives cultivate largely the violet and the rose, which
grow profusely and are exported in large quantities.
Passing by Toulon, the great naval harbour of
France, I reach by rail Marseilles, its greatest commercial seaport, the counterpart of our Liverpool,
boasting 300,000 people all alive and active, and
carrying on an immense maritime traffic with
Africa, India, and Australia. The thing to do is to
mount the rather steep climb of the rock on which
the Cathedral of the Notre Dame de la Garde is
situated, crowned by the gilt figure of the Virgin, the
landmark and object of devotion to the sailors at sea.
From the terrace a grand view of the big city at
one's feet with its huge shipping docks is beheld.
Again a boat should be taken to the Chateau d'If,
where Mirabeau was confined, and the scene is laid
of Dumas' "Monte Christo." Marseilles is fully

exposed to the mistral and is one of the collest places in winter I ever visited. Before leaving the South of France, the land of lemons and oranges, I may just relate a legend which is superstitiously believed in by the lower orders : it is this. When Eve was expelled from the Garden of Eden she carried away with her a fine lemon, which she carefully nursed for a long time seeking a suitable soil to plant it in. At last arriving at Mentone she fixed upon that charming sunny spot as the best she had come across. So she deposited her lemon there, where it took root kindly, and has ever since thriven so plenteously and luxuriantly that the fruit is held in high esteem in Paris and deemed the finest in the world.

CHAPTER XV.

HAVING bid farewell to Marseilles, the *grand ritesse* landed me safely in Paris in about thirty-six hours, which I found in an awful state of confusion and consternation, in consequence of the unexpected failure of Overend and Gurney's bank, which was universally regarded as safe as the Bank of England. English gentlemen and ladies were vociferating loudly over their losses, and scanning eagerly the last news from London. After having had a good look at the beautiful Eugenie, whom I was lucky enough to see walking arm in arm with the Emperor in the Place de la Concorde, I made the best of my way to London to safeguard my own interests, as I was told that the "Bears" were trying to ruin the other banks by making a run upon them. But my bank was forewarned, and had protected itself against their sudden onslaught by getting into their coffers one and a quarter millions of money, and thus could meet every demand. When the settling-day came round the "Bears" had to repay 3 per cent. on the bank's stock; and thus the biters were bitten, and in some cases even to ruin! Here, again, Providence intervened in my favour, and I was thereby enabled to carry out my longed-for plan of settling in London. Beginning with unfurnished apartments in George Street, Hanover Square, I was lucky enough to secure the whole house after I had been there a few months. From the dining-room window I could see, and was often amused at, the splendid weddings which so often took place in St. George's Church, the steps up to which were carpeted with red cloth, generally indicative of a *mariage à la mode* among the aristocracy, and as these were frequently regarded a *mariage de convenance*, the steps were nicknamed "the steps to ruin," and in many instances it was only too true.

When my first London season came round I thought it would be to my advantage to be presented at Court, and as the then Adjutant-General kindly consented to act as my sponsor, I went and was introduced, not to the Queen, but to the young Prince of Wales, who represented her Majesty at the *levée*. I felt disappointed, and so did an elderly officer who had come all the way from India to see his Queen herself. He told me that he was old enough to be the Prince's father, and remembered his being born. But the fact was, her Majesty had been so cut up by the unexpected death of the Prince Consort—Albert the Good, as he was called—that she had not appeared in public for some time. The next best thing that could happen to me was to get a hospital appointment, which I succeeded in doing the first year of my residence in London, which brought me into personal contact with all sorts and conditions of

men, women, and children, from the duchess to the
dustman, from the peer to the pauper, especially with
that perplexing portion of the people since described
as the "submerged tenth." As a hospital physician
I came into close communion with the degraded
classes, and in one's mission of mercy among them
gained their confidence. The fact was very soon and
very forcibly revealed to me, that the drinking of
rough, *cheap* spirits in their raw and immature
character was the cause, as a general rule, of their
pitiful downfall, their deplorable debasement of body
and mind. I don't think the fact is brought home
with sufficient emphasis when the West End talk
glibly of the moral degradation of the East End.
No one would believe the deleterious, the diseasing
effects of these vile concoctions, first upon the body,
then upon the mind, except those who have had
actual experience of such in our public hospitals,
and in the homes—if you can call them such—of
those who apply as outsiders. Those who will closely
look into this perplexing problem as to what can be
done to stem the torrent of evils associated with this
engrossing vice, find themselves hedged about with
many difficulties, though the glaring truth is apparent
to any impartial looker-on, that this spirit-drinking
is the prolific mother of many miseries. When the
man or the woman is once down, and has lost all self-
respect, it seems an impossibility to reason them out
of the vicious and uncontrollable cause. They know
it, they feel it, they confess it with tears ; and it
matters not what position in society they may have
come from, they are all tarred with the same brush,

which marks them as the "devil's own." No blood ties, no social ties, no knowledge, scientific, literary, moral, or religious, in the least degree influences them, and one can only commit them to the gracious intervention of God's good Spirit to move them, come when and where that may.

Under these dire circumstances what can society, what can the nation and its Government do to redeem this pitiable condition of the lower classes and, by self-impoverishment, the very lowest classes? What will the upper middle and aristocratic orders do to ameliorate matters? Go into what is called "good society," and just see and hear for yourself, as one perfectly disinterested and unbiassed. You cannot help observing and feeling that there is some great controlling power at work, obstructing greatly efforts at reform, and encouraging this gigantic evil, this pernicious agency floating freely, without let or hindrance, in every nook and corner of the kingdom. Why is this drink question tabooed? Why is it a forbidden subject in fashionable circles? Why are you treading on delicate ground when you venture to allude to it under your breath? Why are conscientious people put down as fanatics who dare to give their opinion courageously on this momentous subject? The reply to these tangible questions is plain and evident enough to those who are not purposely blind. Vested interests is the answer; interests involving every moneyed class in society; 139 millions of gold invested by thousands of well-to-do people in the higher and middle ranks, who through the medium of huge brewing companies have each

and all a direct pecuniary stake in the manufacture
and *consumption* of intoxicating spirits. The kings
of the liquor trade, counting their millions, who have
made their concerns into *limited* companies, have
immense power in both houses of Parliament, and
exert that influence to protect and increase the
traffic, so as to enrich themselves and their legion of
subscribers, at the expense of the well-being, moral
and physical, of the great mass of the people. That
day is greatly to be deplored on religious, mental,
and physical grounds, when the spirit-lords of the
United Kingdom converted their grand paying properties into limited companies, tempting outsiders by
the inducement of heavy dividends to take shares
in their respective establishments, thus giving each
individual subscriber a direct moneyed interest in the
success of their venture, and what is worse, implanting in their minds a strong selfish motive to uphold a
wrong and to shut their eyes, or assume a silent
attitude, against what is a glaring national injustice,
which if they held themselves aloof and impartial
they would condemn and endeavour to suppress by
supporting the God-blessed Temperance movement
throughout the country. There can be no doubt
whatever that the strong and increasing wave of this
movement alarmed their lordships, and filled them
with fear and apprehension that their fine property
would be depreciated as time went on, so, worldly-
wise, they resorted to the above lamentable expedient
of propping up a falling house.

The magistrates, many of whom are owners of
public-houses themselves, have not the courage nor

the incentive to withdraw licences, not even when the publics are admittedly too numerous and their removal is desired by the local inhabitants—yea, not even when the houses have disgraced their rights by harbouring thieves, and become the resort of prostitutes, betting-hells, and the depot of stolen goods, are they disestablished.

The great majority of the " publics " and gin-palaces are "tied houses" belonging to the wealthy brewers, and these domineering owners and masters can and do exert widespread social and political influence ; so that any one, for example, who aspires to the coveted position of a M.P. has to reckon with and conciliate this powerful caste, which so often turns the scale at elections, and always in favour of that party which will shout the loudest for compensation to the publican, and no Sunday closing, &c. Though this pothouse influence is now becoming more or less counteracted by the Temperance party, which is every day gaining more and more strength in every town and village, the centre of hope, as the saviours of the country, are the Bands of Hope. The children —the rising generation—being secured, the parents become more or less interested in their well-being, and thus this valuable movement rouses their paternal instincts and excites their sympathies.

This is a subject of such vital importance to the commonweal, not only to this England of ours, but to the whole world, that I shall stop here and give it the next chapter to itself.

CHAPTER XVI.

WHATEVER I may have said in the previous chapter, I feel it does not devolve upon me as a layman to give moral advice, or thrust my opinions down the throats of others, as to whether they ought, or ought not, to drink strong alcoholic beverages; but what I do feel I may venture to do, and to do it without offending fixed prejudices, is to try to remove from the minds of the great mass of the people the crass and pitiable ignorance with respect to the misconception of the physiological action of alcohol on the living tissues of the human frame, and the tendency of the spirit to engender a variety of well-known diseases which the total abstainer is not subject to. There is a wonderful concensus of scientific opinion "up to date" that alcohol is a compound of carbon, hydrogen, and oxygen in certain fixed, defined proportions, forming a peculiar liquid, unique, stable, and singularly tenacious—a marvellous agent for evil, without a corresponding minimum for good. The greatest enemy in the universe manufactured by man for man, and the most diseasing of all liquids to the healthy organs of the human form divine, towards whose delicate organism and construction

it yields not the slightest particle of nourishment, or
the smallest modicum for the repair of its structure
by labour or exercise. And why not ? Because when
it is once swallowed, neither the stomach nor any
other organ in our constitution has the power of
digesting it, decomposing, or separating and re-
arranging its ingredients for the process of assimila-
tion ; but we have to submit in childlike helplessness
to its irritating and narcotic and benumbing influences. It is rapidly absorbed into our circulation,
and carried into every nook and corner of the entire
fabric, depositing itself unchanged and unchangeable
in the delicate and sensitive tissue of every vital
organ, notably the cells of the brain, producing
drowsiness, stupidity, and paralysis, interfering with
a healthy train of sound thought and reflection, and
muddling the logical capacity of the mind, rendering
unstable also the spinal movements.

It disturbs and ruffles the quiet, natural and har-
monious function of every organ with its temporary
artificial stimulation, setting up organic mischief in
its sound structure, slowly or rapidly it may be, but
with deadly certainty, in exact ratio to the quantity
collected and stagnating within us, and the inability
of the lungs, skin, and kidneys to expel the burden in
a given time, and the varying strength of individuals
to resist its morbific action. In a word, the frame is
in a state of artificiality in contradistinction to its
condition in a state of nature. It is beside the question here to comment upon alcohol and its uses as a
medicinal drug ; that must be left to the wisdom,
courage, and discretion of medical men, upon whom

must rest the sole responsibility of prescribing it, not as a luxury, but as a curative agent. Again, there is another characteristic peculiarity connected with the introduction of alcohol into our frames, namely, its singular tendency to accumulate by degrees, and fix itself in every part of our structure with an irresistible affinity—humanity bends beneath its despotic sway with absolute submission.

This fact leads us on to ask ourselves the very pertinent question — What are the effects of the gradual accumulation of this narcotic irritant and diseasing agent upon our healthy bodies? Well, the following are some of its disastrous results:— After our patients—it matters not what section of society they belong to—have continuously, daily, and habitually drunk wine, spirits, or beer in what some would deem moderate quantities (an indefinable standard) for a period of time, varying with constitutional differences, they are compelled to pull up, and put aside their alcoholic beverage—be that what it may—and why? because the whole system from head to foot has become gradually overcharged, soaked, we might say, like a sponge, with the continuous influx of alcohol, and the poor body, thus groaning under its intolerable burden, rebels against any further drinking, and a forced abstinence is imperatively demanded, till the bilious or gouty attack, headaches, fever, or other storms of serious sickness have subsided, and the alcohol is more or less washed out of the system by the physician's prescription.

Well, we will suppose the attack is safely over, and

they have narrowly escaped a fatal result in the form of paralysis or "Bright's disease," what do the convalescents do? Do they take a lesson of warning from their oft-repeated attacks? In the majority of cases, not they! No, in vain does the conscientious and patriotic physician reason with his patients, some of whom, perhaps, are blessed with the possession of even the most eminent and intellectual attainments, and disinterestedly reveals to them the real source of their ailment and the danger of its repetition. Some will exclaim in heated language, "What is the use of my splendid cellar of choice and valuable wines, mellowed with age and laid down with anxious care and great expense, if I am not allowed to enjoy them? Am I to abandon my boon companions (friends?), and throw into a state of confusion my recognised position in society?" I heard one man of considerable talent say, "I will die first," and die he did, in the course of time, a raving madman. You may argue till you are black in the face with such thoughtless beings, and others even in their most serious moods only pay passing heed to your remonstrance. Irresolute man, with childish efforts, resolves and re-resolves to be wiser and more circumspect for the future, but generally ends in falling back to his old habits. Now I would ask any practitioner engaged in a large practice in London, whether the above is not a true type of myriads of cases which come before him every year. Is it not very humiliating to a man of any moral or religious feeling to have to record the fact that such cases as above described constitute, at least two-thirds of the labours of every active medical man in our huge metropolis, and also in all our large centres of population throughout our country? There is not a section of society which does not come under this ban!

Such a mode of passing through this life must be condemned as a farcical drama unworthy of a man of common sense and sound reasoning, even taken from a worldly, social, or national standpoint, but how much more less becoming in the professing Christian, who, with his eyes open to its bitter fruits, obstinately refuses to give up his daily luxury (or even its occasional use), which prevents him from keeping the body in subjection to his rational mind and thought, and which clouds over every refined feeling of our nature. Let us look the above facts fearlessly in the face of truth and science, and may we not justly say that they constitute a key-note to the argument against the *continuous* use of alcoholic drinking, and, further, form the basis of our indictment against them as *daily* human beverages. It is to be hoped some good will eventuate to the reader when he reflects that we cannot alter by one iota the peculiar characteristics of alcohol when it is once within us; and, secondly, let him be thoroughly convinced and warned this evil spirit has an irresistible tendency to accumulate within us, and set up disease in our vital organs, notably the heart, brain, and lungs.

Let all those struggling young members who are desirous of getting on and succeeding in either of the professions, or in any of our competitive commercial pursuits, remember and take to heart that nothing tends so much to obstruct their progress as alcoholic drinking, leaving alone excessive smoking. Let them record deeply the stubborn facts which have been laid down for their guidance in the log-book of their memories, so that they will serve them as an unshakable rock upon which they can rest their faith and practice, and also base their replies when asked for their reasons for total abstinence, or, if not total abstainers, for ceasing to be daily and habitual drinkers of an alcoholic beverage.

There are four hundred honest, courageous, and patriotic medical men in London who have associated together to give up alcohol, and not to prescribe it for their patients if possible, and then only as a drug. And I shall be excused if I agree with them, for after fifty years of my life spent amid the sufferings of my fellow beings, and witnessing the fearful evils arising from drink in active warfare and in peace time, also in my hospital and private practice in London, embracing every rank in society, graduating down from the peer to the pauper—the evils involving in their destruction and ruin the high and the low, the rich and the poor, men, women, and children indiscriminately—my large and sad experience will not allow me to sit passively down and do nothing to reclaim and reform them. Before I quit this important subject, I would like to have just a little say in respect to the indulgence in drink, even to a moderate extent, upon the prospects of a professional man in London. This will be endorsed by many a poor talented fellow who has taken early warning by the forelock, but this I shall leave for the next chapter.

CHAPTER XVII.

My last chapter concluded with an expression that I had something further to say in relation to the habit of drinking intoxicants of the stronger sort among the young aspirants to fame in the three learned professions, and among those who intended to gain their bread by brain work. Well, those who have come to the front in their respective professions—some of them, whose names need not be mentioned as they stand out indelibly as household stars, illuminating the unthinking and ignorant masses by their speeches and their lives—these big minds tell us that it is physically and mentally impossible to retain their position of eminence if they did not make a point of being ever on the watch against any indulgence in excess. Nay, further, that they shunned any approach to a quantity that would lead to a state bordering on narcosis, headache, a flushed face, or confusion of ideas, such as would prevent them from rising in the morning with brain refreshed, or induce a feeling of languor and seediness, ill-prepared to fight the day's battle with a cloud of anxious, expectant, and argumentative people, perhaps sickly ones, impatiently clamouring for immediate relief,

and watching every expression on one's face with a
lynx-eyed scrutiny and earnestness. These wise
heads have arrived by personal experience at the
unshakable resolution that an unalcoholised brain
—a brain free from the tainting presence of spirit
in its delicate tissues—is in the most favoured and
active condition for the mind to work upon. And
if this be a logical conclusion on their part with
respect to their prosperity and success in a worldly
point of view, how about the higher classes of thought
and order of things? As the action of the mind
involves the reasoning soul, is not the whole mental
being placed in a more susceptible position for the
presence and active operation and indwelling of the
Divine Spirit, when it receives deeper and more
efficient and sensitive impressions from a material
organism that is not more or less benumbed, nar-
cotised, and handicapped by the presence of alcohol
circulating through its delicate cells? I would appeal
to all Temperance workers and ministers of the
Gospel, and all those who would efface themselves
by doing rescue work among the " submerged tenth,"
to reflect upon this burning question in this light, as
it constitutes the strongest argument in favour of
total abstinence.

But let us come down once more to consider our
subject from a worldly standpoint, as connected with
our every-day life. What facts do we glean from
comparing individuals? What encouragement do we
get from watching those who take strong drink and
those who do not? Do we not find that those who
will make the self-sacrifice and curb their desires are

10

more to the fore in their work, whether we regard
this as the labour of the mind or of the body, or of
both combined. Are they not more precise, more
decided, more ready, more enduring at their work,
and do we not extract out of them the fullest extent
of their natural powers? Let us take, for example,
the artisan, the watchmaker, the engraver on stone or
metal, the electrician, &c., do we not find that delicacy and refinement of touch which is the very
essence of perfect skill, the eye guiding the hand
with unerring rectitude? If the surgeon, for instance, is called upon for immediate action in time
of war, or in a mining district, with its oft-recurring
accidents, we see that he maintains that power of
instant decision and self-command which is the first
quality for the emergency. Then, again, our much-
respected nursing sisters, now faithfully to the front,
will be seen to possess great endurance night and day,
which strikes with wonder and envy those less careful
of their own powers and abilities. Thus, then,
these grand and cardinal virtues—precision, decision,
presence of mind, and physical endurance—are the
outcome of total abstinence from intoxicating strong
drinks to the very fullest extent that the Creator has
implanted them in our mental and physical condition;
hence we enjoy the sweets and the delightful fruits of
those talents with which we are entrusted by Heaven
in their most valuable bearing upon ourselves and
upon our fellow-creatures.

This being so, ought not the authorities regulating
our free education in the Board Schools to insist, as
a very important item in their programme, that the

teachers, male and female, should instruct the little
children—the fathers and mothers of a future generation—in the knowledge that alcoholic beverages,
beginning in moderate quantities, but leading up
inevitably to larger quantities, if *daily and continuously* taken, create in our frames a score of
diseases which would not exist in us but for the
presence and stagnation of the spirit in our vital
organs — besides reducing to a lower standard of
ability our natural gifts of mind and of body?

Let these facts be plainly instilled into our little
ones of every grade and station by parents and
instructors, public and private, so that when they
grow up they will not go astray from sheer ignorance.

I will conclude this chapter by affirming that
alcohol is such a fixed body, and has such a strong
affinity or liking for our tissues, that, as a rule, we
cannot shake it off as quickly as we drink it, hence
its evil effects ; and, to aggravate matters, the raw,
immature spirits drunk by the lower classes have a
strong narcotic, irritating and maddening, and diseasing action on the mind ; and following in the wake
of disease comes the loss of manly strength, of time
and money ; and linked to this sad triplet of troubles
are weak resolves, idleness, and worthlessness.

"And they all began with one consent to make
excuse." This well-known rebuff and refusal to an
invitation to meet others to celebrate a memorial
feast—a feast of reason, is not inapplicable to the
position in which the physician is posed when he
endeavours to call the attention of his patients and
friends to the drink question. It is a lamentable fact

that with one accord they begin to apologise for the daily habit of drinking alcoholic stimulants, and this with an unusual amount of disturbed equanimity and warmth of expression. Evidencing a disposition to shut up the mind and reason against any argument, and a disinclination to be logically convinced upon the subject—they will have none of it. We find little of the openness, candour, and willingness to hear the truth and facts of the case which is usually evinced when conversing on any other matter of daily interest.

An answer which is first and foremost on the tip of the tongue of the great majority is this, "My doctor has ordered me to take some stimulant." One of the most fashionable of these in the present day is whisky in some effervescing alkaline water. Heaven help the poor kidneys which are daily flushed with this and such-like irritating depletants. Well, we will grant that the doctor has done so at a time, perhaps, when extreme weakness and a flabby heart have supervened on a long illness, and he wished to bridge them over the temporary exhaustion. Now, is it not very unfair and unjust to make the poor doctor the scapegoat for the subsequent troubles when the occasion for stimulating has passed away, and they still continue to take alcohol habitually? They would be acting more honourably and generously towards the faculty if they confessed the truth that they went on with the luxury because they liked it, and took all the blame and responsibility on their own shoulders, and thus exonerated the doctors, who at first only prescribed it medicinally.

Again, there is a small community of weakly beings
in this wealthy country of ours, degenerate offsprings
of decaying families, to whom a small quantity of
alcohol appears a necessity of life, without which they
feel, they assert, that they would melt away, and
would be incapable of meeting the small demands
upon their strength—a strength which will not carry
them through half a day's work, or no work at all, or
it may be that they are rusting out their lives in a
state of *dolce far niente*—a condition often seen among
the idly rich, who often bore one with their *maladie
imaginaire*. Such-like beings of both sexes affirm
with no little warmth that they would faint, swoon,
or die away if they did not have their daily reviver—
a " pick-me-up " to tide over the despondency arising
from congenital infirmity or the sinking sensation at
the pit of the stomach. Here the doctor is placed in
a difficult position—he has to choose the lesser of two
evils ; either he must yield with a good grace and
submit to expediency, or lose his moral hold upon his
patients as a gentle persuader and admonisher should
he decline to visit and watch over them.

I have a word more to say in reference to this particular sinking and die-away feeling at the pit of the
stomach, which is almost invariably experienced, now
and again, by those from whom the alcoholic stimulant—the artificial prop—is withdrawn, and which is
temporarily removed by the drinker resorting to
another quantum of his paralysing narcotic. I
believe the sinking sensation, more intolerable in
some than in others, is the cause of more pledges
being broken than anything else. Then comes the

question, how is it to be overcome, and finally disposed of, stamped out, in fact, by those who have made up their minds to abstain. I generally observe that it continues with more or less of severity from two to six months, and then disappears altogether. In those of a very nervous temperament it requires no little patience, perseverance, and moral courage to resist the temptation, the inward crave to fall back on the old pain killer, which is in reality the veritable cause of the sensation and distress.

If the upper ranks of society would sink their pride, and resort to what has been found so beneficial among the working classes, namely, the homely oatmeal porridge well cooked with milk or good beef tea, they would get not only certain relief from their passing distress, but an acquisition of strength truly remarkable.

Again, when common tea is taken as a beverage, the infusion should not allow to brew more than three minutes before it is drawn off, inasmuch as sodden tea in most persons gives rise to a very serious form of depressing dyspepsia; so depressing and painful is it among the poor seamstresses of London, who take it three or four times a day, that it is impossible to relieve them till it be abandoned. It is, therefore, no wonder that they add rum to their cup when they can afford it—thus adding mischief to mischief. " Tea Dyspepsia " was the name I gave to these very numerous cases among my hospital patients. I will conclude this article by expressing a hope that I may live to see the day when the upper crust of society will wave their exclusiveness, and make the self-sacrifice for the sake of the healthy and happy well-being of those below them by drinking stimulants occasionally instead of daily as a necessary adjunct to every meal.

If they would but set the fashion afloat, for strong is the force of fashion, those in the lower social grade would, from sheer love of imitation, follow the good example, which would react again on those of a still lower type, and blessed would be the change all along the line.

Some of my readers will think that I have been rather long-winded over this, to not a few, unpalatable subject ; and yet it comprehends the most burning question of the day in the social economy of our race, not only in England, but in the Greater Britain. Notwithstanding all our grand reforms and boasted civilisation, our scientific progress, our increase of wealth and luxuries, refinement and knowledge, Britain is still left under the ban of its proverbial drunkenness and debauchery, the very scorn of nations. If we look at the horrid sequences of this dreadful system—its curses, its calamities, its huge difficulties, it may well arouse the attention and devotion and earnestness of all our young people, upon whom devolves in a great measure its cure and suppression. Viewing the vastness of the subject from a vital and patriotic standpoint, I don't see that I have said one word too much for the reasoning mind to reflect upon.

CHAPTER XVIII.

HAVING visited nearly every country in Europe, and having time and means at my disposal, I thought it would be advantageous and profitable to go further a-field and "see the wonders of the world abroad," as revealed to us in a tour round the globe. Hence, accompanied by my wife, we took a cabin in that most delightful of the P. and O. steamers, the *Victoria*, and left our shores in November, 1889, when winter was beginning to stare us in the face. Nothing very sensational occurred to us between England and the Mediterranean. Even the Bay of Biscay was in a kind mood and comparatively calm, and did not churn up either sex as is its wont. We had a lively lot of passengers on board, and leaving behind all the icyness characteristic of the British nature, a general thaw took place, and figuratively shaking hands all round, we one and all made up our minds to enjoy ourselves. Every berth was taken up in this favourite ship, the helm of which was under the experienced guidance of the commodore of the P. and O. Company's fleet. We had therefore a large first-class company, which had to be dined at two separate hours—namely, the House of Commons at 6 p.m., and the House of Lords at 8, the captain presiding at the latter more aristocratic hour, when evening dress was the rule and not the exception.

A good deal of card-playing went on, not unmixed with some gambling—an evil sequence not to be surprised at among a lot of idle rich young men ; but the highest stake played was by a bewitching young damsel, chaperoned by an elderly lady, who threw down before an admiring group a most telling trump card, which consisted of an assertion, made through her well-tutored duenna, to the effect that her piquant and fascinating *protégée* had declined sixteen offers of marriage already, but the siren kept back the secret fact that she had speculated in a return ticket to Malta in hopes that she might be fortunate enough in securing a seventeenth which would be to her taste and liking. Now there were many well-gilded and good-looking eligibles on board, but somehow or other none of them came up to the winning post, and Malta was reached without anything of an engagement having been made. It was most amusing to the looker-on to witness the clever way in which she handled the ribbons of her team of admirers—coaxing and wheedling some, and gently rebuffing others. But she was determined to finish her game pluckily by inviting six of her most promising devotees to a champagne dinner ashore, with all the delicacies of the season, and so liberally did the bottle go round, that at midnight, on coming to terms with a cabman to bring them back to the ship, they quarrelled and knocked him down, the issue of which was that our diners-out were taken to the police station, where they were kept in durance vile for three hours till the superintendent was roused out of his bed, who kindly released them just in time to catch the steamer before she left the harbour! Thus ended an escapade, and an unusual spice of self-centred vanity, which served as a subject for a nine days' talk among the young people, and varied the monotony between Malta and Brindisi.

I introduced myself to the Rev. G. M——, going out to Sydney to join the Incumbent of St. Philip's Church. He was a fine specimen of what is defined as Muscular Christianity, and an eloquent extempore preacher. When I asked the captain to allow him to perform the services on Sunday in the first-class saloon, he surprised me by objecting rather brusquely, and stating that he should officiate himself, being, as he said, bishop of his own ship! So our only Episcopalian clergyman on board was forced to be content with holding a service in the second saloon, where I read the lessons for him, and we secured an excellent choir and mustered a good congregation, the waiters crowding the doorways, and others listening through the open skylights to catch the words of a most heart-stirring address.

Brindisi, 2,640 miles from London, was reached on a most brilliant Sunday. There is nothing worth noting except an old Roman gateway and the remains of an ancient fort. No service was held; all seemed busy in the shipping of fresh passengers and luggage, haling from the overland route, and the whole surroundings betokened a working week-day appearance.

After a delightful voyage of two and a half days in a perfect calm we reached Port Said, where I landed just to say that I had trod on African ground. It is a low, dirty place, with equally dirty Arabs, but the rapid way in which this unwashed crew coaled the steamer was a wonder to every one, and at nightfall, when it is carried on under the electric light, their black, greasy, nearly naked bodies frisking rapidly about, passing and re-passing along their to-and-fro gangways, they are more like so many unearthly demons than anything else one can compare them to. Our distance from London is here 3,570 miles.

We passed through the Suez Canal at night under the guidance of the electric light radiating from our foremast, which illumined the water for a considerable distance ahead, and doing away with any difficulty in passing other vessels at the various sidings *en route*. As we neared the pretty French town of Ismalia, quite an oasis in the desert, we witnessed a very interesting sight to the eyes of Westerns. About 500 camels were employed in carrying off in box panniers the sand from a heap forty feet high, which was a source of trouble and expense to the Canal Company, because it kept drifting into the cutting and necessitated dredging out. The sagacious animals quietly lay down to be loaded, and then struggled up to mount the hill in their usually sluggish fashion, in order to deposit their burden at a safe distance from the bank. After passing in review Mount Sinai with its three points, there was little worth recording in steaming down the Red Sea, except that it was not quite so like a Turkish bath at

120 as usual. When we were in it midway, and no
land visible on either side, we were startled by ladies
shrieking on deck, and running hither and thither
shaking their skirts; the alarm being occasioned by
several large locusts settling down on the vessel and
hiding themselves away in any nook and cranny they
could find, even to the crawling up the ladies' legs or
ascending inside the gentlemen's trousers. Some,
two and a half inches long, were secured as specimens, and were furnished with pretty green wings.
We could well understand how a cloud of such formidable insects would soon make a clean sweep of
anything green, and lay bare in a very short time
thousands of acres of agricultural produce. It must
have been a fearful curse on Pharaoh and his people
when the plague of locusts was sent, for it is said
that they filled all the houses without distinction, and
ate up every herb of the land, all that the hailstorm
had left. " Very grievous were they," covering the
face of the whole earth, and consuming every green
thing through all the land of Egypt. The God of
Israel and of Moses must have been sorely tried and
angry in those days. Having demolished our insect
pest, which for a time created so much alarm among
our fair ones, we reached Aden in peace the following
morning. This town, with its fortress, was formerly
remarkable for its huge tanks for the conservation of
rain-water to supply the natives and the shipping,
but these are now obsolete, other means of supply
being substituted. The boys diving into the sea
after some silver coins thrown into it by the passengers
were most expert, for it mattered not how far down

the shining piece had got, they never failed to reach
it and bring it up to the surface triumphantly between their teeth. Imposition is the order of the day
here with Arab purveyors of fancy goods. One very
ordinary article for sale is the long boa made of
ostrich feathers. They began by asking £3, and
kept aloof from any deduction, gesticulating that
they were giving them away at that figure, and that
it was simply ruin to take less, looking as innocent
as they do at a mock auction in London, till the
vessel showed signs of leaving, and just as we were
about to haul up the gangway ladder an Australian
gentleman went down to their bumboat, and, displaying two glittering sovereigns (an irresistible sight
to an Oriental), brought back four of the boas—which
was a bargain certainly, and out of which he could
make a good profit when he reached Sydney. At
Aden we were 4,965 miles away from home.

Crossing the Indian Ocean we hardly encountered
a single sail. Having had a glimpse of the Socotrine
Islands, where much of our medicinal aloes is
obtained, we entered the fine deep harbour of
Colombo, where steamers of any size are safely
anchored behind a grand solid stone breakwater of
about a mile in length, and a fine promenade for
the townspeople. As the Indian mail had not
arrived we had the whole day before us, so we went
ashore to visit this picturesque town, so prettily embosomed in its evergreen trees, yielding abundance of
fruit of many kinds. Declining a ride in the quaint
two-wheel vehicles drawn by a man between the
shafts, we chartered a waggonette and paid the

museum a visit, which contains a fine collection of Singalese objects of natural history, notably the turtles, which I should say are the largest in the universe, and snakes of a prodigious size. Being Sunday, we attended Divine service in the cathedral, a small church of no pretensions to beauty, and while we were inside a violent tropical rain came down, which passed through the wooden roof, warped into cracks by heat, down the walls, and out at the doors, a wonderful sight for English eyes ; but the deluge of water did not distract the attention of the congregation or upset the placid native mind, who entered heartily into the responses and the singing with a correctness of pronunciation which we at home are strangers to. The native portion of the town was very smelly and dirty, with a surface drainage, and appears built on marshy ground, hardened by added soil and regularly dyked and drained, but in the new part the buildings are good and solid—even fine, such as the barracks. All the streets are made to radiate in a straight line towards the park as to a common centre. The public roads are beautifully kept, and as smooth as those made with asphalt. A large body of Lascars left our vessel at Colombo, their three years of contract service being over with the P. and O. Company, and when they left the ship they gave three good hearty English cheers from the barge, showing how well they had been treated by the Company's officers and crews. I was much pleased with the natives, who conduct themselves in a very orderly, quiet manner, and seem well contented under their English rulers, under whom they thrive and have implicit faith. The free-and-easy way in which the local jewellers trust our people is something astonishing, putting a wonderful trust in an English-man's word. In one case I heard of a city man who was entrusted with £15 worth of jewels on approval, and when he got to London had the stones tested and valued, and the tradesman, being an expert, offered him £50 for his bargain, which he declined, whereupon the owner sent off at once his cheque to Colombo. On his return to Melbourne he invested a much larger amount on the same condition, the precious stones being principally sapphires in settings of cheap gold, the usual custom with the Singalese makers, and the same good faith was observed by both parties. It is not an easy matter to distinguish the sexes; the male has a very scanty beard, and both he and his mate wear their coal-black wavy hair long behind, and wind it up into a knot on the head. The cut of the man's features is decidedly feminine. They are both very cheery and amiable, and dearly love money-making. The very lowest are so indus-trious and thrifty that they get on and become rich. We had no time to take a trip by train to Candy, a town in the mountains 8,000 feet above the sea-level, which is cool and beautiful, and where tea planta-tions are numerous. That man deserves well of his country, and indeed of Europe too, and his name ought to be perpetuated by a splendid monument, who first thought of substituting the tea for the coffee plant in Ceylon, when the latter had by repeated cropping exhausted the soil! I must not forget to mention that there is in the public gardens a tree called "the Traveller's Palm," from which, when nicked, fresh water flows out. We need to reside in a hot and thirsty land to appreciate fully this God-sent provision to His people. Our distance here from England is 7,058 miles.

Leaving Colombo at 1 p.m., and steaming down its beautifully wooded coast, green to its water edge with palms and cocoanut trees, we cross the Line at midnight of the next day, and the following morning we are 170 miles south of it, traversing a dead-calm sea without a sign of life on, or in, the water, not even a flying fish disporting itself to vary our monotony. We had not proceeded much further southward before we encountered the South-East Trade Wind, which slightly headed us all the way to Western Australia, and more or less disturbed the equanimity of some of our fair passengers, especially when the deck chairs broke away from their moorings, often causing a ludicrous upset. We had shipped at Colombo a very pleasant and intelligent traveller, Mr. Theo. Davis, our British Vice-Consul at Honolulu, who had been touring through India with his son, a gentleman who took a deep and active part in mission work, especially among the young men and children in the Haiwaia Islands, where he was the proprietor of some very extensive sugar plantations. His cheery conversation, interspersed with most amusing anecdotes, kept our saloon table quite lively; and what with concerts, dancing, and theatricals, we passed away many hours that would otherwise have been very dull and wearisome, and tended to shorten the ten days' steaming required before we could be

landed at St. George's Sound, the first point the mail
steamers touch at on the Australian continent. It is
very remarkable that between Colombo and this point
we never sighted a single vessel, nor had we a glimpse
of any land nor the sight of any living thing, fish,
flesh, or fowl—which is very astonishing considering
the immense expanse of ocean we had traversed,
3,390 miles. We are here 10,448 miles from our
dear old home, and as this chapter has been rather
a prolonged yarn, I shall rest upon my oars awhile
before I begin another which will be descriptive of
scenes and people so widely different to those we have
left behind at the Antipodes.

CHAPTER XIX.

Albany is the name of the town and port in King
George's Sound where the mails are left for Western
Australia. It possesses a fine long pier, supporting a
railway, cranes, &c., but the water is too shallow to
allow large vessels to come up alongside of it, hence
we had to land from a steam-tug. We found the
town a progressive one, with several good buildings,
especially those for public worship. Overlooking the
town and harbour is a steep hill, up which we
ascended, and from the top were rewarded with a
magnificent view inland of forty miles, and with the
sea and shipping at our feet. The ground was
covered with a variety of wild flowers, notably with
the white-blossomed myrtle. Our party returned to
the ship laden with a large quantity of these flowers,
which made the saloon quite gay-looking.

We took on board here an immense quantity of
bananas, which is a regular article of commerce, and
the huge spikes of fruit were suspended by their strong
stalks over the deck-houses to ripen. Albany is the
terminus of the railway to Perth, which is the capital
city of Western Australia. Considering that we were
now, December 19th, in midsummer at the Antipodes,

the air was so cool that we required our winter wraps,
and this, with a roughish sea, continued all the way
to Adelaide, which we reached on Sunday morning,
December 22nd. This city is situated about six miles
from the landing-stage—a stage from which is exported the finest wheat in the world—where we
deposited several of our passengers, whose acquain-
tance had ripened into pleasant friendship during our
voyage, and from whom we had pressing invitations
to go and stay, with characteristic Australian hospitality ; but the heat is intense to a fresh European,
the town being located in a sort of well-like hollow,
backed by hills to the north and east, which seem to
concentrate the rays of the sun into a sort of focus
below. These hills are a very pretty object from the
deck of our vessel, being thickly wooded, and dotted
here and there with white villas peeping out of the
green—residences of the well-to-do merchants who
reside there during the hot months. The railway to
Melbourne zig-zags over them also, and the views,
they say, from this line are very grand. Many
persons leave the ships at this port of call in order
to enjoy the splendid prospects, and get to Melbourne
much quicker than we can steam it. Here we revelled
in the luxurious Adelaide grape, and we took on board
a large quantity of eight different kinds of delicious
fruits to add enjoyment to our Christmas dinner, and
also piles of evergreens and flowers to decorate our
saloons and drawing-rooms. It was at Adelaide that
we received our first Antipodean telegram, hailing
from Sydney, giving us a hearty welcome to the
Australian Colonies, warning us that we had touched

the fringe of civilisation again, though we were now
11,455 miles from home.

Continuing our course northward, we arrived on
Monday night in sight of Melbourne, having been
piloted up the tortuous channel of Port Philip for
forty miles, and reached the harbour of Williamstown, to which we were securely lashed at 10 p.m.
Here we were in deep water, and there is a terminus
of a short line to the city. As we were to remain
there all Tuesday, we took our seats in the train and
went off to pay a visit to this wonderful upshot of a
mushroom town which shows what heaps of gold can
do in a short space of time. It would be simply futile
to try to describe the magnificence of some of its
public buildings. They are on such a gigantic scale
that I do not believe there is a town in Europe
which can boast of so many in so small a space. The
Houses of Parliament, isolated in their splendid public
gardens, and the Town Hall are superb in size and
architecture, and strike the visitor with wonder : and
no less so do also the extraordinary height of the stores
and offices in Collins Street and Elizabeth Street,
some running up to an elevation of thirteen stories,
so valuable has become the ground for building purposes. In Burke and Owenson Streets we met the
fashionables promenading in their Sunday best, it
being Christmas week ; and though an Englishman
would say that the get-up was, upon the whole, rather
loud and vulgar, still one could see that the crowds
were well-off, and no signs of poverty were visible
whatever. Melbourne is a very extensive city, spreading over a large area, with outlying suburbs of con-

siderable size and population—some as much as
10,000—made up of four-roomed shanties in plots of
ground, the occupier being the owner; and when a
man has by industry and thrift acquired one of these
freeholds, he has a vote and a stake in the welfare of
the city, and he becomes a true Conservative in feeling and principle, and you hear no more of socialism
or rowdyism, divide and divide again, &c.; and
though they listen attentively to what Mr. George
has to say, they end in laughing at him. Mr. R., a
well-known and extensive merchant in Melbourne,
asked us to stay with him. He was brimful of information respecting the social, political, and religious
aspect of the city, and he told me that, provided the
wants and needs of the Church were clearly made
manifest to the people, money to any amount was
always forthcoming both for the clergy and the
buildings.

Taking our seats in a cable tram, we came down
Collins Street with a fearful rush to Spencer Station,
where we got into the train for Williamstown, and
on the road down we passed close to the race-ground,
most peculiarly and conveniently situated in a hollow,
with an amphitheatre of hilly slopes around it, so
that men, women, and children can look down, in
their thousands, and enjoy the races at their feet in
comfort and safety. This natural formation of the
land would have been singularly well adapted for the
Olympic games, and only required a canvas covering
to make it a Coloseum on a gigantic scale.

We passed Christmas Day at sea, between Melbourne and Sydney, and at luncheon we had a most

luxurious display of viands, comprising a large boar's head stuffed with minced meat ; a game pie decorated with a pheasant's head and tail feathers ; and in the centre a huge cake three feet high, replete with ornaments on its three stories, and crowned by Old Father Christmas in his own proper costume, backed by dishes of prawns in jelly, crayfish, &c. The big saloon, itself beautiful in white and gold, was rendered still more so by a most elaborate arrangement of evergreens and flowers, the work of our fifty waiters. At 7 p.m. we sat down to a dinner of several courses of delicacies in season and out of season, such as the richest nobleman in England could not have got together for love or money. We had, of course, to thank our refrigerator for yielding, as from a huge ice-house, such things as green peas and ducks, fresh salmon, game of all sorts, brought from home to supply us the whole voyage out—and to top all we had a dessert set before us consisting of eight different kinds of fresh fruits, such as would gladden the eye and moisten the palate of the most exacting epicure.

I got up at 5 a.m. to see the sun rise over the Pacific, and to enjoy one of the most lovely sights in the world, namely, the entrance into Sydney Harbour by the " Heads," a narrow passage between two sharp rocky projections, and a glorious trip up the port for seven miles to Sydney itself. *En route* the scenery is unique, consisting of pretty creeks, and suburban villas on the slopes of well-wooded hills, always green to the water edge, and piebalded with white villas, all protected by verandahs, and some more pretentious with towers or turrets. The harbour was dotted here

SYDNEY.

and there with many yachts of all sorts and sizes (every Sydneyite being a born yachtsman), interspersed with a large sprinkling of huge steamers and sailing vessels hailing from every clime, and as we neared the " circular quay "—the well-known landing place—we passed six men-of-war sleepily at anchor, keeping guard over this, one of the wealthiest and most bustling of ports. Within so small a water area I should opine that there is not in the whole commercial world so much energy and exchange of commodity going on as at this, only one of the quays of the city. The number of landing stages, the repeated going to and fro of the local steamers to the different points of this port, consisting of a multiplication of inlets, each with its stage and adjoining gigantic warehouses, a collection of busy centres most perplexing and confusing to a stranger at first. Not one-half of the extent of these active shipping points can be seen from any one spot on the opposite, or what is called the " North Shore," nor can the harbour be photo'ed as a whole, though what one can take in is a wonderful sight under a brilliant clear sky. Perhaps the grandest view of all is obtained from the top of the lighthouse built near the south " Head." The electric light radiated from this tower is so powerful that it quite dazzled my vision as I was sitting in a drawing-room window four miles away, and from the top of it I saw one day upwards of thirty yachts racing up and down the harbour—a very pretty panorama as they each turned round the light-ship with their white sails glistening in the sun. I will not attempt a description of the public buildings

TOWN HALL, SYDNEY.

in Sydney—they are so many ; but the Post Office,
Cathedral, and especially the Town Hall, stand out
pre-eminently beautiful, notably the latter, which the
Sydneyites may well be proud of, as containing the
largest organ in the largest hall in the world.

The people of this city are a picnic-loving community,
and to carry this pleasure into practice make a holiday
whenever they can devise an excuse. Wishing to see
how a party of excursionists would conduct themselves,
I early one morning joined a train going to the Hawksbury River with about four hundred men, women, and
children, surprisingly got up in their holiday attire of
silks, muslins, and feathered hats, with their brown
arms and hands encased in long gloves to hide their
workaday look. When we arrived at Peat's Ferry
on this river, called the Rhine of Australia, we
boarded a steamer, which took us up a remarkable
serpentine stream, having this singular peculiarity, that
after turning one promontory we get into a sort of
lake-like reach which appears completely land-locked,
and when one gets to the end, and you fancy the
steamer is going headlong into the rock, it suddenly
turns round and gets into another reach of the same
appearance. The banks are very picturesque, and
would yield many a good landscape, the red sandstone rock standing out from thick foliage and the
eucalyptus issuing from the crevices interspersed with
many flowering shrubs—notably the red Christmas
bush—and dotted here and there with wooden villas
for summer residences, which are shut up during the
winter. On our return we had an opportunity of
examining the fine railway suspension bridge consist-

ing of seven spans, each of 480 feet long. It produces quite an ocular delusion, for the further span when viewed from either end appears so small-looking that one cannot believe that it is the same width and height. The engineers have been much complimented on this fine piece of iron trellis-work.—Now with respect to the behaviour of this company of pleasure-seekers. I have never in any country witnessed anything so well conducted and orderly. The characteristic "billy tea tin" accompanied each family, and I did not see any one drink any intoxicating beverage whatever; hence there was no rowdyism, or practical joking, or vulgar brawling, and when they entered the train for the homeward journey of a hundred miles it was done as quietly as if they had been so many lords and ladies, instead of the representatives of every working class in the city—for all are expected to join the fraternity of working men and women, if they mean to hold their own in busy Sydney. Before we left the Hawksbury, I should have mentioned that I saw a catfish caught which has a nail-like spear projecting from its head, and a stab from which is so much dreaded by the fishermen as it is very dangerous, and also what they call the stinging fish, which strikes with its tail and hurts one considerably. It being a hot day many would have enjoyed a good bathe, but they feared the sharks, which ascend this river from the sea. Before proceeding to descant upon the Sydney races and the caves in the Blue Mountains, I shall rest awhile.

CHAPTER XX.

On Saturday, January 4th, I paid the racecourse at Ranwick a visit of inspection. It is situated on a flat with rising ground on one side, so that the whole circle can be clearly seen without going on the grand stand. Racing is quite an institution among the Sydney people, they are a regular horsey class. Every colonist is born, as it were, in the saddle. The races occur about once a fortnight, the prizes are of small amount. I saw both flat and hurdle races. The bulk of the horses differ from ours about the rump, which slopes downwards like a barb, and tends to bring the hocks closer together; but they have the advantage over English horses in having deeper chests with very muscular forelegs and well-developed large joints, with the head small and stag-like. I saw twenty run in one race and eighteen in another, and they were all so fleet that they ran throughout in such close quarters that one might have covered them with a sheet; no one horse beat his opponent by a length or two, as one sees so often in England. The two-year-old stands up in as good a form as our three-year-old does, thanks to the climate and the grass. In one race I saw twenty horses jump the hurdles

almost simultaneously, and came to the post in a
ruck together like a flock of pigeons, and coloured like
a bed of pansies—one of the prettiest sights I ever
beheld. I cannot say much for the betting ring: it
was about as noisy as Epsom, differing, however, in
this, that many ladies came down from the grand-
stand and joined the groups of gentlemen in the
gambling ground, and it is to be hoped acted as
checks to bets of extravagant amount. The crowd
outside were very orderly and good-tempered, and
the book-keepers, being all publicly registered, confined the stakes to the small sums of one shilling or
half-a-crown. I saw no drunkenness on the course,
nor any strong drink taken in the booths, but there
was a large demand for fruit, which was excellent
and cheap, and the " billy tea tin " was not forgotten.
There was none of that " rough " element present
which is so prevalent on English race-grounds; and as
I walked back with the crowd to the city I saw no
disorderly horseplay whatever. The women and
children were quite safe from insult or molestation of
any kind. I could not help asking myself, are all
these people, the outcome of every class, really the
offspring of English people? Well, all I can say is,
I wish their relatives at home would behave as well.
I can bring in a word here about Sunday closing; in
Sydney they have it, and one Sunday night I was
returning from the north shore, and passed along the
streets in the principal thoroughfares, and I found all so
quiet and peaceful that it might be well compared to
a city of the dead! I was told that if a man is seen
zig-zagging along in a state of drunkenness in the

public streets, he is immediately "run in" by the police, when we, in our large towns, would let them alone to find their way home, provided they were not disorderly ; but in Sydney, whether disorderly or not, the authorities are down upon them sharp, and will not look on with indifferentism upon such a reproach to social morality.

No visitor should fail to take a tram-ride of six miles to see the pretty little bay of Coogee, a sweet nook nestling in shrubs, and rapidly becoming a popular sea-bathing resort for the citizens. It would be well also, in order to judge of the wide extent of the other outlying suburbs, all in touch with one another as far as the large town of Paramatta—a distance of sixteen miles from the mother city, and forms a very interesting ride by railway, which gives also a good idea of the huge area upon which this widespread city is built, each suburban villa or mansion being surrounded by its own well-wooded grounds. Balmain, so well seen from the Observatory Gardens in Sydney, is situated on a spur of land running into the port, and is now a large municipal town of itself ; there one can see how the thrifty artisans are building houses for themselves, and very near may be seen a new grand dock, which is excavated out of the solid sandstone rock on one side of Cockatoo Island, which will take in the largest steamers afloat. Having obtained an introduction to Major ——, the manager of the Mint, he kindly showed and explained to me the whole process, from the assaying to the blocking out of each sovereign, which, if it were two-tenths of a grain too light was cast aside by the working of a very singular automatic piece of machinery, the amount of alloy being 11 per cent., as in England. I was asked to take a seat on the platform and give an address to an audience of several hundred men at the Young Men's Christian Association Hall. which the working-men put up at a cost of £40,000. It contains a library and reading-room, a gymnasium, and a coffee-room, &c. I was told that I should have to face a large body of sceptics, who would not attend any ordinary place of public worship, but would slip into this hall and listen to its bright and cheerful music, and tolerate without a sneer or interruption the short addresses from different *laymen* on the subject of morals and religion.

Rising up early one morning, I took the train to the Blue Mountains, at the foot of which we crossed the Nepean River, that supplies Sydney with water—a distance of forty miles—irrigating also the Emu plain, noted for its extensive orange and peach plantations. Our train begins the ascent by zigzagging, being drawn up one incline, and pushed up the next by the engine and carriages going into a siding at each angle, thus reversing the order of going at every gradient, till we reached the plateau, or dividing ridge, when we went along a slight rise till we got to Mount Victoria. Finding that I had time to spare, I continued on, to see a grand engineering feat—the "Great Zig-zag," which terminates the mountain railway and brings one down to the town of Lithgow, in a valley boasting of four valuable colleries and a large pottery manufactory, the manager of which was kind enough to show me the whole pro-

ZIG-ZAG RAILWAY, BLUE MOUNTAINS, LITHGOW VALLEY N.S.W.

cess. He complained of the competition and other difficulties the company had to contend with, by the old country deluging the Sydney market with its condemned goods, the imperfections of which the squatter could not detect.

On my return journey, the scenery from the Zigzag was even grander, and I had plenty of time to dwell upon it, as the ascent is a slow affair, and done on the same system as I have already described. Mount Victoria was my resting-spot for the night, in a fairly good hotel, but the bed was very hard. This mount is covered with villas and a few restaurants, and is the resort of residents from the hot towns during the summer month. Here the climate puts one in mind of Scotland.

The next morning we were up to an early breakfast, and took our seats in a coach, which carried its eight passengers to the "Half Way" house, as it is called, where we lunched, and having changed horses, continued our journey, through dense forests of eucalyptus, till we reached the Caves, now named "Janelon," at six o'clock, in time for dinner; the constant jolting over the ruts having made us desperately hungry. The one hotel here, occupying, with a road and a small brook, the whole of a pretty little creak, is styled "The Accommodation House," but was not very accommodating, it being crowded with tourists, twenty-nine of whom had to make the most of twenty-four beds. Professor L——, of the Sydney University—a most learned and agreeable companion —and myself were fortunate in getting a small bedroom, with two beds in it. Mr. Jeremiah Wilson, the

12

proprietor and discoverer of the caverns, gave us most excellent meals, considering the distance we were from any stores. The next morning I made one of a party of ladies and gentlemen, overflowing with life and good-humour, to pay the right-half of the Imperial Cave a visit, which is lightened up by Government with electricity, and our guide illuminated the more beautiful parts with the addition of the combustion from the magnesian wire, each person having to pay five shillings towards this item of expense, otherwise everything else is free. I will not attempt to describe minutely the splendid dazzling beauties of this huge underground cavern. The white and red colouring in distinct divisions of what is called "The Shawl and Curtain Drapery" is most peculiar, and as transparent as hanging sheets of porcelain. Again, another remarkable feature is the singular shape of the stalactites in the Mystery Cave, where they assume most fantastic forms—some like twigs of trees pointing sideways, and some even upwards, which is quite inexplicable considering that the accretion from the carbonate of lime in solution is from above, and the natural gravitation downwards. The bones of wallambi and other animals are found here encrusted in the deposit, and when the crust is broken the bone within is found intact. A good specimen was shown to me of a small vertebra and a jaw-bone, with alveolar process complete, and these in a cavern six hundred feet below the surface. Another wonderful sight is the "Broken Column," the upper part not being in line with the lower, which can only be explained by an earthquake breaking and diverting the column from its original position, how many thousands of years ago I will leave geologists to determine! The cavern called "Lucinda," after the wife of the discoverer, is sweetly pretty, and it boasts of a fine specimen of the shale-formation. After a good deal of stooping and corkscrew ascents and descents, we regained the iron gate which bars the entrance, and returned to the hotel to luncheon, after which refreshment we started again to explore the left half of the Imperial Cave. This is very much a repetition of the right half, with this very important exception, we had to visit the Underground River, which was to be reached by descending a dark shaft of 50 feet by means of a wire-rope ladder of thirty-two rungs, which vibrated most alarmingly. The first round had to be seized in a doubled-up position, and in this cramped attitude we made the first step downward and feel our way from rung to rung till we got into a pit of Egyptian darkness, for we could not carry lights. When once at the bottom, we found ourselves at the side of a quiet, flowing stream of pure limpid water, cool and refreshing to the taste, down which the visitors amused themselves by sailing on its surface wooden floats, on which were fixed lighted pieces of candle, which gave to the sides and roof of the tunnel a weird, unearthly aspect, and only wanted a blue sulphur flame to make it look like Dante's Inferno! Now one would suppose that this feat would be difficult enough for men to do, but four ladies of the party had sufficient strength of nerve to accomplish it, and seeing this, though many years their senior, I made up my mind not to be beaten by women, colonial or otherwise. Hence I summoned up courage to face the peril, and descended safely, amid applause. I need hardly say that our ladies did not hail from Belgravia. These afternoon explorations were rather fatiguing, and we emerged again to the light of day with intense appetites that made a deep impression on Mrs. Taylor's dinner, the cloud of flies notwithstanding. In the evening we entertained ourselves with music and singing, and I recited some anecdotes connected with my Crimean war experiences, which amused the colonists not a little—the Baby Incident exciting much sympathy in the minds of the fair sex. The next morning we paid a visit to the Lucas Cave, which is remarkable for the huge dimensions of its cavities. The Exhibition Cavern, as it is called, being two hundred yards in circumference, and required two hours to see it properly. The winding zig-zag descent to it is weird looking in the extreme, when you look back and upwards and see the visitors coming down in single file, each with a candle in hand, stumbling and falling now and again with a horrid, ghost-like screech, and enveloped in pitch-like darkness, they resembled so many shapeless demons going down into the bottomless pit. The swaling of the candles over the dresses of the ladies and the coats of the gentlemen, gave rise to much laughter, as the spots of grease on each person gave them the appearance of a spotted hyena, but they all took it in good humour, as it was impossible to hold the candlestick straight when one's attention was directed to all sorts of curious sights. The bespattering of your neighbour went on in perfect innocence, while you in your turn were served exactly alike,

because we were all on different levels. In the afternoon we visited the " Devil's Coachhouse," an immense cavern, 200 feet high, open to enter at both
ends, and lighted by a large opening in the centre
of the roof. I could not throw a stone with all my
force one-third of the way to its ceiling, and a
wooden gallery made round its roof for visitors to see
the interior the better, looked very queer—their
bodies resembled midgets in size and their voices
sounded as if they came from the skies, and calling
out to me, said that I looked like a small fly seated
on a rock at the bottom. There were other caves to
explore, but I had had enough ; and I left the next
morning at 5 a.m., having had a high time of it ; though
it did rain a good deal I was sorry to leave such
a pleasant company. I drove back alone in a buggy
and pair, and passed through the Hartley Valley,
where the hares are so numerous that an English
sportsman is asked as a favour by the farmers to
shoot them. And the wallambi, a sort of small
kangaroo, is met with frequently, for whose scalp
fivepence is given and for the skin sevenpence. They
boast also some pretty feathered pigeons and parrots,
but no rabbits trouble them in the mountains. The
grass is so rich and nourishing that the oxen are as
sleek and fat as those stall-fed at home. When we
arrived at the ridge of the hills I was shown two small
rivulets, one going west and originating the River
Murray, and the other passing eastward and forming
the Nepean River, which supplies Sydney with water.
I could not help remonstrating with my coachman for
driving his horses so fast, and never slackening rein

on hill or dale. They are nearly thoroughbred, and
they are strained most unmercifully, for they only last
about four years, and then turned over to the cart or
the plough. They are replaced by fresh young horses
which are cheap, costing £4 or £5 a head. This
plan the coach proprietors find pays better than feeding the poor animals on corn to keep them up to their
work; fortunately for the poor beasts the grass is very
nutritious. The wind and endurance of the colonial
horse strikes an Englishman with wonder—a British
horse in harness could not stand such work for a
week—and their surefootedness is astonishing down
or uphill, along rough roads full of ruts, sludge, and
loosened stones they keep on their legs, which are as
fine as racehorses'; their great strength lies in the
shoulder and in a very muscular forearm. On
returning to Victoria Mount I had an opportunity of
admiring the celebrated Victoria Pass, which consists of a gulf between two precipitous cliffs, bridged
over by a wonderful piece of masonry of great ingenuity. It was constructed by the convicts in days
gone by, one of whom cut his name on the rock. The
gorges visible on each side the bridge are 1,000
feet deep, and looking down from the stone causeway
the big fir trees at the bottom look like so many
blades of grass. I was shown the building in which
the chain gang were confined during the night, and
also the court-house where they were tried for mis-
behaviour. These places are now used for better
purposes. In the valleys coal is found, and at the
pit's mouth is sold at four shillings a ton. Shale is
also present, from which they distil kerosene. Some

of the trees are very large, and of great age, the rings
in some indicating a thousand years. When the
squatter wishes to clear the ground for grazing, he
kills the trees by removing a ring of the bark, then it
dies and stands up denuded of leaves, and the grass
grows up at the foot. The old trees often rot in the
centre, and in the cavity thus made the people make a
fire to cook their food, and take shelter from snow and
rain. Before I take leave of this land of caves I must
just parody what the Book of books says with regard
"to those who go down to the sea in ships, and see
the works of the Lord and His wonders in the deep,"
by stating that they who go down into the bowels of
the earth at the Janelon Caves see also the wonders
of the Lord hidden from sight in the midst of the
rocks! for these mighty hollows ought and should be
seen by every visitor to New South Wales, for it is
impossible for any one to exaggerate their superb
grandeur.

CHAPTER XXI.

Before leaving Sydney, I must not fail to state that the best mode of seeing this beautiful port, with its numerous harbours, is to charter a steam launch, and begin at Manley Beach and the middle harbour, then cross to Watson's Bay, and so work upwards, crossing and recrossing till every inlet is seen and admired, finishing up with a trip along the Paramatta river, whose banks are picturesquely dotted with the villas of the rich and their woody inclosures. Having left my card and address at Government House, his lordship being away in the mountains during the summer, I left this charming city with great reluctance, and took my passage for the Island of Tasmania, which is a two days' voyage due south from Australia. This colony rejoices in two large prosperous towns, one at the north end, and the other at the south, 130 miles apart. Launceston, at the north end, is prettily situated on rising ground, sloping down to the Tamar, a tidal river, and a brisk trade is carried on in tin and wool and apples. Here I resided for some time at the house of an old magistrate, who was well up in the history and commerce of the island. On Sunday we attended

FERN TREE VALLEY, SCOTSDALE, TASMANIA.

Divine service at St. John's Church, built of stone by the convicts in days gone by. The sermon and service were decidedly sluggish, the temperature in the shade being 97°, so it was excusable. On Tuesday we took our places in a train which went zig-zagging through the mountain wilds to a township called Scotsdale, passing *en route* some exquisitely beautiful creeks and water-gullies, with lots of tree ferns in them. Here we had an opportunity of walking into the primeval forest, and examining the huge trees, some upright and some fallen, centuries ago. Avenues of dead trees most weird in appearance, produced by "bush fires," and bounded on each side by the green eucalyptus, extend to a great distance. These dead monsters are called skeletons —looked ghostlike—and when the interior, which is like tinder is ignited, it goes on burning to the very top, then falls from its own weight. I should say that these monster trees, from their origin to their fall, would be at least 2,000 years old. In this locality grows the wattle tree, the bark of which yields three times as much tannin as our bark, and is largely exported to the tanyards of England and America. At Waverley, a short drive from Launceston, there is a woollen factory in a pretty creek among the hills, where an enterprising Scotchman, with the aid of a well-directed water-power, and supplemented by a Government subsidy, has succeeded in erecting some modern machinery, which will turn out all kinds of cloth, good enough for volunteer uniforms, trouserings, shawls, and blankets. I was surprised to see that the proprietor had got the

electric light laid on for the works, and also to hear
that he could not put up with the free-and-easy way of
the local colonials, and found it paid better to import
his employés direct from Scotland. The great sight
which the Launcestonians are so proud of showing
the visitor is the wild-looking Gorge. A tortuous
path leads up the hill commanding the Gorge, through
which gushes the turbulent river Esk, and when a
similar pathway is completed on the opposite side,
and the two rocky banks are united by a suspension
bridge, a view will be obtained of rock, wood, and
rushing frothy waters, as can hardly be surpassed in
any part of the world, enhanced as the prospect is
by the pretty upstanding town and shipping harbour
at one's feet. The tourist should not fail to pay a
visit to the tin-smelting works close at hand, and see
the ingots of metal moulded, and which are shipped
in large quantities to Europe. The heat from the
furnaces is intense, and the fine body of men were
streaming down with perspiration; and on my inquiring whether they quenched their thirst with beer
or any alcoholic liquor, they all replied unreservedly
that they had tried it over and over again, but found
from experience that they could not do with it at all ;
and that oatmeal and water was the only thing that
could support them under the fearful strain of such
physical pressure. Finally, I must mention that in
the Museum will be seen, a fine, clever picture by
Dowling, a native artist, representing a group of the
aborigines—very repulsive, but life-like : also some
good specimens of one from the Bischoff tin mines,
which should be visited if any one is desirous of

seeing for himself the richness of this colony in
minerals. It would be ungrateful not to mention
how I enjoyed the delicious apricots, peaches, and
plums, from standard trees, so refreshing in the hot
weather, and which adorn the tables at every meal,
accompanied, as in Australia, with tea, coffee, and
cocoa, but no stronger drinks whatever. Receiving
a pressing invitation to a friend's house in the centre
of the island, we left the hospitable roof of the old
magistrate, and made our way by the main line to
Ross, where we were met by our host, and driven in a
carriage a few miles into the country, where a new
experience awaited me. This gentleman lived on his
own estate of 5,000 acres, which fed 3,000 Merino
sheep—400 of which were a stud stock, several having
taken valuable prizes at the agricultural show. One
ewe especially had distinguished itself, having taken
a silver cup twice over, and yielded a fleece weighing
22½ lbs., a fact difficult to believe in England, where we
get only 7 or 8 lbs. of wool from a sheep; but thanks
to the climate and the nutritious nature of the grass,
these heavy fleeces are not uncommon in Tasmania.
A large river runs through the property about 500
yards from the house, and an American windmill
pump sends the water up to the house and gardens,
which, by irrigation, yields an abundance of the usual
fruits with the addition of cherries, strawberries, and
grapes. The rabbits were the great plague on this
station; it might be defined the irrepressible rodent,
as its fecundity and multiplication is so rapid that
our friend had to keep going two men throughout the
year, who were paid £1 each per week, to suppress

the nuisance. It was but small pay for that colony
as they had to find their own ammunition, but they
liked the sport and stuck to it. I believe they get
some small capitation fee for each scalp from the
Government. I only saw one live kangaroo on the
estate ; they are gradually being exterminated, as
they eat up the grass, and, besides, their skins are
valuable. A great domestic inconvenience in the
home life of the island is the difficulty of obtaining
female servants, and when you have got them to
retain them, for if they are at all nice looking and
capable, they are sure to be snatched up by the men
and married. And in a country place this family
trouble is still more felt with regard to men servants,
since nothing, love or money, will induce them to
work indoors, their whole heart is bent on an out-of-
door life. One day we drove off to pay a call at Mona
Vale, one of the grandest mansions in the colony,
where the Duke of Edinburgh was entertained.
There I fully expected to see a butler and two foot-
men at least ; no, nothing of the kind, only a quiet-
looking young woman answered the door, but in the
gardens, which were beautifully kept up, I observed
three gardeners at work. We then paid the Principal
of Horton College a visit, where young men are
educated, and there also female domestics waited
upon us. Though our host was a member of the
Legislative Assembly, a magistrate and warden of
his township, and the owner of a flourishing estate,
such was this difficulty and worry in connection with
indoor servants experienced by him and his household, that his wife and daughters, ladies in every

sense of the word, were obliged to give an active
hand in many little domestic arrangements—in fact,
while one moment they would be helping to clear
the dining table, the next they would be amusing us
with some excellent classical music in the drawing-
room, for parents as a rule in Tasmania, as in
Australasia generally, make it a sacrifice and care to
give their children the best education money can
command. Though in the estimation of many self-
made colonials money makes the man, knowledge,
notwithstanding, is held in great respect, and stands
forth as a dominating power. The neighbourhood of
Ross is well adapted as a residence for sportsmen,
there being fishing and shooting in abundance, and
the horses are very fine and swift; and as each man
and lady is brought up as it were in the saddle, riding
exercise is very much to the fore as an every-day
pleasure. Picnic parties into the mountains amid
lake scenery is a common source of bringing young
and old together—social gatherings which are carried
on without stiffness or formality, thus knitting together in one sympathetic bond all the families for a
circuit of many miles. We were loath to leave our
host and his happy and cheerful surroundings of wife
and children, but we had to move on, and our next
stay was at Hobart, the capital of Tasmania; but we
were not allowed to enter as strangers, our friend
accompanied us, and he being a M.P. knew everybody
and everything, hence we had a most useful and
instructive cicerone. We were shown the Houses of
Parliament, Government offices, the Museum rich in
curios connected with the natural history of the

island and its minerals, the quay where much active
commerce was going on with all parts of the world,
and the very extensive and beautifully situated public
gardens on rising grounds overlooking the harbour
and Government House. I called upon the Dean of
St. David's Cathedral, and read the lessons for him
on Sunday. This building is not yet completed,
though the foundation stone was laid by the Duke of
Edinburgh twenty years ago—in fact, the Nonconfor-
mists are much more in advance of the Church of
England as to their buildings, especially the Congre-
gationalists, who have a very fine freestone Gothic
building with a high spire in Elizabeth Street.
Hobart is in a lovely situation, at the foot of Mount
Wellington, which is often capped with snow even
in the summer time, and which should by all means
be ascended, especially as half way the coaches land
you at Ferntree Arbour, a charming spot shaded
with large tree ferns. Now having explored the city,
I will just relate as shortly as possible what the
traveller ought to see. Let him go down to the pier
and take the excursion steamer to what is called the
"Eagle Hawk's Neck," a narrow strip of land
which joins the Tasman peninsula to the mainland.
This point was guarded formerly by dogs and soldier
sentries, to prevent the convicts from escaping into
the open country; their penal settlement being on
the peninsula, located at a place called Port Arthur,
now falling into ruins. The courageous and daring
attempts to pass the dogs and sentries by the convicts
were quite romantic, but they invariably ended in
disaster by a well-directed shot, or if they escaped the

bullet starvation stared them in the Bush, where
food was scarce and difficult to get without firearms.
Those who would wish to read these harrowing
accounts, so sensational and blood curdling, should
get a book entitled " For the Term of his Natural
Life," written by a convict, a gentleman who had been
transported for a crime for which he was quite innocent. In those days many persons were exiled for
very slight offences. It is rather a stiff walk from
the " Neck " to the " Blowhole," a natural curiosity
in the shape of a tunnel through a rock through
which the sea rushes with a deafening roar !

Another trip worth taking is to go by steamer to
the viaduct which crosses the Derwent river some
miles above Hobart, and then take the train to
Plenty Station, then get out and walk to the
artificial ponds, where salmon and trout are hatched,
and when matured turned out into the Derwent,
where they afford capital sport to the angler, who
uses a live grasshopper on a bare hook, and soon fills
his basket. The curator kindly supplied our party
with tea at the side of the pools, where we amused
ourselves watching and feeding the young fish which
were quite tame, and the keeper could whip out any
of the larger ones with an artificial fly for our inspection, and then throw them back again. ' In this
valley we had a good view of some luxuriant hop
plantations, and thousands of acres of apple orchards,
bearing some most tempting fruit grown to a great
size in a well-irrigated loam soil. The jam factories
in Hobart are quite an institution, and are supplied
to any extent by fruit from these prolific valleys

yielding peaches, apricots, and plums, from *standard* trees, pruned down to about 12 feet. There is now a large export trade of apples to London, since they have learnt how to pack them properly. Thousands of cases of this fruit in the green state are shipped off to England in chartered steamers, where they fetch a high price, as they arrive in our country in the winter time. I doubt not it will not be long before a plan is discovered of exporting the fresh apricots and peaches as well.

Before we part company with Hobart and our dear kind-hearted friend, I must make a remark upon the young women. They are well formed and strong, tall, and walk uprightly, with complexions and good looks which will bear favourable comparison with those we meet with in any of our own large towns. The men are tall and well set up, and it is not an uncommon thing to see men on the streets who stand 6 feet 2 inches or 6 feet 3 inches in height. We bade adieu to Hobart on a Friday, taking our passage to New Zealand in the well-equipped steamer *Mararoa*, in rather gusty weather which sent the ladies to their berths. This continued all Saturday, and more or less on Sunday, in consequence of which we had no religious service, though there were three clergymen on board. On Monday night we neared the coast, and as it was not safe to enter the Bluff Harbour at night, we kept outside till morning dawned, then steamed on and reached the pier at breakfast time, after which we ascended a steep hill of 600 feet, flying the signalling flag, and from thence we had a magnificent view over sea and land. On Wednesday

13

we had reached Port Chalmers, where our steamer
was put into a dry dock, so we had plenty of leisure
to make our way to Dunedin, eight miles off by train,
where an international exhibition was being held of
colonial produce and manufactures. If we wished to
see evidences of the astounding progress our colonies
have made, we could not have had a better opportunity than the fine display at Dunedin, a Scotchified
town, where the people of any other nationality were
boycotted till a few years ago, so jealous and selfish
were its founders. They may well be proud of their
grand stone buildings, especially their churches; one
in particular, standing out pre-eminently so, the
Presbyterian, which is like a noble Gothic cathedral,
with a splendid tapering spire. The town is prettily
situated on steep hills and well-wooded dales, up and
down which rush cable-trams at a furious rate, which
the residents state were the first ever started in the
world. The views from these various suburban emi-
nences are simply charming, grasping in a bird's-eye
prospect the long port and island opposite, the
public park, the University college, and other large
prominent buildings which the industrious, thrifty,
and canny Scotchman has erected. And, though
last not least, the sight of its wide streets, lined
with large shops and high plate-glass windows,
displaying their elegant wares from every country;
its banks and hotels, to compare with which there
is nothing so English-like in any other town in New
Zealand.

CHAPTER XXII.

No one should leave Port Chalmers without ascending to the cemetery, which is well laid out as a flower garden and public recreation ground, situated on a rocky plateau overlooking the harbour and pier, and dominating also the peninsula on which the town is built, and around which a good drive has been made yielding pleasant views in every direction. There is also a striking object in the form of a very fine stone-built Presbyterian church, in the Gothic style, with high-tapering spire, perched on a pinnacle of rock, such as one sees in some Roman Catholic towns in Europe. We are here 1,034 miles from Hobart, and continuing our course along the eastern coast we arrive after a passage of 200 miles at Lyttleton Harbour, the port of supply and export for the city of Christchurch, which is eight miles inland. This short distance was difficult to traverse, leading as the winding road did over a high mountain, and was a great impediment to commerce till it was tunnelled by an enterprising and popular superintendent of the province, Mr. Sefton Moorhouse, and a railway made to connect the port with the city. Christchurch is

the centre of life in the magnificent and fertile
Canterbury Plains, a fine and extensive view of
which may be had from the Lyttleton hills and
from the spire of the cathedral which I ascended,
though the ladders are rather rickety. The plains
overflow with fruitfulness irrigated as they are from
the watershed from the hills which bound it on all
sides, and are 100 miles apart, all the tributary
streams centring in the beautiful silvery Avon, in
which trout do abound, and takes a pretty serpentine
course through this rich land, yielding an immense
quantity of corn, wool, flax, and fruits, but especially
horses, which are bred here in great numbers and then
exported to India, where they produce a valuable stock
for the cavalry and artillery by interbreeding with
the native stud.   I met a gentleman who, with his
partners, owned 17,000 acres of fine pasture land; he
told me nothing paid so well as the breeding of horses
—cheap on the spot, but fetched a good price when
they reached Calcutta. No immigrant need imagine
that he can purchase land in these plains at a low
figure, and unless he has a long purse he had better
stay at home. The visitor should not fail to pay a
visit to the splendid Museum with its large and unique
collection of objects of art and of natural history;
the lovely Public Gardens, through which meanders a
river teeming with trout; the noble Cathedral; the
old Provincial Council Chamber, the most perfect of
its kind in New Zealand; the Government domain
and the Botanic Gardens. As a tourist I can only
summarise by saying Christchurch abounds in
public institutions of every kind and need, and

especially places of public worship of every known
sect, even down to the Salvation Army. A very
pleasant time may be spent here and in its eight
extensive suburbs, some of them with 10,000 people.
If the traveller desires to go further a-field, let him
take the coach to Nelson through the Buller Gorge,
or to the west coast by way of the Otira Gorge, or
he can diverge and visit the Gold Fields at Hokitika
if money fascinates him. Cook and Son help one
well for boating and fishing and local excursions.
Returning to Lyttleton, I may just mention that the
men occupied at the shipping business don't do amiss,
provided there is no loafing and shuffling. They get
one shilling and threepence an hour, and with thrift and
sobriety can occupy a cottage of their own in three
years. The union men pay four shillings and sixpence
a month to their club, and for this get during illness or
incapacity for labour £1 a week for six months, then
ten shillings a week for a month, and finally five
shillings till they are well. The climate is delicious,
like our English summer, and barring the apprehension of a coming earthquake would be a charming
place to settle in and be content. A tourist fond of
enjoying a picturesque sight of unusual beauty could
not do better than mount one of the low hills above
the town which is so prettily built on the slopes of
the gullies leading down to the harbour—the streets
being in terraces one above another—every square
yard being utilised.

Taking a steamer, and continuing our passage along
the east coast for 175 miles further north, we reach
Wellington, since 1861, the capital of New Zealand.

in which we land on a fine, but dusty and windy
day, characteristically windy, hence its nickname,
" Windy Wellington." The large Government buildings, the Houses of Assembly, and even the Governor's
palace, are so many shams. In the distance you
exclaim what splendid freestone structures, and when
you go up to them and tap them with a finger you
find that they are nothing but wooden erections,
painted and rough cast with sand to represent stone ;
but they are very handsome, being ornamented with
pillars having Corinthian capitals well carved, and
elaborate cornices, and surmounted by towers or high
spires. They are regarded by the citizens with great
pride, and a wonder of the world as the largest buildings of wood in the universe. A Roman Catholic
church perched on a pinnacle of rock high above
the town was enough to deceive any one, but on going
up to it was found to be wood also, but sculptured
with figures at great expense. It has been discovered
that it is safer to live in a wooden dwelling than a
stone one in case an earthquake should pay them
a visit. Their grand harbour is land-locked and has
deep water to its very edge, capable of floating the
largest iron-clad war vessel. The town is confined to
the space between the hills and the port, of a horse-shoe
shape, so that the people have been obliged to build
their houses up the steep hills, and in the gullies, and
on any flat available space, natural or artificial, that
they could stick a building on, hence the quaint
aspect of the city from any high point is picturesque
in the extreme. This being so hemmed in by the
guardian hills has prevented the city from spreading

landwards, and it boasts of being the most compact
town in New Zealand, the Empire City as they
love to call it. To see its extent the visitor should
take a train ride from one end of it to the other, a distance of three miles for a penny—the cheapest ride
in the world—then he will be able to judge what
a bustling, busy place is Wellington. A very good
bird's-eye view of the town and the beach where the
fashionable promenade and bathing goes on may be
obtained by ascending a winding road which leads up
to Mrs. Rhodes' house, built on a spur of the mountain at the east end of Wellington. Then again
there are other " lions " to see, such as the Botanical
Gardens situated in a creek, dotted on each side its
little streamlet with high tree-ferns, and crossed now
and again by rustic wooden bridges. English trees
have been planted here between the native, reminding
us of home. The walks are so tortuous and inter-
lacing that the garden may be compared to a Rosa-
mond's Bower, in which we might lose ourselves.
On our return through a singular looking suburb, we
noticed how curiously the villas appeared perched one
above another on plateaus of rock blasted to get a
flat basis to rest upon, and behind them the bare
mountains denuded of trees. Again an outlying
district called the " Lower Hut " is the centre of
amusement for pleasure parties ; there being a racecourse, and tea gardens for picnics, &c. Before I
leave this delightful town I must not forget to say
that it is lighted with electricity ; that the " publics "
are closed on Sunday ; that I did not see any
drunkenness on that day, or rowdyism or brawling :

that there were no signs of pauperism nor any pawn-
shops visible. General contentment seemed to prevail. Earthquakes had not visited this locality for so
long a period that the speculators had taken courage
and built some very grand stone and brick stores,
while the authorities had erected a very fine post
office and customs house on the quay. These
with the huge meat-freezing factories gave the
town an aspect of great commercial importance,
which it merited. As at Christchurch so here, the
places of public worship and schools are so numerous
that every phase of religious sentiment is represented,
and though the citizens may be called worshippers of
Mammon the sabbath is well observed and orderly.
Thus I have given a very short summary of this
pleasant resting-place, which in my opinion is sufficient for the passing tourist. And now we leave
Wellington and proceed not by steamer to Napier—
oh! no, certainly not—the right thing to do is to
take a railway ride of a hundred miles over the most
interesting part of the colony, namely, over the
Rimutaka Mountains to Palmerston, on the west
coast. It cannot be compared to a trip over the
Rocky Mountains, nevertheless, the wild scenery
we meet with and the Fell engine with its central rail
working up the steep gradients is a sight worth some
trouble to inspect, and implies great engineering skill.
At Palmerston, situated in a well-wooded and fertile
district, there is a break at present in the Wellington
Manawatu railway, and we had to take a coach and
four, which was a pleasant change, through a well-
cultured valley till we reached the Manawatu

Gorge, a fearfully dangerous pass of three mile in extent, up which we were coached with a perpendicular rock overhead, and the same below, and traversing a roadway made by blasting the face of the rock, so that if a wheel came off or our horses shied we should have been sent down into the abyss below, in which roared a perfect "hell of waters." There was no railing on the side, and the wheels would go as near as eighteen inches to the edge, the look-out was fearful, and shook the nerves of even the old hands present! We were, therefore, very much relieved to find ourselves out of it. On the other side of this gorge they are making a single line of railway by blasting the rock for a road, and tunnelling through the projections here and there, a very slow, expensive piece of cutting. A few miles further on, our coach stopped at the flourishing town of Woodville; here we had a refreshing lunch, and then proceeded by train to Napier, 95 miles off, through a fine well-watered country pasturing thousands of sheep and cattle. This was a hard day's travelling, and we were glad to find ourselves at the Masonic Hotel at Napier, where our Scotch host gave us very excellent rooms. Napier is the chief city in the Hawke's Bay Province, one of the best agricultural districts in New Zealand. It is a diocesan city and the residence of the Bishop of Waiapu, who, when he attended the synod of bishops at Lambeth Palace, was greeted with the pun, "Here comes the representative of church free sittings, *Why a pew?*" The town rests on a lovely site, which neither the pencil of the artist nor the photographer can do justice to. The houses of the well-to-do stand brightly forward on a succession of rounded hills and their intervening valleys, embosomed in evergreens and flowering shrubs, a very paradise of beauty and serenity. The glorious peninsula of villas ends in what is called the "Spit," where there is a fine basin for ordinary sized vessels; but the spirited authorities are making, at great cost, a splendid breakwater to accommodate the largest steamers. I should advise a tourist to walk or drive round this peninsula, a distance of five miles, as he would be well rewarded. The roads and pathways in and around Napier are excellent. Again the thing to do is to drive to Taradale, a native village seven miles off, in the midst of English civilised dwellings and cultivated fields. We entered the chief's principal lodging—a large room, on the floor of which matting was laid down for men, women, and children ; here his family and retainers slept, each having a proper allotment. We were warned not to go too far into it by our guide because the "live stock," as he called them, were too numerous, and would be unpleasant mementos to take away with us. The centre props to the room were ornamented with idols, carved in wood, hideous looking monsters. This dwelling was surrounded by less pretentious ones made of wattle, reeds, and clay like wigwams. Outside these were seen the Maoris squatting and cooking their meals, and who took very little notice of us. They are a very fine athletic race with an intelligent aspect, and some of the young women were quite good-looking with olive complexions, oval faces, and coal-black eyes, with long wavy dark coarse hair.

On our return journey we passed the racecourse, an institution so characteristic of this horsey people, and is here located in the midst of thousands of acres of garden-like land, yielding abundance of every produce. Horses, cows, and sheep, looking sleek and fat, amidst a people thriving and smiling, a veritable land of "milk and honey." Hovering above we saw several hawks, hence the name given to this district!

On Sunday we went to the Cathedral, a fine brick and stone building, which is strengthened in the inside by heavy buttresses in case of an earthquake coming. While we were examining the interior, the dean came up to us in a most affable manner, and gave us a very excellent account of the church from its beginning, and the difficulties he had to encounter to get it erected, and the danger and risk of a possible earthquake that he had to provide against. The dean has a very pleasing, expressive face, very like that of the Saviour, especially the one painted by Count d'Orsay. Although a spare-looking man, he has a powerful voice and an excellent extempore delivery, just suited to the place and its people, hence he is very popular. He asked me if I would read the evening lessons for him which I did, and afterwards invited us to the deanery to tea with Mrs. Hovell, his son, and two daughters, with whose amiability and courtesy we were much pleased. Dean Hovell is cousin to Mr. Mark Hovell, the specialist who attended the Emperor Frederick with Sir Morel Mackenzie. There is Sunday closing in Napier, and the streets are remarkably quiet; and on Saturday night the promenades were crowded with well-dressed people, English and native converts alike; and the Salvation Army were busy at the corner of our hotel doing their level best to induce their listeners to think of the higher life.

CHAPTER XXIII.

On Monday we left Napier at six in the morning to commence the wonderful inland coach journey of about two hundred miles to Oxford, *via* Taupo. We carried the mail, and each passenger was only allowed one portmanteau. I don't think the ladies had the least idea what they were going to encounter in the way of roughing it. For the first twenty-five miles we drove up and down hills, and through about forty creeks, having 2 feet or 3 feet of water in them, with a shingly bottom. Down into these the five horses dashed with as much impetus as they could muster in order to get up the opposite slope, urged thereto with much shouting and whip-cracking by the driver, conveying a most unpleasant jolt to our bodies. Then we would slowly ascend some high mountain, we men getting out to walk; but when once on the summit we were rewarded by some really very grand views — notably from the tops of Mounts Tauranga, Kuma, and Titiokura. Then we would have to descend some fearful ziz-zag road cut out of the side of a hill, with a precipice on the other hand looking down gorges 400 feet to 1,000 feet deep, with rushing torrents. At the sharp turns in these awful roads our Jehu would amuse himself with shouts and flicking of his whip, which sent the nerves of the strongest of us into a most unpleasant state of tremor. To watch our dismayed looks was, I dare say, fun to him, but it was decidedly painful to his living freight. Hence we were very glad to find ourselves at the half-way house, and get a little respite from the continued jolting of our heads against the roof of the coach, and the thuds to our nether ends by bumping down on the hard cushions. In the short space of four hours I never, in the whole course of my life, heard so many exclamations of oh! and no wonder, our very spines felt like a mass of jelly. Having had a refreshing lunch and changed our horses we all got into a good humour again, especially as we were told that the track would now become less perilous and distressing, with less screeching from our fair companions. We passed a most interesting sight *en route*, and that was the collecting together on the side of a hill by stockmen and their collies 10,000 sheep, an immense flock, reminding one of what Israel had in patriarchal days. Again we met a party of Maoris filing along on horseback, the ladies riding cross-legged, like their lords. We dropped some letters into an old box stuck on a post close to the road-side, and this was the primitive depository for the correspondence of a township some distance off, not a habitation of any kind being visible anywhere, and there could have been no thieves, certainly.

The evening of the first day found us at Taravera, having traversed a distance of fifty miles. There we had an excellent dinner and spent the night; the daughters of the host waited on the guests, and then amused them with some music, and in no way felt it *infra dig.*, in New Zealand. The next morning we started afresh to traverse another fifty miles, principally over a desert-like plateau, without a vestige of life on it, and for twelve miles no water for birds or animals to drink. Hence we passed carcases of dead bullocks and sheep, which had succumbed in their journey across this waterless track. The plateau, as far as the eye could reach, was wearisome in its perpetual sameness: a barren wild of fern and small shrubs of the Tei tree growing in loose soil of powdered pumice-stone, the only relief being in front of us a high volcanic mountain of 8,000 feet in full activity, and the snow-capped Ruapehu. At the half-way house there was another luncheon and a change of horses. A wide stream passed through the grounds, and on this we threw large flat pieces of pumice-stone, which floated away on its surface—contradicting the usual saying, that a stone sinks in water. Starting once more, we descended by a tortuous dusty road, from which we enjoyed splendid views of the grand inland Lake Taupo, and the valley beneath us, from which issued here and there from the green bush white clouds of steam, indicating the spots where the hot springs were located. Having run along the shore of the lake for some distance, we arrived finally at Joshua's Spa, in the midst of this valley of geysers. This is the most extraordinary situation for a sanatorium I ever saw or heard of. This spa, called Joshua, after the name of the pro-

prietor, consists of a number of separate wooden
buildings erected in a land-locked hollow, naturally
excavated in a valley of pumice rock and soil, through
which passes a small stream of hot sulphurous water
from a neighbouring spring, supplemented by hot
ebullitions in the grounds, which are diverted into
baths for the use of invalids. Of course we did the
singular sights of the locality. A short walk leads
you down to the celebrated Waikato River, which
takes its origin in the lake. Near its banks we
look with amusement at the geyser called the
" Crow's Nest," with its peculiar border of sticks
encrusted with white silicate of lime. These sticks
were said originally to have been placed round the
edge to prevent the Maoris' children from falling in,
and become fossiled in time. Next came the " Witches'
Caldron," belching up its steamy contents at a temperature of 180° F. Further on we came across the
" Paddle-wheel Ben," in which the sulphur gas issues
forth from a rocky cavern with a gushing, hissing
sound—a blow-hole I called it. On returning we
started a brace of red-legged partridges. As to our
meats, the mutton, our only flesh meat, was very
stringy, because the weather was so hot, or the gas
did not agree with its keeping, for what we had to eat
at dinner was killed in the early morning of the
same day. The sweets were excellent, and we had an
entrée of wild ducks brought in by the Maoris, who
shot them by self-made shot. We passed two days
very pleasantly with our friend Joshua, a most
obliging and gentlemanly host, at whose expense I
made an innocent pun. How came it about that

Joshua had no father? because Joshua was the son
of *Nun!* The Lake Taupo is the largest in New
Zealand, being twenty-four miles long by fifteen
broad, but we did not take our excursion on it in the
steam launch, as we could admire its broad expanse
and its smoking volcano at the further end from the
hills, which the next day we had to ascend on our
coach. We were told that there was some very
good gratuitous shooting here of wild duck, pheasant,
and partridges during the winter months, which it
was not our pleasure to wait for. Early in the
morning we took our leave of the Spa and our seats
on a coach and five horses, and continued a jolting
journey northwards through a most uninteresting
wilderness of fern and bush, till we reached Rotorua,
a distance of fifty-six miles, where we were refreshed
by a really good dinner, followed by sound sleep till
five in the morning, when I went out and had a
delightful swim in a bath, in the grounds of the
Palace Hotel, which was only slightly impregnated
with sulphur. Subsequently we walked a short mile
to the regular baths connected with this world-famed
health-resort. These are on an extensive scale,
under Government control, with a regular doctor
engaged, and in every other way the organisation is
perfect. The use of the "Rachel" bath softens and
smooths the skin, while the larger amount of silicate
of lime in the celebrated "Priest's" bath excites the
surface, producing strongly a prickly feeling and
intense perspiration, and being at a temperature of
103° F. the patients do not remain in it more than
fifteen minutes as a rule. They say these two baths

have cured some most obstinate cases of chronic
rheumatism and inveterate skin diseases.   Knowing
that I was a physician from London, the authorities
took good care to give me every information, and
praised the sanatorium as the best in the world, and
statistics would show that its reputation was well
sustained by Australasia, at any rate as the sick
flocked from all the colonies for relief when all
medicines had failed.   There is a good Maori settlement adjoining the colonial town, possessing an
English church.   There is an excellent understanding
between the natives and the English, the former
highly appreciating the education their children get
in the colonial schools, and the clergyman makes
many converts to Christianity through the medium
of the Church services, where they receive instruction in their own language; but he complained sadly
of the obstacles thrown in his way by the English
selling the Maoris strong drink.   I remarked to a
resident who had been there fifty years that I seldom
met a Maori with grey hair, and he replied that he
had never seen one with a bald head.   I asked him
if there was any truth in what I had heard, namely,
that the English settler would marry a Maori girl,
and after living with her for several years and
getting lots of children by her, would, when he
had prospered and become rich, desert her and his
children, though she had materially assisted him in
getting the wealth.   He replied, "I am sorry to say
such is the case in many instances within my own
knowledge."   To show how very fertile the soil is
about the hot springs, Mrs. Macrae, our hostess, told

us that some of the onions in her garden weighed 11lbs., and two pumpkins scaled respectively 103lbs. and 120lbs. Mrs. Macrae, who kept the hotel in the vicinity of the pink and white terraces, the pride and glory of New Zealand, gave me a most graphic description of the volcanic eruption of mud which destroyed them and her residence, and from which so few escaped alive, and left the traveller to mourn over the loss of the sight of these lovely silica incrustations.

If one did give up making the usual excursions from Rotorua, it would be a great mistake not to pay a visit to the native village close at hand, and study a little the peculiar customs and habits of the Maoris. It comprises a collection of native huts called whares; also rather a fine meeting-house, well carved and painted outside, with a statue of our Queen in the interior. There are boiling pools where the villagers cook their food, and warm pools where the men and boys do bathe. They manage very cleverly also to divert the hot stream from these pools into a variety of holes, which act as ovens, and thus obviate the necessity of making a fire. We will ask our readers to follow us, as we ought to have done before, along this wonderful inland drive, through the very heart of the North Island of New Zealand, as indicated on a map. We were now *en route* again on a mail coach, drawn by five horses, as usual, and our destination is Oxford; the drive proved to be the most dusty I ever experienced. Talk of swallowing a peck of dirt in a lifetime, I should say that a month would be quite long enough to inhale that quantity if we had to traverse this road daily. First of all we had to zig-zag up a series of hills and dales till we reached a mountain ridge, along which we travelled for some miles, with precipices on each side, and in the gorges below a depth of hundreds of feet could be seen the trees of a primeval forest, and though huge in size when looked at from above, appeared like so many saplings. This was really a superb sight when the clouds of dust would permit us to enjoy it. We came across many bush fires, where the trees are cleared by burning, and English grass seed is sown and covered with the charcoal dust, and a fine crop arises in a few weeks, to the great joy of the settler and the success of his sheep run. Our journey was only one of thirty-five miles in extent, and yet till this space is covered by a railway the excellent health resort at Rotorua will not be patronised as it deserves to be. We arrived at Oxford in good time for a thorough brush down, and our clothes to have the thick layer of dust brushed out of them. My long brown coat was as white as a miller's. It was quite refreshing to see a railway again, and to find one's self in the vicinity of ordinary civilisation, while the surrounding farms and homesteads looked like dear Old England, barring its characteristic hedgerows. We were up betimes the next morning, and after break-fasting at 6.15 took our places in a train which landed us at Auckland by 2 p.m. There, indeed, we did meet with a welcome change from the rough life we had been comparatively leading for some time past. We put up at the Star Hotel, where we were accommodated with some fine lofty rooms, while the table was luxuriously supplied, conjoined with an efficient staff of men waiters; the essential bath-room on every floor, and the whole house conducted in as good a manner as a first-class hotel in London; a few minutes' walk from the port, and other centres of life and amusement, but I will leave a further description of beautiful Auckland for another chapter.

CHAPTER XXIV.

A DESCRIPTION of beautiful Auckland painted in the
most vivid word-colouring would fail to give the
reader a fair idea of its varied loveliness. It is
situated on an isthmus with a sea view nearly all
round, and unique in its bright grandeur, surpassing
anything of the kind I have ever seen. The sight of
Naples and its bay, with Capri and Vesuvius in the
distance from the Mount St. Elmo is not to be compared to it, and any one of the views that the eye
can grasp of the separate harbours of Sydney does not
match it, and if one's mind is recalled to the sight of
the entry into the Bosphorus at Constantinople, or
the passages up to New York and San Francisco with
the morning sun glowing on those splendid cities,
still Auckland bears the palm, and stands out pre-
eminent in a situation of beauty so extensive and
comprehensive that nothing in my opinion can come
near it. I would ask the visitor to go with me to the
top of Mount Eden—a rise of 650 feet above the
town, and only three miles off, with a winding road
to its summit. From this historic old crater and
Maori fort, in excellent shape and preservation, a
panorama unique in extent and sublimity is to be

19*

seen which the citizens may well be proud of. From
its base to the sea we have the lovely city with magnificent buildings of halls, churches, museum, hospital,
and huge warehouses, with harbour crowded with
shipping from all nations, and further out numerous
yachts with their white sails like so many butterflies
flitting about, backed by the opposite shore, with
Mount Victoria clothed in verdure, dotted with
suburbs of elegant villas. Right and left of Mount
Eden there are extensive suburbs also nestling in
pretty nooks, clothed in evergreens, reachable by a
tramway. Now let us turn round, and an extraordinary sight faces us. No less than twenty-four
volcanic cones on as many round hills dot the
landscape, extinct for ages past. Again, between
these hills are located large mansions in parklike
grounds, interspersed by homesteads and even hedgerows, putting one forcibly in mind of old England,
and the simile is enhanced by a railway winding
its way through the dales. Before we descend let
us face the city again and admire the well-kept
central Public Gardens, the big building to the
left being the Provincial Hospital on a high site
dominating the public domain. The Museum, Law
Courts, and Government House are nearly obscured
by trees. It is very difficult to get a good photo
from Mount Eden of the city and its surroundings. We will now take the steamer constantly
going to and fro to the north shore on the opposite side of the harbour, and take a ramble in
Davenport, the fashionable summer resort, much
prized by the Auckland people. Rising from the

centre of this suburb is Victoria Mount, about 200 feet high, with a well-shaded wooded walk to its flagstaff top, from which a view of the city opposite is afforded of the most splendid nature, far surpassing that from the north shore at Sydney, especially in the afternoon, when the sun's rays are in full play upon it. Having now admired this exquisite bit of scenery, we can take a cab or the coach and enjoy a most agreeable drive of four miles to the Lake Takapuna, another favourite resort, along the road to which and on its banks are springing up numerous dwellings in their snug grounds, rejoicing also in a large popular hotel, with boats on the lake. This lake is very deep, and has no outlet, contains fresh water, though only a narrow strip of ground separates it from the salt water of the ocean. If we continue along the north shore we come to Northcote, another very pretty suburb, and near to this a popular settlement called Birkenhead, in which there is the Colonial Sugar Company's Works, an extensive refinery. On the side of the hill, one above another, are the rows of cottages belonging to the work-people, exceedingly picturesque. Auckland and its western suburb is a thing to be seen and not forgotten from this elevated quarter, and no visitor or tourist has done himself or the lovely city due justice who has not rambled at his ease along the north shore, and taken in his fill of such a delightful prospect. We will now return to our hotel, and to-morrow charter a hansom cab and pay St. John's College a visit, so interestingly associated with Bishops Patterson and Selwyn. There we shall find an extremely pretty, but quaint-looking, old wooden church, with memorial brasses and windows to those good self-denying men. On the road back I called on Dr. Cowie, one of the handsomest of bishops, to whom I handed my letter of introduction, and was heartily received. I was shown over the large Selwyn Library, and over his most singular wooden palace, fixed to the side of a steep ravine, with the bedrooms below and the reception rooms on a level with the ground above, but all the windows overlooking the harbour and north shore; a grand picture, truly—nestling in peace and quietude—a soul-inspiring spot for an ecclesiastical student. The bishop had one feeling at any rate in common with myself, we had both been in active warfare; he as chaplain to the forces in India, where he had been actually engaged in carrying shot to our men in the midst of the din and danger of a fight. What a contrast to his present position! Now that I am on the subject of Colonial Bishops, I will here introduce a rather weird story told by Sir George Bowen when he was Governor of New Zealand. A very good heading to it would be this, " A New Zealand Chief's Preparation for the Higher Life."

Among the loyal Maori chiefs invited to meet the Duke of Edinburgh was one of the original signers of the treaty of Waitangi in 1840, and who had ever since been a firm friend of the English. One of the Anglican Bishops afterwards said to the Governor, " Do you know, Sir, the antecedents of that old heathen ? " " No my dear Bishop," was the reply, " but I do know that he brought five hundred of his

clansmen into the field to fight for the Queen, so
I invited him to meet the Queen's son." " Well,"
continued the Bishop, "when I first arrived in New
Zealand that chief came to me and said that he
wished to be baptized. I knew that he had two

NEW ZEALAND CHIEF.

wives, so I told him that he must first persuade one
of them to return to her family. He said he feared
that would be difficult, but that he would see what
could be done, and came back to me in two months.
When he returned he exclaimed, " Now, missionary,
you may baptize me, for I have only one wife."

I asked, "What have you done with our dear sister, your first wife?" He replied, smacking his lips, "I have eaten her!"

The Maori priests were the scholars of the tribes, and to them were entrusted the important business of tattooing. This was considered a very grave undertaking by the chiefs, each of whom indulged in special patterns, which distinguished them from one another in the same manner as our coats of arms do our aristocratic families. I give a sketch of an old chief who gloried in a kind of shawl devise which marked his particular rank, and the little kingdom he reigned over. This disfigurement is supposed to overawe his enemies with fear, and to hide the wrinkled traces of old age. Girls before they marry are not honoured by a tattoo, and the married very slightly so on the lips, chin, and eyebrows, but all this custom is fast passing away from those who join the English community. The Maoris as a people merit a few further remarks, but I shall make them as brief as possible, just of sufficient interest to instruct the coming tourist. They are not supposed to be the original natives of New Zealand, but immigrants from the South Sea Islands. Captain Cook when he visited the country reckoned them at 90,000 double what they are now. They could weave coarse cloth from the native flax; work and polish their sacred green stone, and very hard work it is; make canoes and ornament them with rude carving; make battle axes and spears and fishing nets, and grotesque personal decorations.

Some of the best specimens of this handiwork

may be seen in the Auckland Museum, and the
Dunedin Exhibition, where a fine chieftain's tomb
was on view. The white spots are bunches of
feathers from rare birds. The carving is really
wonderfully skilful, considering the simple tools employed. Primogeniture is a recognised law. The
spell called "Tapu," acts as their principal mode
of government, and the cast of the spell over anything was sufficient to make it sacred—not to be
touched, and hardly to be looked at except with
veneration and awe. The influence of "Tapu"
strengthened the hands of both chiefs and priests in
their dealings with the people. The Maoris believe
in a future state, though it required the aid of
Christian missionaries to convince them that God
was omnipotent. They love pleasure, and have many
sports, the principal being horse-racing. They erect
their storehouses on piles to keep away the rats.
They are naturally a war-like race, and when the
Anglo-Saxon first invaded their country he found
them no mean enemy to contend with. Their
fortresses, called "Pahs," were most ingeniously con-
trived to keep our soldiers at bay ; protected as they
were with rifle-pits, ditches, and stockades in front,
we were often defeated in our attacks upon them.
As to the sale of land or other property which is
common to the individuals composing the different
tribes, this cannot be effected without the consent
of all concerned, hence a good deal of trouble has
arisen to Europeans buying their lands in consequence of some individual objecting to join the
majority, somewhat like one juryman not falling in

with the other eleven in our country. Then angry
feelings and contention arose, and force has been
used to settle the conveyance. The Maori of to-day
has not much to thank the English for, since he has
learnt all the evils of civilisation without acquiring
its virtues. The only wise thing they have learnt in
coming into contact with us has been the giving up
of the hideous tattooing; but against this we must
set their artful cunning in over-reaching us in their
bargains, and we have taught them to be ardent
smokers and heavy drinkers, whenever they can
purchase the " fire water," hence they become lazy,
given to cheating, and mulish in obstinacy.

Can we be surprised, then, at the population decreasing and the whites increasing ? Can we feel
otherwise than that the Maoris are doomed ? though
it is a crying pity that we don't influence them for
good, for they are a fine manly race, and deserve
better things than being made bad imitations of
ourselves. Why are not our missionaries and
temperance workers to the fore ? The Episcopalians
did, single-handed, much good work among the
natives for several years, then crept in the Roman
Catholics and Wesleyans, introducing their creeds,
with the result that they quite bothered the Maori's
intellect, which is fairly shrewd and quick, and they
were unable to understand the religious divisions of
the three churches, and remarked very sensibly and
pointedly, " If these learned priests cannot agree
among themselves which is the straight road to
Heaven, and the correct religion to follow, how can
we poor unenlightened Maoris be expected to know

how to choose?" Can we be surprised, then, that
between these three stools the puzzled native falls
to the ground and relapses into paganism? The
Bible was translated as far back as 1837 into the
Maori language, and it may be asked how many converts has it made? The Maoris struggled against
us for eighteen years, and stopped all progress, but
in the year 1840 the chieftains agreed to the following
treaty, namely, "The Maori chiefs ceded to Queen
Victoria the right of government over the whole of
their country." The Queen, on her part, gave the
chiefs full right over their property, but ceded to Her
Majesty the right to purchase the land if they were
willing to sell. And, thirdly, "the Queen agreed to
protect all her Maori subjects, and granted to them
the same rights and privileges as if they were
Englishmen." Notwithstanding this treaty, quarrels
and angry passions were roused in connection with
land purchases, and fighting went on between the
natives and our red-coats, which seemed to excite
them like the red cloth does at bull-baiting; and
matters did not mend till our soldiers were withdrawn and the colonists were left to settle their own
affairs with the Maoris.

We will now take leave of the Maoris, and hark
back to Auckland, and for an hour or so seat ourselves
on its large pier and landing stages, which I reckon
could not have cost less than half a million of money.
Let us just dwell on its busy scenes, with Mount
Eden in the background. What is the occasion of
this lively sight? Why, in the first place, one sees
huge ocean steamers taking their cargoes of

thousands of carcases of sheep, frozen in an immense factory adjoining the pier, which communicates with the shipping by a railway, so that there is no time lost for the meat to thaw before it gets into the refrigerator of the vessel. Again you will see hundreds of bales of fine flax, which the colony yields in immense profusion, and with it sacks of hops and bundles of merino wool, all of which are exported to England. As to the cereals, the oats are grand, weighing 45 lbs. to the bushel, and much appreciated in our country. Then come packages of Kauri gum from the Kauri trees, very precious, while the wood is plentiful and valuable, taken from the Thames Valley, down whose beautiful river the logs are floated during a "freshet," and caught by booms.

Of all the precious minerals which New Zealand yields—gold, silver, copper, antimony, manganese, and coal—gold is the only one I shall allude to, as it is that which is most interesting to those already there, and to those about to go. £45,000,000 of gold was the amount of the find from 1853 to 1889. A splendid outcome, and it is no marvel, therefore, that the colony has flourished so well since it was first constituted in 1840. Personally, I feel an unusual interest in this matter, because a friend of mine, Mr. Charles Ring, of Ringcote, Auckland, was with his brother the original discoverer of gold in New Zealand. In prospecting for the precious metal he first came across it at Coromandel in 1852. The Government had offered a reward of £5,000 for the first discovery of "available" gold, and when

NEW ZEALAND VEGETABLE CATERPILLAR.

Messrs. Ring applied for the reward, it was refused on the ground that the Maoris objected to the spot being worked, hence it was not "available." Notwithstanding, the Government instigated these gentlemen to go on prospecting in order to ascertain to what extent the auriferous deposit existed in the colony, and they did so at their own expense, and they continued to make discoveries, and because they were not "available" through the obstinacy of the natives, they still kept back the reward. A mean and shabby thing to do—thus utilising the time, talents, and money of these public-spirited men for the public welfare without a just recompence.

I now come to speak of the most extraordinary thing I met with during my tour round the globe, namely, the New Zealand Vegetable Caterpillar. Our old scientific teachings are completely upset when we insist that a vegetable production must of necessity take its origin and extract its nourishment from the soil: that it is through the medium of gases dissolved in water, constituting what is called "sap," which ascends the plant till it reaches the leaves, where circulating through the cells, it becomes subjected to the influences of light and heat, and deoxidation is effected, oxygen being set free to purify the air, while the carbon descends, constituting woody fibre and vegetable growth. This physiological explanation is of no avail to us in our efforts to explain the nourishment and growth of the Vegetable Caterpillar—a most startling phenomenon—a singular freak of nature! Remarkable to relate, this plant fulfils its destiny by possessing the power of reproducing itself by means of minute

seeds, which are massed like so much red sand on the
ends of the twigs. They are clearly seen by an inch
magnifier, packed together firmly somewhat like the
maize in the cob. These small seedlings find their
way into the interior of the caterpillar through the
pores of the animal's breathing apparatus, represented
in the drawing by the round marks. Once inside its
body hair-like roots are sent out, which ramify into
every nook and corner of its soft tissue, absorbing no
gases in the usual way of soil-growing plants, but
directly taking up the albuminous fluid from the
body of the grub, which, as the plant bursts outside
and develops itself, gradually sucks dry its very
existence, starves out in fact its very life, and the
caterpillar shrivels up by degrees and dies of inanition.
In this condition they both fall down to the root of
the tree, when it is said the Maories collect them into
bundles, boil, and eat them—quite as palatable perhaps as fat snails consumed as a relish by the natives
of other countries. This very peculiar and interesting specimen of creative genius is indeed unique, and
like many other created things, at present beyond our
comprehension. We must be content to await patiently
the greater developments of scientific research. We
must remain students all our days, and keep our
scientific eye open to the reception of new laws, and
the rejection of old conclusions. This perpetual going
to school, this attitude of honest and humble study,
will tend doubtless to keep the mind fresh. Thinkers
must all admit that God works in a mysterious way,
and because we cannot at once understand and explain
His wondrous marvels, let us not shut ourselves up

in our own vain conceits, and say that there is no
Creator. "We are fearfully and wonderfully made,"
so says the Psalmist: but he goes on to say, "and
that my soul knoweth right well." Do we know it
right well? Do we really and practically feel it? Do
we humble ourselves at the sight of God's grand and
indescribable developments? Do we confess our intellects very small, very midgy-like, veritable pigmies,
when compared with His magnificent intelligence. If
we do, then we may venture to say and to feel that
our faith and hope is based upon a solid rock which
cannot be shaken by the attacks of sceptics, be they
ever so sharp, delusive, fascinating, and plausible.
Sometimes I give a lecture on this singular phenomenon so inexplicable to the scientist of the day,
and end by drawing some useful moral reflections
from it, such as the following:—

The introduction of these seedlings into the caterpillar, and the gradual destruction of its body and the
extinction of its very life, may be very aptly taken to
illustrate the effects of the smaller sins into the hearts
of men and women. In a thoughtless and unguarded
moment we permit these little evils to penetrate into
our minds, where they take deep root—a tenacious
lodgement—till they gradually expand into some besetting sin, monopolising the whole soul, which we
cannot of ourselves shake off. And if we do not apply
earnestly and vigorously for the power of the Holy
Spirit to come to our aid and help us to weed it out,
it will take as firm a grip of us as this plant does of
the grub which it cruelly kills, and hinders from per-
fecting itself for the higher life of a splendid insect, a

beautifully coloured moth, soaring upwards to the skies in self-delight and the admiration of all beholders. It shows also very forcibly how necessary it is for us in going through this world, replete with temptations and traps to catch the unwary, that we should be steady and unswerving sentinels, wide awake and ever on the watch against the insinuating arts and wiles of the Evil One, going about seeking where he can drop his seedlings of sin and mischief, and also knows so well our salient points of weakness. Whether these be the outcome of our various positions, high or low, rich or poor, old or young, or not, none are exempt from attacks. As we pity this unfortunate caterpillar which is shrivelled up into a mere shell, and even as a grub looses its comely aspect and its chances of a higher development, so must we pity the human being whose soul is so perverted and disfigured by continuous sinning that it is not fit to mix with the company of the angels in heaven. We lament over the being who is so careless and slumbering that a little evilly-disposed wish is allowed to enter a corner of the heart, where it finds congenial soil till it expands into a masterful giant! To get this wish gratified all the cardinal virtues are sacrificed and ignored, such as truth, temperance, self-respect, honour, justice, humility, and faith, and all the helps to the acquisition of these virtues are set at nought, even voted a bore, or tolerated only for social appearance sake, such are prayer, bible reading, public divine worship, and all that belongs to the formation of the Christian character. As men and women in the image of our God we rob ourselves of our higher life

and dignity, and become not unlike this caterpillar
and its parasite, which thinks only of sensual gratifi-
cation. We may well take this warning lesson from
the New Zealand caterpillar. Let us strive to safeguard ourselves against the first insidious entrance of
the small seedlings sown by the Evil One in our minds,
which grow so big and formidable, and create in us
such a cruel injury. But should we in an unguarded
moment have allowed one to penetrate our hearts, let
us quickly search and weed it out before it has time
to take deep root within us, and thus hinder our spirits
from soaring heavenwards, and mounting from strength
to strength, and from glory to glory, till we have
reached that spiritual peace which passeth understanding. Finally, let us bethink ourselves how such
a depraved mind prevents our shining here as lights
and helpers to others, and checks our ascent to God's
glorious home, clothed in our beautiful resurrection
bodies, which He has promised to those who love and
serve Him steadfastly and faithfully.

I cannot take my leave of beautiful Auckland without
a word with respect to the social aspect of the upper
classes. They are so thoroughly English in their ways
and feelings that it is difficult to imagine oneself out of
England. They are very fond of music, and though
their assembly room was burnt down twice by an in-
cendiary, they have now erected a third one of stone
and brick, which has 1,800 sittings. All the concerts
are by amateurs, who invite their friends, and most
agreeable evenings are spent. There is a great deal
of quiet sociability going on among the families, without any pretence at anything grand or expensive. The

AUCKLAND YOUNG LADY.

excellent tramways running in every direction tend to
bring friends cheaply and conveniently together. The
churches are large and well attended, mostly evangeli-
cal. At one of these where I read the lessons for a
popular preacher, who was giving his farewell sermon
before leaving for England, every seat was taken, and
in the vestry afterwards I was surprised to see that
there were in the collection of £8 17s. 10d., 256 threepenny pieces, and only four coppers; so I asked for
an explanation, and was told that the working classes
look with contempt on copper coins, and consequently
give the lowest silver one. So well understood is this
at all church collections, that when the clergyman's
daughter wanted small change from John Chinaman,
who is the greengrocer in every colony, he drew out a
handful of copper. "Oh, no, I don't want that," said
she; he immediately replied with, "Ah, I sees what
missy wants, churchy money," and handed over a
quantity of threepenny bits. The young ladies' complexions are singularly fair and smooth for so sunny
a climate, and their growth is precocious, a girl of
fourteen being equal to one of eighteen in England.
The young people are naturally fond of picnic gatherings, the lovely climate and picturesque neighbourhood
being well adapted for such pleasures. We will now
close this chapter, as we are leaving the land and
betaking ourselves to sea again, with the following
remarks on strong drink in its bearings on the work-
people. This splendid seaport, one of the most
bustling in the colony, boasts of very extensive
suburbs of wooden cottages, each containing four
rooms, with necessary outbuildings for animals, all

enclosed in a quarter or half an acre of land. I inquired who they belonged to, and I was told that they were freeholds, and were owned by the occupants. Now, a good, steady, hard-working man will get his shilling an hour for eight hours a day, which would amount to £2 8s. per week, and I was informed such a man would, in about three years, become the owner of one of these cottages. Then I inquired, how about the drink? The reply was very suggestive. "It can't be done, it is quite impossible." The man who drinks stagnates or is lost, and, if they are not up to time at the shipping business, they are turned off without the least compunction by a lynx-eyed foreman. Hence if a working man is to get on in the colonies it is by sheer hard, sober efforts, and no drink. No one need emigrate and expect to succeed who cannot make up his mind to follow these rules; abide by them, and prosperity and independence is the result, without failure. No one, be he a temperance advocate or otherwise, can be blind to the fact that this colony's welfare and progress is intimately bound up with the Englishman's resistance to alcoholic liquor, while he has the constant warning before him that the Maoris are gradually being exterminated by it.

CHAPTER XXV.

HAVING already secured our passage in a deck cabin
while in Sydney, and had our heavy luggage placed
therein, for a voyage to San Francisco by the mail
steamer *Mariposa*, we had nothing to do when she
arrived at Auckland but say farewell to our numerous
friends, and to enter comfortably into our berths and
possessions. The vessel being altogether under
American management, and manned throughout by
Yankee officers and crew, was not nearly so agreeable
and luxurious as an English ocean steamer would be;
in fact, the food was atrocious, the flour had turned
sour, the meat very tough, and even ship's biscuits
were tainted. I pitied the poor children who were
deprived of good bread and milk. And the waiters
were a scratch lot. However, we had to put up with
it, as there was no competition on this line; but there
was one consolation, the *Mariposa* was a good sea-
boat of 3,000 tons and 3,000 h.p. It was rather
monotonous steaming for 1,700 miles, only varied by
some good concerts of an evening, when we sighted
Tutuila, one of the Samoa Islands. There a schooner
came out to us with letters in exchange for some we

gave, but no passengers landed. Accompanying the
schooner was a swarm of canoes, very cleverly paddled
by both female and male natives ; some of the girls
were quite pretty looking, and the men with straight,
well-knit, athletic frames, with reddish skins and
expressive features, good teeth, and wavy black or
brown hair—nothing of the negro type about them,
but decidedly of the Malay stamp, and I can well
believe that the Maoris descended from them. Both
sexes were quite at home in the water, reminding one
of the Arabs at Aden, swimming and diving like
amphibious animals. They brought carved sticks
and bludgeons and fans on board for sale, and seemed
quite *au fait* in striking a bargain. These islands
have a nominal king, but are really under the protection of America, England, and Germany, which
gives them a code of laws. Hence the inhabitants
are rapidly becoming civilised and christianised by
missionaries. We saw on one of the group a church
with a tower to it, and some school buildings. A
passenger, presumably Irish, wanted to know how
long we should be before we reached Halleluja, meaning Honolulu. Before we could get there we had to
encounter some rough wind and rain, which disturbed
the peace of some of our party. Such changes are
very sudden in the Pacific, which at such times much
belies its name. After leaving Samoa there was little
to record till we reached Honolulu, where we arrived
at two in the afternoon, and were greeted and welcomed
by an applauding multitude and the music of the royal
band, which played us into the harbour. Honolulu is the
capital of the Hawaiian Islands, and though governed

by a native king and a representative constitution, is
virtually under the protectorate of the United States
of America, which keeps a watchful eye over its doings.
On landing we called on Mr. Theo. Davis, recently
our Vice Consul, and were advised to take a buggy
and drive up the winding road to the top of the hill
called the " Punch Bowl," which dominates the city.
From this old extinct crater a very splendid and
extensive view is to be had of the town, harbour,
and pretty suburbs, embellished with flowering shrubs,
and on the left, rice fields, now waving with corn. In
the valley between the foot of the hill and the town
are situated the Chinese vegetable and fruit gardens,
irrigated in a marvellous manner, by diverting the
mountain stream into rills. The cleanliness of the
white-robed Chinamen, together with their thrift and
industry, is most praiseworthy, and, as shopkeepers,
most successful. They constitute, with the Japanese,
a large and important section of the population, about
20,000—the whole of the Islands numbering not much
more than 80,000. From the " Punch Bowl " hill one
cannot see well the line of the streets, they are so
shrouded in leaves, but the king's palace, the Government buildings, and the two spires of the Cathedral
stand out in strong relief. The natives proper put
me very much in mind of the Maoris in face and
form, but they are sadly decreasing in numbers,
while the Americans and English are increasing,
and no wonder, for the babies fade away and die
early, because the parents on both sides smoke and
drink heavily, the late king setting the example : but
it is said the reigning queen is a great temperance

advocate, and will not allow any intoxicating drinks
in the palace. On Sunday we went to hear the bishop
preach in the Cathedral, and in the same grounds we
found the old pro-cathedral now given up to the Chinese
converts to Christianity. As a service was going on,
we entered, and heard an English sermon being in-
terpreted, sentence after sentence, to the Chinamen.
Though the clergyman could read the Bible and say
the prayers in their language, he would not trust himself to preach, for fear, he said, of being misunder-
stood. They sang their hymns to our tunes in good
time and voice. There is a good attendance of women
in the morning, but not at night, as it is not the custom
for Chinese women to go out at night into the streets.
Being desirous of seeing the limits of the city, we took
our seats in the tramway, which bisects the town in
every direction. On the tram we entered into conversation with a very intelligent lady, who spoke
English perfectly, yet she had never been out of
Honolulu. Her vocation was that of mistress at the
Chinese school, where she had to teach English to the
boys in the morning and the girls in the evening.
She told us that there was not much difference in the
capacity for learning between the two sexes. As a
rule they were quite as quick as the English children.
Education was free to all classes; but the daughters
of the upper ranks attended school with their feet
contracted, the small toes being bandaged under the
great toe, so as to bring the foot to a point. This is
the outward sign of the fashionable Chinese lady of
rank. The girls from the working classes do not thus
disfigure their feet; they do not presume to be *à la*

mode. Besides, the poor are apt to despise their
daughters, especially with regard to education, and
to favour their sons only. There are extensive sugar
plantations in the other neighbouring islands, the
value of the several estates being worth a million of
money. The lines of railway intersecting the plantations are thirty miles in extent. America is the
principal market for the sale of this commodity. Mr.
Theo. Davis, our upright, honourable, and intelligent
Vice-Consul, has been the life centre of this great industry for a number of years, and the public fetes
which have been held in his honour when he left for
England, speak eloquently of the great good he has
been to the Hawaiian community; and well he
merited all the applause, for he has thrown himself
most actively into all philanthropic and Christian
works, and is one of the most popular men in Honolulu. Before leaving Honolulu and its delightful
climate, the tourist should take a trip in a local
steamer, and visit one of the group of islands where
there is a very fierce volcanic eruption going on, called
the Kilanea, one of the craters passing under the
name of the " House of Fire," which the title gives
one a fair idea of.

On leaving the Honolulu Pier we were again
entertained with music from the royal band to
"speed the parting guests," but the quiet, serene
life we had been enjoying was soon to be interrupted
by a dreadful storm at sea, and that sea the Pacific;
Heaven forgive those who gave it that name ! For
two days and nights we did not have our clothes off,
for the rolling and the rocking was so violent and

jerky that we could not keep in our berths. Those poor ladies who had cabins on deck could not get out, and no stewardess was allowed to go to them, as it was not safe to walk the decks, which were being swept fore and aft by huge waves, and the wind was so high that the cabin doors could not be opened. The officers of the ship had never been in such a hurricane before, and it was a question for forty-eight hours whether the good ship could weather it out or not. No meals could be had because the cooks could not keep the pots on the range, and no end of crockery and glass was broken in the saloon racks. However, there is an end to all troubles, even to those at sea; hence, after a stormy passage of six days, we all most gratefully hailed the sight of land with a thankfulness, the sincerity of which was depicted on every face, pale and haggard indeed, but expressive of a deep feeling of gratitude to the Giver of all goodness, and to that Mighty Power which could still the waves of the troubled deep, and command it, as of yore, to be calm!

After passing through that narrow passage called the "Golden Gate," we were soon warped to the side of the quay at San Francisco. After some little delay at the customs house in connection with the examination of our luggage (which I must say, to the credit of Cook and Son's agency, we were helped not a little), we took a carriage, and drove off to the Palace Hotel. Oh! the difference between this exquisite sort of luxury, comfort, and enjoyment, and that of the vessel which we had just left was something to calm the most ruffled feelings, and to

soothe the most sickly and woebegone passenger
after such a sea voyage. We were soon revelling
in rooms most exquisitely furnished, in which every
possible convenience was present which talent could
devise and money accomplish. Arranged on a dial
in the sitting-room were a series of knobs to press,
which by electricity would indicate to the porters
whether you wanted ice-water, a fire, refreshments,
an out-door porter, or a laundress. Hot and cold
water was laid on into the marble baths and wash-
stands. It is a monster building of eight or nine
storeys, containing 1,800 rooms from basement to
attic. It has a central court covered with a glass
roof, in which several carriages can wait at a time,
and visitors can sit in easy-chairs, smoke, and con-
verse. There is a balcony round each flight, ornamented with hanging creepers and flowers; from
each of these you can look down on the court below
and listen to the band playing. There are double
corridors on each storey, and these are so wide and
high that they are called streets; ours was called
Market Street, after the main street in the city.
There were velvet-seated lounges at the side for the
visitors, and plenty of room in the centre for a
carriage and pair to drive along if need be. The
vista was such a length that you could not distinguish a person at the further end. Imagine, therefore, six of these double thoroughfares one above the
other, and communicating with each other by "lifts,"
or "elevators," as they call them, smoothly running
up a party of twenty or more at a time, and stopping
without a thud at each stage to let them out in

squads to their several apartments; and this up
and down work went on from early dawn to midnight. Of course, there were many staircases with
marble steps covered with soft carpeting, independent
of the elevators, for those who liked this mode of
taking exercise. There could not have been less
than 4,000 people under the roof of this little town
when we were there, all well fed and housed in the
lap of luxury and ease, without confusion or worry;
every one thing and every one person had its place,
and in that place they were always to be found, like
well-disciplined sentinels. San Francisco is said to
be built on a hundred hills; anyhow the visitor
must see for himself that the streets are all up and
down, and yet cable and horse-trams bisect it in
every possible direction, and most convenient they
are, at 2½d. a ride, running to and fro every few
minutes, varying in colour according to the district
they go to; they pay well, as they are the common
conveyance of the masses, who foot up to the number
of 300,000. Though this city of gold is said to be
the most abandoned on the face of the earth, religious liberty is in evidence to a remarkable degree,
for there are no less than 113 denominations, including the Chinese, who form a very important
part of the population, counting up 30,000, and
occupying a square half mile, which they monopolise
in the very heart of the city. They are very closely
packed, the lower orders sleeping in bunks one above
the other, as on board ship, with a narrow alley
between of about two feet in width. So the visitor
to Chinatown must be prepared to find it not a little

smelly, and swarming with "live stock," some of which he might carry away on his person. Domestically speaking, Johnny is a very important personage; 6,000 Chinese are domestic servants to the Yankees, and very honest and reliable they are. Three thousand are laundresses, 15,000 are common labourers, and the rest are shopkeepers and well-to-do merchants, some of whom may be seen driving in their carriages and pair, and reputed to be wealthy. In every living room, large and small, high and low, good and bad, may be seen altars and idols, candles and incense, and much praying goes on. All their food is brought in a dried state from China—mushrooms, ducks' eggs wrapt up in clay, pork, fish, potatoes, &c. When the tourist visits the Chinese quarter he had better take a policeman as an escort. Fortunately we had a friend who had been a citizen of San Francisco for many years, and he was very kind, not only in taking us about to many places of note, but in supplying us with much interesting local information. For instance, he took us to Nob Hill, where all the rich merchants live, hence its nickname. It must be understood that there are thirty millionaires in the city, whose possessions vary from three to twenty millions each; hence they have erected mansions on Nob Hill at a fabulous cost, marble and polished granite entering largely into their structure. From this spot we passed on to a cemetery occupying a singular but picturesque position on a sand-hill, from whence there is a good view of the people's pleasure park and public gardens, with the racecourse adjoining, where our friend's son was killed by a race-horse bolting and jumping the boundary rails, falling upon him and crushing him to death, leaving a young wife and baby to mourn his loss. From his monument in the cemetery could be seen the exact spot where he was killed, the sight always acting as a reminder to the father of the uncertainty of human life. Our friend was the composer of the "Grand Entrée March" for the Knights Templars when they congregated at San Francisco in 1883 from all the States of America. It was performed by thirty performers of the Native Hawaiian band, which had taken the first competitive prize against all American bands. It was played every evening in the court of the Palace Hotel, where thousands of ladies and gentlemen came to listen to its lively strains, and also to give a hearty welcome to this pilgrimage of Knights Templars, who monopolised every room in the spacious building. Every official grade of masonry was represented from every State of the Union. It was at this celebrated congress of noble and benevolent men that the Rev. Dr. Clinton Locke, of Chicago, said in his address to them, " You read of French gallantry, Italian refinement, and English breeding; but it will not for a moment compare, as far as the sacrifice of one's comfort is concerned for the sake of others, with the unvarying respect American men ever show towards a woman or a child. . . . To the woman unprotected and of good character, is passport sufficient, even in the wildest West, to ensure to her the devotion and the loyal devotional service of every man she meets." As a rider to this gallantry I may just add that when

the ladies and gentlemen entered the "lift" at the
Palace Hotel, the ladies took their seats in these
elegant miniature drawing-rooms, while the gentlemen stood up and invariably took their hats off out
of respect to the fair sex. But to continue our
sightseeing we will charter a carriage, and drive off
to The Cliff, where we can see a colony of sea-
lions disporting themselves on the rocks, and from

SEALS ON THE ROCKS AT SAN FRANCISCO.

thence to Telegraph Hill, from which is obtained
the best view of the city, its bay, and surrounding
country, and finish up our outing at Golden Gate
Park, where there is a beautiful conservatory to
admire. There is no Sunday closing in San Francisco. It is sad to see all the theatres and shops
open as on a week day. Amusements of every kind are
the order of the day. When persons are migrating
from other parts of America to this city, it is a

common saying, "that they are going to leave God behind them." Divorces there are quite common, even among those *recently* married, and easily arranged. The shamefacedness with which young girls talk of the matter, even to their elderly lady friends, is simply astounding to an Englishman, and would make him blush in his own country. We went with our friend and his family to spend an evening at the house of a millionaire—a self-made man, originally haling from Ireland. Among other precious and valuable elegancies which his large mansion contained, was an onyx marble mantelpiece, the upper slab of which was truly splendid, and was said to be cheap at £10,000. Of course our host was very proud of showing off this unique piece of rarity, and turning round to me, said, "I guess that beats anything you Britishers can show in your country." Then we ascended to the flat roof of the house, from whence there is at night-time a grand panorama of the city at one's feet, with its wide thoroughfares illumined with gas and electric lights quite dazzling like a pyrotechnic show. Yet with all these glorious surroundings, and with a handsome queen-like wife to boot, he did not strike me as a happy man, and that peace did not reign in his dwelling.

We attended one Sunday evening a service at Trinity Church, and heard Mr. Reed give an eloquent extempore discourse to a crowd of working men, on the subject of capital and labour, and the inequalities between man and man, and his struggles to get the necessities of life. He also pleaded for temperance workers on the dual basis, stating the remarkable fact that fifty-six bishops of the American Episcopalian Church had decided to be total abstainers, in order by force of example to advance and support this grand work among their countrymen.

CHAPTER XXVI.

Having already secured our railway tickets and sent on our heavy luggage to New York, by that admirable system so slow on our own lines to adopt, we drove down to the ferry, where a huge transfer steamer was ready to convey us across the bay to Oakland, a very beautiful suburban town. On arriving at the pier we enter a most imposing wooden structure which serves the purpose of a ferry-house and a railway station. Here we find the great overland train with its long line of sleeping cars awaiting us. We enter it without confusion or fuss, and every one settles down in its sumptuous saloons with its soft velvet-covered seats and convenient tables. We travel along the valley for twenty-eight miles, and then we arrive at Port Costa, where there is something to surprise us. Our long train of eleven carriages, each 84 feet long, has to be carried bodily across the Carquinez Strait to the town of Benicia opposite. This transfer boat, called the *Solano*, is said to be the largest in the world, and is so constructed that it will hold on its immense deck forty-eight cars and two engines divided into parallel portions. Let us descend from our saloon for a moment, and see for ourselves the easy

and remarkable way in which the train leaves the
rails on the land to meet those on the boat on a perfect
level. Then the whole ponderous mass moves off so
smoothly that those inside the carriages do not feel
the movement. When we reached the other side, both
sets of rails again approximated to a nicety, and we
trained off again as if nothing very important had
happened. To say that this is a grand piece of
engineering skill is to say little. Only in America
would one see such gigantic works carried out, and yet
we are only at the commencement of that wonder of
wonders—the passage of the Rockies. Night coming
on, we undressed and settled down for a sleep in our
berths and sofas. Early the next morning we were
greeted by the sun shining on the snowy top of the
Nevada range of mountains, which we had reached
by our train zig-zagging to a height of 7,000 feet
above the valley we had left behind the evening
before. These snow-clad hills are covered here and
there with fir-trees, and in order to protect the railway from avalanches of snow long timber sheds have
been erected at the most exposed situations. Some
of these are so long that they resemble long wooden
tunnels, lighted at the side by portholes, through
which we get a pretty glimpse now and again. It is
said that the measurement of the covered ways, when
put end to end, would reach one hundred miles, a
prodigious work in such an inhospitable region.
Sometimes they catch fire from the engines, which
leads to much expense to the company; but they are
indispensable, as they support sometimes eighteen
feet of snow on their roofs. Now the scene completely

changes. We descend the eastern slopes of the Nevada range, so different to its western side, which is so full of gold that two hundred and fifty millions have been extracted from it in forty years, and which has enriched California far above any other State of America, till at last we reach the great American desert, and its arid plains yielding only sage-brush and grease-wood. Hour after hour passes by in wearisome monotony, till the eyesight tires over the desolate waste, destitute of the lowest forms of vegetation—and all this from want of water, for it is found if it be irrigated it will produce almost anything, but at present it is all sand, varied with here and there a surface of alkali, which shines in the distance like water, simulating lakes with its deceitful mirage. In this Great Basin, surrounded by mountains, a natural curiosity exists, namely, the river Humbolt runs for 380 miles, and, failing to find an outlet, buries its water in the arid sand, within view of the passing train. Having traversed a run of 460 miles, we leave the State of Nevada behind, and enter the territory of the Mormons, and we soon are looking down upon the Great Salt Lake, which we keep in view for the next one hundred miles. This mysterious inland sea, called also the "Dead Sea" of America, has no outlet. When its shores get dry in the summer, a large quantity of crystallised alkali is collected. At last we reach Ogden, 894 miles from San Francisco, and the journey was accomplished in thirty-six hours, continuous travelling—rather slow, especially for America. A Baptist minister, hailing from the Golden City, told me in the train that the old

Friscoites, who boasted of their being the "Pioneers" and founders of the city in 1849, considered themselves so pre-eminently good and moral on that account that they never need trouble themselves on the score of religion, its duties and needs; and some even replied, when asked what denomination they belonged to, would say that they were "forty-niners."

At Ogden we drop our passengers who desire to visit the Yellowstone National Park, and we put our watches on one hour, it having been found by the Government more convenient to make three changes only in the time between Frisco and New York of one hour each. Continuing our journey for another thirty-six miles, we reach Salt Lake City, and take up our quarters at Cullen's Hotel, where we luxuriated in most delightful rooms, sitting, bed, and bath-rooms *en suite*, with electric light, most excellent cuisine, and good service, which was a surprise to us in the "City of the Saints." The next morning we were greeted with a splendid view of the opposite snow-capped hills in a pink halo of sunshine, somewhat like the Pyrennian range from Pau, in France. These glistening peaks of the Wahsatch Mountains run up into the skies from 9,000 to 13,000 feet high above the sea-level. To a casual visitor no difference would appear in its outward aspect between this city and any other. Everything in the streets seemed to be conducted in a most orderly and peaceful way. The first objects which a tourist seeks for are the Mormon Tabernacle—The Temple—and close by the Assembly Hall (*vide* sketch). First, then, we enter the Temple, with its curved roof like the back of a

SALT LAKE CITY.

turtle. It sits at ease 9,000 people, yet it is only 250 feet long, by 150 feet wide, and 100 feet high, contains a huge organ with 57 stops and 2,846 pipes. The acoustic properties are marvellous. One can hear a pin drop or the hands rubbed together across a space of 200 feet. It is an extraordinary building, all of wood, and every visitor should attend the afternoon Sunday service, and look down on its vast congregation, and hear the organ and choir sing the hymns with astonishing enthusiasm, the breaking of bread by the priesthood, the fervid addresses to show with astonishing plausibility the identity of the Latter Day Saints' Church with that of the Zion of prophecy, which, as one writer has said, " must impress every thoughtful visitor more or less powerfully as the instruments of a gigantic imposture, and his moral nature recoil from them as the spiritual cloak of a carnal church—the perfumed drapery of an ecclesiastical seraglio." We now turn to the magnificent Gothic Temple, all built of granite, 200 feet by 100 feet, and 100 feet high. It was commenced in 1853, and has cost millions upon millions of dollars, and it is not yet completed. A stranger will naturally ask, How do they get the money? Well, it is a fixed law with the Mormons that they prove their faith by their works, by giving 10 per cent. of their profits to complete the Temple. Again, the first Thursday in every month is set apart by the shopkeepers, so that their *employés* may attend a religious service and contribute donations for the relief of the poor and needy. The Assembly Hall is a pleasure resort for all classes— reading, dancing, and concerts.

We will take our seats in the electric tramway
along Main Street to the foot of the hill two miles
off, and then a short walk brings us to Fort Douglass,
where there is a battery and artillery barracks. From
thence we get a good bird's-eye view of the city below,
containing its 30,000 inhabitants, the streets inshrined
in green foliage, obscuring the line of roads, as in
Honolulu, but all the grand buildings, including the
Holy Cross Hospital, stand out in bold relief, backed
by the Salt Lake and the mountains beyond. We will
now return and take a carriage drive through the
wide thoroughfares shaded by poplar and acacia
trees, and visit the late Brigham Young's house,
called the " Amelia Palace," after his favourite wife,
who lived there with him, while the other wives
resided in a large house named the " Bee Hive ; " but
we were told by the daughter of one of Brigham
Young's servants that his other wives had each a
separate house and a separate establishment quite
distinct from one another. I got a capital photograph
of Brigham Young, who died in 1877. He was
President of the 142 hardy " Pioneers " who entered
the valley in 1847, who suffered many privations, but
who, with extraordinary religious zeal and pluck,
have succeeded in founding a beautiful city, making
what was once deemed for ages a barren waste into a
most fertile country, where every luxury can be obtained, and where useful factories abound.

Brigham Young's tomb should be seen. Our
previous informant told us that many of his devotees
still believe that he is not dead, and that others were
so superstitious that they placed sentinels over his

grave for some time; and recently they affirm that his gravestone has shifted; therefore, to make things more secure, they have placed a more weighty slab over the original, and one can see the stone ready for fixing. The visitor should not fail to pay a visit by train to Lake Park bathing resort, a sort of Brighton to the citizens, situated on the shores of the Salt Lake, about twenty miles off. and by all means try a bath in the buoyant water, which contains 22 per cent. of pure salt, in which it is impossible to sink. Care should be taken that none of the water gets into the mouth or nostrils, otherwise there would be danger of suffocation. To the porter who busied himself in getting our luggage into the train I put the question, with as little offensiveness as I could muster, "How many wives have you got?" He replied, very readily, "Only one, and I find some difficulty in maintaining her. It is only the rich nobs and higher classes who can afford to have a lot of wives." This answer recalled me to the social condition of Turkey, where the rich pashas only can indulge in a harem. We will now resume our journey eastward, and before we reach the mountains we pass through a grand valley some miles in extent. full of Mormon settlements smiling with fertile fields and orchards in the highest state of cultivation, brought about by the persevering industry of the people, who, through hard work and irrigation, have turned this valley from a wilderness into a garden that blossoms like the rose. Just look at the bright-eyed and healthy children who meet you with baskets of fruits, strawberries, raspberries, currants, apples, &c., and

you will be convinced that you are in the land of
milk and honey. A very pleasant little town on this
route, and a summer resort for the well-to-do, is
Provo, where you can get an excellent dinner at the
station.

A short distance to one's right we see the beautiful
Lake of Utah, a large body of fresh water, which the
Mormons call the Lake of Tiberias, and from this
lake runs a fertilising stream they name the River
Jordan, flowing into the Salt Lake, styled by them
the "Dead Sea"; hence the Latter Day Saints desire
to draw an analogy between this disposition of nature
and that in Palestine, and that it is in accordance
with the Divine plan and purpose that this beautiful
valley should be blessed as the abode of the Mor-
monites!

Now we will commence the romantic story of the
route from west to east of the Rio Grande and Denver
Railway, 700 miles in extent. Passing through these
gigantic barriers, necessitating the ascent of our
train to elevations of 7,465 feet, 10,852 feet, and
7,238 feet. These have to be surmounted, and then
we have to penetrate through awful gorges, or cañons,
as they are called, which are such remarkable features
in the Rocky Mountain railway system. Soon after
leaving Provo we begin the ascent of the first of
these tremendous bulwarks, and by all sorts of
twistings and zig-zagging gain what is termed the
"Soldier's Divide," the summit of the Wahsatch
Range, which sends up its tall spires of rock high up
into the skies. After traversing a certain amount of
plateau we begin to descend, and get some scenery

which, though picturesquely fine, is but a faint fore-
shadowing of that which is soon to be our delight to
gaze upon. The first and foremost object to astonish
and fascinate our attention is the Castle Gate
entrance to Price River Cañon, one of the grandest
single objects in the entire mountain world. It consists of two immense projections from the sides of the
gorge of solid rock, dyed with a rich colouring of red,
while the pine trees growing about them reach only a
short way up, but serve to intensify the varied hues
of rock and shrubs. These two huge pillars are
respectively 500 feet and 800 feet high, and guard,
like sentinels, this narrow passage through the heart
of which the railroad runs side by side with the
river, one pressing closely upon the other in fearful
proximity. The train is brought to a stand here that
we may all admire and take away such a recollection
as never can be forgotten. After passing through
the winding cañon with its lofty and precipitous
walls varying in colour at every turn, showing a
strife with the elements over thousands of years of
time, we debouch at last upon the broad valley of
Green River, a stream of good size, which fifty
miles further on joins the Grande, to make up the
far-famed Colorado. The valleys between these two
rivers are rich agricultural lands, extending over a
hundred miles. After this our train has to traverse
a weird piece of country, reminding one of the Nevada
desert, the dreariness relieved only by the sight of
a remarkable formation called the Book Cliffs, resembling piles of books on a shelf, and in the distance
the glistening mountains of Serra da Sal and San

THE ROYAL GORGE, PASSAGE OF THE ROCKIES.

Rafael. Soon after passing Montrose, we arrive at the Black Cañon of the Gunnison river, considered one of the most stupendous and awe-inspiring scenes in the world, penetrating a gorge of several miles in extent, with perpendicular walls of solid granite on each side, rising from 1,000 feet to 2,000 feet, between which tears along an impetuous torrent, splashing and foaming over its rocky bed; and by the side of this gushing stream has been blasted from its granite side a sufficient platform to lay down a single line of rails. Upon these our train passes through numerous windings and projecting rocks, adding an overpowering impressiveness to the scene. On the bottom of this deep gulf the sun never shines. One of the special features of this magnificent cañon is the Currecanti Needle, a huge granite monolith that rises from the gorge with all the grace and symmetry of an Egyptian obelisk, which is red from base to summit, and stands like a grim guardian in watchful solitude.

As we emerge from this weird chasm we welcome the sunny quiet of the Gunnison valley, which affords a happy relief to one's over-wrought feelings, for our hearts have been standing still for some time with the awful grandeur of this wondrous pass. Leaving Gunnison behind, we now begin the ascent of all ascents—the most exhilarating and surprising railway ride in the world. We first of all have our long train divided into two portions, each to be drawn by two powerful ten-wheeled engines, and we begin our climb to the "Continental Divide," called so because it separates the eastern from the western

17

side of America. As our rise becomes steeper the
engines puff out a sullen roar, indicating: the tremendous strain upon them; and then, as we get
higher we begin to wind round the mountains, and,
after struggling by steep gradients for four miles, we
find that we have only got upwards about half a
mile above the railroad we see below us, on which,
comes, following in our wake, the other portion of our
train, apparently going in an opposite direction. We
wave our handkerchiefs one to another as a passing

RAILWAY OVER THE ROCKIES.

salute. On and upward we go into the skies, with its
rarefied and exciting air, along narrow ledges of rock,
through cuttings in the solid stone, and passing banks
of snow and stunted pines. The track frequently
doubles upon itself, and slow is the progress till we
begin to think that we shall never reach the top; but
everything comes to him who can be patient, and so
we reach at last the Marshall Pass, which is covered
with a long wooden shed. Here we come to a stand
after a gradual climb of 10,852 feet above the sea-

level, and yet we are at the base of Mount Onvry, which is 4,000 feet still higher. On each side of the ridge arises, on the eastern, the River Arkansas, which goes to join the Mississippi, and on the western, the River Gunnison, which flows into the Colorado. We are not kept long on this, the backbone of the Rockies. A cry of "All aboard!" is shouted, and we have to resume our seats, and, having detached one of our engines, we go down very slowly and cautiously; but this gives us more time to gaze upon the magnificent scenery of the eastern slope. The grand Sangre de Cristo range stands boldly out against the skies right in front of us, and below us are the peaks of hills with green valleys and sparkling brooks between them, till we reach the Arkansas plains. At every turn we must admire and laud the great engineering skill which could devise this railroad and overcome its varied difficulties, and yet one never hears his name mentioned. Our descent is by grades of one foot in twenty-four. We soon reach a dining-station, and for a moment our thoughts do not go back to the glories of the Marshall Pass. After this refreshment we were better able to enjoy a trip through the Royal Gorge, the Grand Cañon of the Rockies, whose wonders and superlative magnificence surpass anything we have yet seen, and that is saying a great deal. To make a passage through this gorge the engineer's hand has surpassed itself in ingenuity. No photographer, or writer, or painter, can convey to the eye of man a tithe of its awful and fascinating grandeur. The skill and dogged perseverance of the Anglo-Saxon is here very apparent. With the dashing, foaming River Arkansas rushing through this chasm, the engineer has carved his way by its side through the living rock, and constructed a roadway for a single line of rails. There was scarcely room for the river alone to get through it, and granite projections blocked the way with their mighty bulk. When one reflects that this gorge extends fourteen miles, the very thought was enough to make any man's heart sink within him ; but he faced the difficulties with superhuman efforts, and the numerous obstructions were gradually blasted out of the way, and, following the contour of the rocks, a thoroughfare was at last pierced, and its hidden glories revealed, which, once seen, can never be effaced from the mind of the fortunate tourist who is permitted to behold these mighty works of the great Creator and His inspired creature—man.

We come to a stand at the entrance, and our conductor goes through the train, informing the several passengers that the Denver and Rio Grande Company have, in order that they may see the gorge to greater advantage, placed at the rear of the train an " observation car," into which about a hundred and fifty persons pack themselves ; it is all open top and side, like a long truck with seats in it. From this point of vantage we can see at our ease the extraordinary wonders of this rocky cleft. We pass down very slowly with the Arkansas river, a very " hell of waters " by our side. The deeper we go, higher and higher become the perpendicular walls of granite, without a shrub to mar their smooth surface, towering to a height of 1,000 feet to 1,500 feet, between which

we see an arch of blue sky, but no sun ever pene-
trates to the bottom of this abyss. No sign of a bird
or any other living thing, and the noise of the rushing
torrent only breaks the awful stillness.

Overhanging crags overshadow the track here and
there, and threaten to fall down and crush us. If we
could but mount up to one of these and look down,
what a veritable pigmy our train would appear amid
such overmastering surroundings! With this fancied
picture on our minds, we will now emerge from this
grand undertaking of which the Americans may well
be proud of as their country's *chef d'œuvre*. As we
are now re-entering civilised life again, we will defer
its description for another chapter.

CHAPTER XXVII.

EMERGING from the Royal Gorge we next come to the Cañon city, where may be seen a monster building, like two or three of our workhouses rolled into one, with a well-armed guard pacing up and down its grim walls. On inquiry we are told that this stronghold is the Colorado State Penitentiary. After a further run of forty miles we reach Puebla, an old Spanish town, full of life and activity. Continuing our journey northward for 120 miles, we arrive at Denver, our road having run along the base of the Rocky Mountains. On our left, from which may be seen issuing peaks, 12,000 feet to 15,000 feet high, while on our right we behold an interminable plain or prairie, which is like an ocean with nothing but the horizon in the distance, unbroken by hedges or trees, but whose fertility by irrigation from the watershed of the Rockies is unbounded. Those who have money to spare and well-lined pockets should strike off at Puebla for Maniton, described as the Saratoga of the West. There they will find large, sumptuous hotels, with every elegance and luxury for wealthy summer visitors who are in search of health or pleasure. The beauty of the surrounding scenery cannot be surpassed in America. The ascent of Pike's Peak is easy for ladies or gentlemen, though it does run up 14,000 feet into the heavens. From thence they better can see the boundless plains, giving a grand sweep of vision towards the east; and though this peak is so high the American Government have erected an observatory on its summit. It might indeed be justly said that no trip to the Rockies can be considered complete which omits a stay at Maniton. Again, another chief attraction is a carriage drive to the "Garden of the Gods" and Glen Eyrie, where one will be fascinated by a series of coloured rocks of fantastic, unearthly shape, which impart to the scenery a weird aspect in the midst of the most peaceful surroundings.

We will now hark back to Denver, one of the magic wonders as a city on the American continent. Many another has sprung up in mushroom fashion, but none have come up to Denver in the rapidity of its rise; the population having increased from 5,000 to 125,000 in eighteen years. It is the commercial centre for the mining district of Colorado, and here are situated the great smelting and reduction works, and some good mineralogical specimens can be purchased. The hotels are excellent, and the trams run in every direction. We attended divine service at the cathedral, which has been erected through the untiring zeal of Dean Hart, formerly of Blackheath, near London, who came here for the benefit of his health, and is now well and robust, and very popular

as an extempore preacher, the only kind of preaching
that goes down in the States. The suburbs of Denver
are very pretty and neat, and easily reachable by
train. The houses are most comfortably built, and
very picturesque in the Queen Anne style, each in
their own separate grounds. Such satisfaction and
contentment do these residences give the people that
Denver has been called "the city of homes." The
citizens are a rich and go-ahead race. We passed
the huge town-hall and state offices with its central
dome, and which is to cost when finished one and a
half millions sterling. The station buildings are
immense, and it is quite a sight to see the grand
baggage depôt for passengers' trunks, &c. We now
take our places in the train starting for Chicago,
shortly called "Sheego," by the people. This is a
run of 1,025 miles, and to get there we have to pass
the three great States of Nebraska, Iowa, and Illinois.
In Iowa they are prohibited from brewing or selling
spirits, consequently there is not such a demand for
maize (corn) for the purpose of distillation, hence
they say the corn trade is depressed in that state, yet
to the tourist it seems as flourishing as any of the
others. We traverse for miles and miles a more or
less undulating prairie with an everlasting sameness
of aspect, the chief features of which are its rapid
agricultural development, varied with towns and
villages cropping up in every direction, shaded by
woods and plantations. The farming produce is
truly remarkable; for instance, it is said that the
maize crop, or corn, as it is called, alone in these
fertile plains would fill a goods train 2,000 miles in

length, or if we placed the corn on our English
waggons it would constitute a procession of trains
that would reach round the world. In Iowa the
maize is so plentiful, such a veritable glut in the
market, that they use it for fuel to heat their ovens.
The eye wearies over this never-ceasing land of
plenty, "this grand republican valley, watered and
drained by its huge republican rivers," the mighty
Missouri, and its still mightier brother, the majestic
Mississippi, the "father of waters," as the Americans
so proudly call it; and we are glad to reach Omaha,
the most populous city we have seen since we left
Frisco. It has an immense wholesale trade, large
smelting works, extensive stock-yards and packing
houses, and the visitor might do worse than break
his journey here, after his wearisome passage over
the prairies, where his patience has been not a
little tried. Buy a photo of a settler's family on the
plains entitled, "Getting a Start." Mounting our
train again we soon reach the bridge which crosses
the Missouri, a splendid structure of 3,000 feet in
length. It is a grand piece of engineering skill, and
as graceful as it is substantial. It may be seen to
great advantage from the left-hand windows, supposing that you are approaching it from the western
side. The volume of water which is calculated to
flow under this bridge in the winter-time is immense;
viz., 750,000 gallons per second; but it decreases so
rapidly in June that it shrinks into comparatively
small dimensions, hence at that season one would
little imagine that large steamers navigate the river
for 2,300 miles above this point. At Burlington,

which is a picturesque city on the banks of the
Mississippi, we cross that river which never becomes
as shallow as the Missouri, and has a finer appearance because its sides are more richly wooded. The
bridge which spans the river is also a very magnificent one of 2,237 feet long, the draw span being itself
362 feet in extent. Between Burlington and Chicago,
which are separated by 200 miles, we get into a most
prosperous and highly-cultivated country, and as
interesting as it is beautiful, more like England,
being better wooded, and with clean, white homesteads standing in cozy nooks surrounded by green
shrubs and trees. The huge red barns indicate the
prosperity of the farmers, who ought to be well content living in the midst of such Arcadian loveliness.
Thus we pass onward through the granary of the
world until at last we come to a very pretty suburban-
like series of villas, through the centre of which our
train runs, and on inquiring as to our whereabouts
were told that we had entered the outskirts of
Chicago, and that we had yet twenty-four miles to
travel before we reached the heart of the city. This
will give the tourist a fair notion of the extent of
this famous metropolis. It is the most wonderful
of modern cities in its rapid strides, as a great centre
of population, combined with its world-wide commerce
as a meat-producing community. Its growth since
it was burnt down about fifteen years ago is quite
phenomenal. To give an instance of the rapid
way in which they can build, I may mention the
"Auditorium." This remarkable building was begun
and *completed in the short space of two years.* Its

frontage is 710 feet, is 270 feet high to the lantern, it has eleven storeys, contains a theatre, opera house, hotel, library, museum, and an observatory on the top, &c., and up to which one goes in a "lift." The weight of this monster is 110,000 tons, and, wonderful to relate, fifty million pieces of ornamental marble were put down by the human hand. As there will be an immense gathering of people from all parts of the globe to visit the "World's Fair," to be opened in May, 1893, at Chicago, I must be excused if I enter a little more into detail respecting the greatness of this wonderful mart. I will begin by saying that when the Queen ascended the throne the population of Chicago was only 3,000, now it contains one million and a half of the most energetic and enterprising people on the face of the earth. The length of the city is $24\frac{1}{2}$ miles long by $11\frac{1}{2}$ miles wide, and stands on an area of 175 square miles. With the advent of railways it soon became one grand centre for railroads from all parts to focus in, which are kept very busy in transmitting to every corner of the civilised globe its live and dead stock, and its unlimited stores of grain. A visit to its stockyards, many acres in extent, into which thousands of hogs and bullocks are carried by rail every day, is a wonder worth going thousands of miles to see. The day we went there, and there is no difficulty in getting a ticket of admission, there were nearly 8,000 pigs to be slaughtered and packed away. During the twenty minutes that I was on the platform of observation, I saw sixty hogs killed, the carcase dropped into a tank of scalding water, where all the bristles were shaved off by the

fans of a water-wheel constantly revolving in the
trough, and the body passes out over a slide as clean
as a new-born babe.   One carcase follows another in
quick succession into the cooling gallery without the
hand hardly touching them, and almost noiseless, so
that each pig is killed, cleaned, cooled, cut and
quartered and quite ready for the cook in thirty-five
seconds !   This sounds too ridiculous to be true, but
I can vouch for the truth of it.   Otherwise I would
ask, how could 8,000 hogs be disposed of in one day
if this expeditious mode of killing, &c., did not exist ?
In the packing-houses 6,000 men are engaged, and
what is quite incidental to this business is the small
one of 50,000 lbs. of sausages made daily.   Now I
will take the visitor back through the busy streets,
as thronged as London Cheapside, to the immense
pile of buildings of ten storeys high, with polished
granite pillars, which they call the Board of Trade
Buildings, in which is held the Bourse, as noisy as
that in Paris, a veritable Babel of tongues.   Here we
saw on the notice board as one day's sale—700,000
lbs. of lard, and innumerable barrels of packed pork,
ready to go to the ends of the civilised world.   There
is rather a remarkable sight, and in the very heart
of the city too, such as one would not meet with in
any town in Europe, but everything must give way to
the general good of the many in a republican place
of business—every sentiment is swallowed up by the
trading deity.   This ugly monstrosity is a huge iron
revolving bridge, which turns on its axis to allow of
large steamers passing along the River Chicago.   It
is amusing to watch the sudden cessation in the

traffic in a wide bustling street while this proceeding
went on. Every class of vehicle and every style of
person had to submit patiently for about fifteen
minutes on both sides, and then ensued a rush as if
to catch up so many dollars that had been lost by the
delay to the traffic ; fancy all this at the bottom of
Ludgate Hill in London, then you can imagine the
concourse collected at every stoppage. I met a
gentlemanly-looking man who was wearing a tricolor
decoration in the button-hole of his coat—blue, red,
and white, and getting into conversation with him on
the subject of the American War, and knowing that
Americans looked down with contempt on war medals
and other insignia of distinction, I asked him what it
signified, and he said it was the Military Order of
the Loyal Legion of Americans, instituted by the
officers who had been engaged in the War of the
Rebellion ! They have a club, and they meet once
a month. If a tram be entered in the centre of the
city, where the large hotels are situated, the visitor
will have a good opportunity of seeing its long, wide
thoroughfares, bristling with grand stores and shops
for about eight miles, which will bring him to
Lincoln's Park, a most lovely promenade, very
prettily laid out with flowers and shrubs, and within
which is a good zoological collection of wild animals ;
the elks, buffaloes, and red foxes being very fine
specimens. The young people seemed very happy
with their boats and swings, &c., all free and unfettered, apparently without a sign of a keeper to
keep guard over its proprieties and protect it from
any breach of its privileges. A pleasant restaurant,

with simple refreshment and mild, cooling drinks,
was there, with plenty of seats and nothing to pay.
The want of beauty and grace in the womenkind both
in Denver and Chicago is very remarkable. In the
latter the men are well-made and tall; but the pallor
of the face and the dark rings under the eyes denote
that the place and surroundings are not health-giving,
and the strongest feel a sense of weariness and have
a washed-out look. I heard it said that if a man did
not make his fortune in ten years in Chicago, the
wear and tear is such that the constitution gives way!
It would be unjust and ungrateful to take leave of
Chicago without a word in favour of that splendid
hotel called "Sherman House," with its four hundred
rooms, and its pretty central hall with its promenade
gallery looking down on its bustling floor, and from
which issues of an evening some delightful music and
singing. The dining-room is on a large scale, the
cuisine is first-rate, and the waiting unexceptionable;
the variety of dishes to choose from quite puzzles an
Englishman. Of course, being in the very heart of
business life and places of public amusement, it is not
a dead calm at any time of the day, and what it will
be when the Exhibition is on it is not easy to imagine.
We therefore leave these nice luxurious quarters with
regret, and proceed on our journey to the Niagara
Falls. *En route* we pass through a grand fertile
country again, with numerous ranches of wide extent,
in which we saw large herds of cattle, and the proprietor was said to be fortunate if he could boast of
having a thousand head or more, the lot being defined
as a "fine bunch" of cattle, in the same manner as

NIAGARA FALLS.

they would say in Australia when a lucky squatter
rejoiced in a large " mob " of cattle, where the wives
of the aborigines, called " Gins," are such adepts not
only in collecting the animals, but as drovers also.
We rattle along in a most superbly appointed train,
in which we are regaled with most sumptuous fare,
cooked " on board " in a wonderfully small space, and
waited on by obsequious black attendants in white
caps and jackets, with soft voices and noiseless tread,
with luscious dessert of strawberries and cream, and
especially of peaches, which are indeed the boast of
the State of Michigan, where they grow to such per-
fection ; and not only its fruits, but it is proud of its
splendid crops of corn, its output of copper, and the
production of a large quantity of salt.   Traversing
this state to its northern end, we reach its handsome
commercial capital containing 250,000 inhabitants,
Detroit by name, and there we cross the river, and
on the other side enter the province of Ontario, where
we find ourselves once more under the British flag ;
but now nothing more of interest worth recording
takes place till we get to the " Welland Canal," which
has been constructed to unite the Lakes of Erie and
Ontario together, a union rendered necessary in consequence of the Falls of Niagara and its whirlpool
making the stream unnavigable.   We are soon
startled by the conductor, warning us that we are
approaching the greatest of waterfalls, where the
train pulls up for about three minutes to give the
passengers an opportunity of seeing from the carriage
windows this wondrous roaring cascade ! After making
a slight curve we pass over a cantilever railway

bridge, a great height above the Rapids, and on the
other side we find ourselves once more on American
soil and soon in a large commodious station, where
we descend from our car and drive off to the Prospect House Hotel, where we took up our abode for
three or four days. This hotel is said to have been
patronised by the Prince of Wales, Duke of Con-
naught, and Prince Leopold, &c. All very well for
such high folk ; but an ordinary tourist, whose purse
has its limits, it would be as well to think twice
before entering such expensive quarters. The best
thing for a tourist to do is to get a public conveyance
with a pair of horses, and, after having settled as to
the charge, then to take first the American side and
drive off to see respectively the " Goat," " Bath," and
" Luna " Islands, then the " Three Sister " Islands.
And descending the steps to where the tower stood
before it fell down, one gets very near indeed to the
edge of the Cataract, and if the visitor has nerve
enough he will see a sight which passes far beyond
all human description or painter to depict. He will
see a volume of water 15 feet thick rush over a
rocky precipice 120 feet high, and some hundreds of
feet in width, and finally take a bird's-eye view of the
whole from a corner of Prospect Park, and then the
visitor has something photoed on his brain that will
never fade from it. Now we will take to the carriage
again, and drive down the right bank till we get to
the Inclined Railway, a sort of lift such as one sees
at Scarborough, which takes us down easily to the
edge of the whirling torrent ; thence we can look up
at the Falls, and the boiling waters at our feet,

18

THE BRIDGE OVER NIAGARA RAPIDS.

and on returning to the office on the bank a good
large photo can be purchased as a shadowy reminder
of the great original. Driving further on we come to
the Whirlpool Rapids, where Captain Webb lost his
life in his endeavour to swim them; it was supposed
that he got stunned by striking his head against a
projecting rock. The wire on which Blondin crossed
the Niagara may be seen. Now we will cross the fine
suspension bridge, 1,268 feet long, and get on to the
Canadian side again, from which a still grander view
of the Falls may be obtained, and even a water-
proof dress hired, with a guide who will pioneer us
behind the fall of water, if you feel so inclined. It is
quite safe even for ladies, who often do it in perfect
safety. On returning over the suspension bridge stop
the carriage midway across it, and gaze at your ease
on this "hell of waters," *à la* Byron, in front and
beneath you, and that from a mid-air standpoint,
because the bridge is 190 feet above this raging
tumultuous stream. The "publics" are open on the
American side, but there was no rowdyism or brawling on the Sunday. We attended St. Peter's Episcopalian Church. The service was of the higher order
of ritualism, and in the evening all was choral and
no sermon was given. The congregation was a thin
one. I have omitted to mention that the huge volume
of water which passes over the Falls is the concen-
trated collection from the Lakes Superior, Huron,
Michigan, and Erie. All this rushes down the precipitous sides of the River Niagara and empties itself
into the Lake Ontario, which is the head-spring of
the great River St. Lawrence. Having now seen

and notified everything worth describing at Niagara, we will proceed onward to New York. Our first halt is at the bustling town of Buffalo, where we changed our carriage, and for two dollars extra each we have the privilege of riding in the "vestibuled car," which is without an equal in any country. The superior style in which it is furnished is only comparable by the excellence of its viands, which taste the more delicious amid such elegant and refined surroundings, and the look-out over the charming scenery as we sit at ease and glide smoothly but swiftly along, must be done to give a fair idea of the position. There is, however, "no rose without its thorn," hence now and again our peace was disturbed by the loud clanging of a bell and the bray from the engine before reaching a level crossing, or a run down the centre of the main street of a town, to give out a tremendous vigorous warning to the inhabitants that the traffic must be temporarily stopped. As there are no bridges over the line as we have, the carriages can be built any height. Passing along this run of 462 miles we come to the great cities of Rochester, Syracuse, and Albany, interspersed here and there with pretty towns and country villages of smaller note, but infinite in number. Large manufacturing buildings, like the cotton mills in Lancashire, crop up constantly, with the everlasting steam-engine predominating everywhere and for everything over the handwork of man; but all this is diversified and beautified by the intermixture of some splendid agriculture, which makes the New York State so worthy of its title, "the Empire State." But before we reach that head centre of commercial vitality and incalculable wealth, I have to describe and admire the last but best bit of our journey since we left the Rockies, and that is the delightful run from Albany to New York, a distance of about a hundred and fifty miles, along the left bank of the Hudson River, which may not only be compared to, but stamped as of superior beauty to the Rhine in Germany. The traffic is so immense that it has a double line of rails, and the iron road follows the windings of this grand river, about two miles wide, and bounded on each side with picturesque scenery of the most fascinating character conceivable. After passing down the line for thirty-five miles, the famous Catshills are seen to great advantage, and on reaching the Fishkill Landing, the gorge known as the Highlands is entered, rough and grand, at the northern end of which the " Storm King " commands one's attention. Again, six miles further down on the same side, standing out on a most romantic site, is the United States Military Academy of West Point. Steaming on another twenty-five miles we get a sight of the basaltic columns, known as the " Palisades." Besides these sights we pass the "river cities" at various intervals, some of which have an exceedingly picturesque appearance. We may note Poughkeepsie, with Vassar College in its rear; Tarrytoon, with its quaint old Dutch church, and Yonkers. The Hudson has some sad tales to tell in connection with the Revolutionary War; for instance, Major Andre's trial and execution. We lose sight of the river at Spuyten Duyvil as we turn eastwards, and

Harlem Bridge is the next object of our attention, and then the terminus of the Elevated Railway, and behold we are in the heart of New York before we can realise it! But we have not quite done with the beautiful Hudson, with its shining surface speckled over with large white paddle-steamers, some for pleasure, others towing half-a-dozen long barges in double line like a big duck convoying a brood of small ducklings, interspersed here and there with yachts carrying high white sails, flitting across the water like so many butterflies, a bright, lively sight and no mistake, and "good for sore eyes," as the Scotch would say. Another very striking feature to a tourist is a number of large buildings on the right bank at frequent intervals on the very verge, and even overhanging, the water. These, we were told, were factories or depôts for ice! Enough, one would suppose, to supply the whole world; but no, iced water is such a favourite drink with the residents of New York that it is placed at your side at every meal, and even supplied to every bedroom—no doubt a great luxury when the temperature in the shade is at 100° Fahr.; but it does seem extraordinary to an Englishman this crave for ice. Every bit of vantage ground that a house can find a lodgment on is secured at a fabulous sum to erect a residence for some city millionaire or other; and no wonder, the prospect being lovely in every direction, which a combination of rock, wood, and river can give to the exquisite picture! a view seen at every turn in the river, with a train on the right whisking along round the corner between two projecting rocks and the shipping in the centre of the stream.   Just imagine it—picture it to your mind if you can.

My last chapter I shall devote to my recollections of New York.

CHAPTER XXVIII.

Landing at the Central Station, well known as the grand central depot in 42nd Street, it is difficult to give any foreigner an adequate idea of the scene. Supposing we rolled the Euston, Midland, and Charing Cross stations into one, it would be no exaggeration to say that its two façades of 1,000 feet each would be equal to those three combined, and I don't think then that those stations stand on so large an area of ground as this gigantic building. I must here premise this description as only a start, because as we go on we shall find that everything in the building line is on a tremendously exaggerated scale in the city of New York. The rooms for the reception alone for the trans-continental luggage are immense, and here we found our baggage quite safe and uninjured, which had been forwarded from "Frisco," and which they will, for a small fee, keep in hand and transmit to your steamer when you have made up your mind to take your passage home. Just as we were getting our wraps together a respectably dressed lady-passenger asked us if we were going across the city to join our Atlantic steamer that night, and on replying in the negative we were

NEW YORK.

surprised to hear her say that she knew we were *foreigners!* As both parties were speaking good plain grammatical English we were rather startled, I must say, at being called foreigners! But the fact is the people feel a certain pride in being Americans, and do not look upon it as any compliment to be regarded as English. The native born views his country as the first and most go-a-head of any in the whole world. In New York at any rate an Englishman soon feels himself rather " boiled down " from a puffed-up estimation of himself or his country. First of all, then, we must suppose ourselves settled in a good hotel in Broadway, the focus of liveliness, where we can secure a good room and every luxury, barring intoxicants, from 12s. to 14s. a day ; but if we desire to put up at a more fashionable one, in the Fifth Avenue for instance, we must expect to pay more, the fare, however, would be no better. The city has so much increased in size and changed in its appearance since my last visit to it thirty-eight years ago, that I was puzzled to know where to start from with a visitor who wanted to see everything and had not much time to do it in. I was told if I wished to ascertain how very much New York had extended itself, that I could not do better than take a seat in the Elevator Railway at Castle Garden and run up the city on one side and then down the other, which we did, and after traversing numerous streets and avenues we reached the terminus at 129th Street: there we descended, and took a horse tram across the city to the terminus of the " Elevator " on the other side and ran back to Castle Garden, a distance

TERMINUS, ELEVATED RAILWAY, NEW YORK.

of twenty-two miles there and back, at the small cost
of 7½d. each. A cheap piece of sight-seeing truly!
for our vision was simply glutted with the numerous
church towers and spires, public halls, monster
hotels, and still bigger warehouses, public gardens,
and squares, &c.; but what astonished us not a trifle
as we passed along was the singular sight of ladies
sitting calmly and unconcerned in their drawing-
rooms, into which we could plainly peep as we glided
past from the carriage windows, but everybody and
every interest must give way where it clashes with
the benefit of the masses! Just fancy carrying an
" Elevator " along Piccadilly or Pall Mall in London,
who would dare to introduce the Bill into the House
of Commons! When I inquired whether the
" Elevator " had not been the ruin of the owners
of the mansions in the fashionable avenues, they
replied, " Oh no, no, not at all, just the reverse had
happened. They paid better when let for stores or
offices than they did as residences, especially those
near the stations, which brought the merchants into
touch with one another at every quarter of a mile or
so." Underneath the " Elevator," which was erected
on a delicate-looking iron trellis-work, was a horse
tramway, which could deposit one at any inter-
mediate point. This convenient mode of locomotion
to commercial men to whom time is gold, is of course
everything, for they can time their visits to each
other to the half minute.

Having reached Castle Garden again, we descend
the stairs and walk about the pretty grounds, which
are historically interesting. Here are deposited all

the immigrants from Europe, representatives of every nation and speaking a diversity of tongues, it is a curious Babel of sounds. A thousand can be sheltered within the walls, but they do not remain many hours but are sent up-country to their various destinations. They must all show that they have means of support otherwise they are not allowed to land but sent back to their own country: at any rate they are not permitted to loaf about New York as our immigrants do in the East End of London, often adding to our list of pauperism. In Castle Garden was formerly a fort which subsequently became the basis of a concert hall, in which I heard an opera at my last visit to New York. Jenny Lind sang here under Barnum's management and was a great success, very unlike the place as it now appears. As we are now near the lower end of Broadway, we will walk along that renowned commercial highway, with its great variety of architecture, its shops and throngs of people. The first monster building which attracts our attention is the Equitable Life Office, got up in the most expensive style, its marble hall and wide staircase are faced with all kinds of precious stones, notably onyx and yellow marble—very bright and beautiful, nothing like it in London. Next comes the New York Life Office, hardly second to it in beauty and grandeur. The proprietors of these expensive buildings say it is a cheap way of advertising their business. Old Trinity Church must be visited and its many quaint inscriptions in its yard be read; the many shrubs and flowers form a singular oasis in the midst of such a desert of granite, marble, and

BROADWAY, NEW YORK.

sandstone. Opposite the church is Wall Street, so often quoted in money transactions, a busy thorough-fare, and looking back from the bottom of it, the spire of Trinity stands out nobly through the narrow vista of tall houses. Continuing our walk along Broadway we next come to the Post Office, with its fine solid frontage of granite, triangular in form, each of its four stories being ornamented with columns, and near here we see terminating many lines of horse trams, while others are passing to and fro in Broadway, and here we can best study the moil and turmoil of New York Street traffic to the fullest extent—the crossing is actually dangerous. Behind the Post Office we see the Houses of Assembly, now dwarfed into insignificant dimensions by the side of the tallest building in the city, which boasts of fourteen stories of brick and stone, and on the top of these three more stories of iron trellis-work inclosed, and in which the printing and editing of the *New York World* paper is carried on. The proprietor was determined to outdo even Cyrus Field's huge edifice of twelve stories, upon which it looks down and on everything else for miles round. It makes one quite giddy to look up at this pretentious erection, which is a high-standing evidence of the extent advertising is carried on by means of buildings of exaggerated size and outward show: for every one naturally asks, What is that? Taking our places in a tram-car we pass on till we arrive at Grace Church, the most elegant Gothic structure in the city, having a high tapering spire of white marble which glistens in the sun, and is a very prominent feature at the turn which Broadway makes at this point. Joining our friend the tram again, for it must be known that Broadway is five miles long and hard work to walk its length. We get down in Madison Square, one of the chief centres of American amusement and fashion. It abounds in theatres and concert halls, several first-class hotels and restaurants and half-a-dozen clubs, all on a grand presumptuous scale. The gardens of six acres is very prettily laid out with shrubs and flower-beds, and on summer evenings is a pleasant resort to smoke a cigar in, while during the day it is overrun by no end of nursery maids in charge of well-dressed children—plenty of benches with backs, and the sexes keep well apart on separate seats, and don't intrude one upon another —an instance of gallantry which we might well copy from. As the ever-convenient tram skirts the square we mount it again, and continue our journey now to the end of this extraordinary, crowded, bustling thoroughfare, replete with its diversified wondrous sights, a tithe of which cannot be depicted by the pen of the most gifted ready writer, and we are dropped at the entrance to the Central Park, a pleasure ground now justly termed the most beautiful in the whole world. This I feel is no Yankee boast, for in all my travels I have never seen anything to be compared to it in either sphere of the universe. Twenty years ago it was little more than a swamp with projecting rocks in it, and it shows what an energetic, wealthy, and *unfettered* community can do in so short a time by the aid of skilful engineers and landscape gardeners. Though the size of this park is only two and a half miles long and half a mile wide, there are nine miles of carriage drive 60 feet wide, and bridle-paths five miles long, 17 feet wide, while the footpaths varying from 13 feet to 40 feet wide are twenty-eight miles in length. As to the seats, these are for the million, and count up to ten thousand and not a cent to pay: how different to our parks in London! There are some lovely bits of artificial scenery with picturesque peeps here and there from its five hundred covered arbours. The lawns are kept green and smooth like a bowling ground, and no one is allowed to walk on the grass, but rigidly confined to the walks and drives. It is the fashionable promenade for the superbly appointed family equipages and fast-trotting horses. The water area covers forty-three acres, and one lake of twenty acres is divided by a narrow channel crossed by a bridge. On this lake may be seen flitting about in all directions pleasure boats at 5d. a row round its lovely shores. The next thing to see is the menagerie, containing a fair collection of birds and animals. A very fine specimen of a bison and some prairie wolves well rewarded our visit. On leaving the Park we soon enter the renowned Fifth Avenue, in which one can admire some of the handsomest private mansions in America. Foremost is the one belonging to Mr. Vanderbilt, the wealthiest man in the city, said to be worth twenty-five millions of pounds. There is one thing in particular to be noticed in the front of his house, and that is a huge flagstone in one solid perfect piece, 24 feet by 18 feet and 6 inches thick. This remarkable monolith was quarried without

a crack, and conveyed on special rails and then
on trollies and fixed down as a pavement before the
house ; and would pass unnoticed, but it is well worth
examining, and fills one with surprise that such
a large flat piece of brittle freestone could be safely
laid down without a flaw—it only shows what money
can do. Nearly opposite Vanderbilt's is St. Patrick's
Cathedral with its two fine spires of white marble,
rather prominent objects in the sunshine. We will now
leave New York and go over the East River to quiet,
sleepy Brooklyn—a city of families and a city of
churches with high spires, which has a million of
people. Should one happen to be there on a Sunday
morning one can follow a surging crowd which will
take us to the late Mr. Beecher's church, a simple
building, but containing 2,800 seats. These used to
be put up to auction annually, and have realised as
much as £12,000. He certainly was a wonderful
leader of men. But what takes the visitor more practically over to Brooklyn is to see the splendid and
magnificent suspension bridge over the East River.
The whole length of this grand structure is a few feet
short of 6,000. Between the towers the span is 1,595
feet. It is 85 feet wide ; this gives a central space of
13 feet for foot-passengers, underneath a double
railway track for passenger cars, worked to and fro
by a fixed engine, and on each side of this track is a
carriage way. The total length above high water is
272 feet. Its cost was some 15 millions of dollars.
It was opened in all its parts in September, 1883, and
in the first nine months its railway alone carried
5½ millions of people. The fare is three cents and for

pedestrians one cent only. It is of a light airy appearance compared with that of our Forth Bridge, which strikes one as so heavy and cumbersome. The visitor had better walk one way over it and return by the railway.

If the visitor would really enjoy a delicious treat he should not fail to make his way again to Castle Garden, and then take a steamer across to Bedloes Island in the centre of the harbour, on which is erected Bartholdi's statue of "Liberty," the pride of America! Its height is 305 feet from the base to the torch, which represents Liberty enlightening the world. I give some of its dimensions, which will convey a fair idea of its great size. For instance, the head from the chin to the cranium is 17 feet, and in which forty persons can comfortably stand. The length of the right arm is 42 feet, and in the gallery round the torch, which is held in the hand, twelve persons can stand comfortably. The tablet in the left hand is 23 feet long and 13 feet wide. The steps of the ladder up the centre of the body are very slippery, the metal being smooth and polished by constant use; hence it is easier to mount if the shoes are taken off. I need hardly say what a splendid bird's-eye view of New York, Brooklyn, its bridge, and the great length of seventy quays with ships not countable is to be had from the top. Fail not to see this grand national monument. The High Bridge is well worth a visit. First take the Elevated Railroad from Sixth Avenue to 155th Street; then a horse tram will carry you to the bottom of a wooded, sloping hill (Washington Heights), up

which there is a path. Along it you walk till you
reach the bridge. This bridge was built to convey
the Croton Aqueduct across the Harlem river and
valley. It is 1,460 feet long, and has thirteen arches
resting on granite piers. From the footpath along
its side, 116 feet above the river, a very fine prospect
is to be had. The fresh water it supplies to
New York passes over it in iron pipes 7 feet in
diameter, inclosed in a tunnel of brickwork. A short
walk further on brings one to a splendid doubled,
arched-iron, cantilever bridge spanning the same
valley, with a grand carriage roadway 75 feet in
width. It well deserves the name of " Washington."
On Sundays crowds of excursionists visit these two
bridges, near to which are several tea-gardens and
convenient hotels. I forgot to mention that the
Croton Reservoir, which receives this water—1,000
millions of gallons in quantity—extends the whole
length of the Central Park on the left-hand side,
that is, two miles at least !

I think I may venture to conclude now by saying
that I have written a small illustrated account of all
those " lions " of New York such as a visitor *en
passant* would care to explore, and which, in my
opinion, are worth a voyage across the Atlantic to
see, to enjoy, and to admire. And especially so is it
worth a week's or ten days' sojourn *en route* to, or
from, those tourists going to visit the Chicago Exhibition. If, however, any tourists, men of leisure and
of money, are curious to see the seamy side of human
nature, they can do some " slumming " by taking a
detective, whose charge would be £5 ; then they can

imitate the freaks of London society in our East End. Thus safeguarded, evening parties of men can pay a visit to all the miserable dens of iniquity which will occupy the whole night. Passing from water "dives," the home of the "Border Gang," to Sebastopol on the east side, and then on to "Battle Row" and "Hell's Kitchen" on the west side. May it be to their moral edification!

Before I finish, it would not be out of place just to give a few characteristics of the New Yorkites. First, then, comes the cab and its driver, extortionate as our own when they have a chance; hence make your bargain before you enter. As they are painted black and yellow, they are popularly known as "black and tan." The charges are 1s. a mile or 4s. an hour. A trunk outside is charged 1s., and each parcel 5d. — very dear in comparison with London. Now for the mode of living. Americans are exceptionally fond of hotel life, and at all the hotels large numbers are permanently boarded, at a considerable discount to what a passing guest would have to pay. Again, those who cannot afford the hotels go into boarding-houses, which abound in every quarter, and meet the needs of every grade in society, the charges varying from £1 to £2 a week; but the better sort in the avenues go up from £2 to £10 or more, all depending upon the style and position of the room or rooms one occupies, but the meals are alike for all—breakfast and dinner at night. The women-servants, or helps, are not obliging. It would be better for the stranger that he or she should be slow to make acquaintances, and take rooms

week by week, for fear of meeting disagreeable
neighbours. The "Norman" and the "Earle"
hotels are of moderate dimensions in comparison
with some. Let us not forget that the charge for
cleaning a pair of boots in the hotels is 5d., and
not to walk abroad in dirty shoes, otherwise the
shoeblacks will bore you at every corner with
calls for a "shiner," for which they demand
2½d. I don't know whether my readers have
ever been to Petticoat Lane in London, but if they
have not they would see a great resemblance to it at
the Bowery in New York. It consists of rows of
cheap stores, mostly displayed on the sidewalks ;
numerous low concert and beer saloons ; stands with
fruits, pea-nuts, and soda-water. You are greeted by
the vendors of every article of every variety by
the call of "A great bargain!" The rumbling
sounds from four tracks of horse-cars below, and the
noisy puffing of the Elevator Railway above, produce
a sight so unique as not to be seen in any other part
of New York, and to the uninitiated is indeed most
bewildering. There are four hundred churches of
every denomination in New York, which afford a
sitting capacity for 250,000 persons out of 2,000,000.
Where do the great majority go to on the Sabbath ?
Strangers are welcome to all the Sunday services,
and there is no collection, each church depending
on its pew rents and subscribers. The free-school
systems give to the children of parents in all grades
of society the opportunity to acquire a good education,
second to none in general excellence. No separate
schools *now* exist for coloured children ! There are

evening schools for those who are obliged to work during the day. The cost to the city is four millions of dollars, or £800,000 of our money. Beer is fast superseding all other beverages *except water* in the affections of the citizens. The breweries—151 in number—are colossal in size, and yield three millions of barrels in a year. It is sold everywhere at five cents the glass, or ten cents for a larger one called a "schooner." If you ask for foreign beer they will charge at least double for it.

From what I have seen I should say the New Yorkite working-class are abstemious in comparison with the same grade in London, and especially may this be said of their women. The Society for the Suppression of Vice is ever on the alert, and the laws are very rigid in regard to any obscene or immoral publications. The acuteness of the trading community is of such world-wide notoriety that little need be said, other than to remark that they deal in imports to the extent of 500 millions, and of exports to the value of 400 millions of dollars! They must be all wide-awake and to the fore, especially on the Stock Exchange, where the transactions are prodigious. 250,000 to 300,000 shares of stock change hands daily and the value of the railway and other bonds dealt in range from two to three millions of dollars! This Exchange has 1,100 members, and the market value of the seat is worth £6,500, transmissible to the members' heirs! The Produce Exchange, held in a magnificent building, has 3,000 members, who deal in every kind of food. Then, again, there are the Cotton and Petroleum Exchanges, at all of which bustling, seething crowds, buzzing like so many bee-hives, or creating a noise and confusion resembling a veritable Bedlam, are speculating with the almighty dollar—that dollar which holds its own with such despotic sway!

Before leaving America and the many friends who have been so kind and courteous, and enlivened our visit with so much pleasure, a few remarks respecting the ladies who have locked hands in matrimony with so many Englishmen during the past few years would not be out of place. As soon as we enter the " Empire State" we cannot fail to observe that the looks, dress, and style of the women is notably better than those we have left behind. In New York itself this change is very perceptible. The height of fashion predominates, and it is nothing singular to see " sweet sixteen " in three or four different gowns during the day. The girls in their teens are not only very attractive in their attire, but piquant and fascinating in their manners and address. They can hold their own and queen it in their mothers' drawing-rooms in a way that outshines English girls of the same age; and what is more, their handsome faces, beaming with a lively expressiveness, and their conversation, sparkling with wit and repartee, far surpasses a like number of girls in any of our large centres of popu-lation. The American father will slave away at home in order that he may give his daughters a liberal education in accomplishments, backed by an expensive tour in Europe, while the girls in their turn get well posted up in all the passing news and popular literature of the day, and convey the information to their parent, who is too busy hunting up the dollars to spare much time for book-learning. In a word, the child becomes a kind of domestic encyclopædia to the father, who is often a self-made man, and has had few scholastic advantages.

Hearing that the White Star line of steamers were the largest, swiftest, and most admirably equipped of any crossing the Atlantic, we asked a friend known to the company to secure for us a passage in that splendid ship, the *Majestic*, 10,000 tons and 582 feet long, with twin screws revolving with little or no noise or thudding. Our cabin, called a " saloon " room, was 10 feet high, furnished with two berths soft and easy, delightful marble appliances for washing, with electric light and bells. We had, all told, 1,536 souls on board, but it can accommodate 2,136—quite a little town in itself !

Having ordered our heavy luggage from the Central Depot to be sent down to the pier No. 45, where the steamer lay, we had nothing to do but to walk on board and take our places. Easier said than done. We were quite staggered to see such a crowd of people, friends of the passengers, who brought with them quantities of floral decorations in different designs, some of them worth £5 or more, notably two most beautiful little yachts, with the rigging covered with roses and geraniums, &c., and when placed on the saloon table at dinner-time were the centres of admiration. Indeed, the large saloon was literally overdone with the load of flowers, hiding, as they did, the gold and white gorgeous ornamentations of the room itself. After a good deal of handshaking and kissing, amid much arriving and departing of carriages, the pedlars shouting their wares, and all the hurry and skurry of departing friends, the bell rings, and the gangway is removed; then the truly majestic vessel swings itself out into the stream, amid the cheers and waving of handkerchiefs of the assembled crowd, and the answering shouts from the passengers. Then we have spare time and free space to scan and admire the splendid appointments of this magnificent floating hotel, its smoking, card, and retiring rooms, its well-stocked gratuitous library, its delicious writing- and reading-room, where one can quietly read and write in ease and comfort, for there is little noise or motion during the steaming of this great monster of the deep. The vessel being so unusually steady, a good deal of dancing was enjoyed by the young people on board. One would have supposed that this simple, innocent amusement could have been carried on without any reflections of a mercenary nature emanating from their elders, looking on, and apparently admiring the lithe figures and handsome dresses. Not so. Money calculations seem deeply engraved on the minds of fathers and mothers in general, and on those of the American in particular. Hence one was amused by the following remarks originating in the fertile brains of two financiers present, lost to all social sentiment, who were footing up the probable amount of capital which the parents of those dancing possessed :—" Now, I say, Nobbs ; I calculate that there lot represents 200 million dollars. What think ye, old boy ? " " Well, I should say that you are very near the mark."

"And I say again, Nobbs; if the M. girls " (these rich young ladies stood aloof) "had joined the others, then there would not have been a cent less than 250 millions." "Ah well," said his friend ; " I guess you are about right now." So they turned on their heel and left the lively scene, perfectly satisfied that they had done a good stroke of business for future development on the stock market.

We reached Queenstown in six days and sixteen hours, and I saw no sickness on board. Our food was delicious, consisting of every conceivable luxury, as if we were on land. As to the attendance, well, we had a waiter to about every third chair, hence that department need not be praised. We reached Liverpool that night, and the docking of the huge steamer by the aid of two tugs was a sight worth seeing.

THE END.